Kowalski's Last Chance

Kowalski's Last Chance

LEO SIMPSON

Clarke, Irwin & Company Limited,
Toronto/Vancouver

Canadian Cataloguing in Publication Data

Simpson, Leo, 1934-
  Kowalski's Last Chance

ISBN 0-7720-1281-4

I. Title.

PS8587.I44K69   C813'.54   C80-094170-5
PR9199.3.S54K69

© 1980 Leo Simpson

ISBN 0-7720-1281-4

1 2 3 4 5   JD   84 83 82 81 80

Printed in Canada

This is a work of fiction.
No resemblance is
intended to any persons
living or dead.

The author wishes to
thank the Canada
Council for its support
during the writing of
this book.

For Julie

One

The Magic World

1

"Theft under fifty dollars," Joe Kowalski said to the manager of The Magic World toy store. "He's a grandfather, Mr. Sieracki, for God's sake. Why don't we forget about this one?"

Sieracki was a man in his late thirties, a lanky man with black hair combed straight back, peaking in the middle of his forehead. He had a satyr's ears and in fact he looked a lot like Count Dracula, a malignant person. At the moment he was angry.

The shoplifter was a tiny Italian man in a black suit, a Mr. Bulgari. He had tried to walk out of The Magic World with a dump-truck priced at $14.95 under his suit jacket. Mr. Bulgari was simultaneously a defiant and scared immigrant. He was working on the losing idea that he could make a defensive smoke-screen of the strange North American customer credit system.

"My son has the card," he said to Kowalski. "Can't I buy some things and bring a card in tomorrow? Go out in the store, sir, and tell me how many people you see paying money. No one. They are giving the little cards. I promise I will bring in a card, my son's card."

"It's the same with the God damn Greeks, it's always the

same with these God damn people," Sieracki said, his own speech thickly accented, his eyes rolling in anger. "One Greek kid comes in here and thieves an egg of Silly Putty. So for ninety-eight cents I don't bother him. Then the next day the store is full of God damn Greeks, stuffing my merchandise into their pockets. If I don't charge this thief I'll have Italian families in here all next week. What the buggers do," said Sieracki aggrievedly, "is they talk to each other in their own language. 'Go downtown to The Magic World, help yourself, nobody will bother you.' "

"Have mercy on me, friend," Mr. Bulgari said to Sieracki, grasping his lapels and staring up into his face. "Have mercy on me and I'll pray for the repose of your soul."

Sieracki's office was a desk and two chairs in the corner of the stockroom. The dump-truck was on the desk. Kowalski sat down at the desk and wearily pulled his notebook and pencil out of his breast pocket, pushing the toy to one side with his elbow.

"I hate this," Kowalski said. "You know, Mr. Sieracki, it's practically a rule of life that a grandfather should be able to give a birthday present to his grandchild. That's almost a law of nature."

"All right, Mr. Kowalski," said Sieracki. He freed his jacket from Mr. Bulgari's tiny hands and sidled behind the desk. "Where does it say in the law of nature that every grandfather should be able to give a birthday present to his grandchild at Albert Sieracki's expense, hey?"

"You could give this little guy a break."

"I don't even know his grandchild. I'm in the toy business, that doesn't mean I'm Santa Claus. Now I'd like to say something personal to you, officer. Next time I call the police station I don't want you handling the case. I have stomach problems. But I bet you feel great. Why not? You're a good guy. What I'd like when I call the station next time is a real policeman. I pay taxes to have my property protected by the law of the land, not to hear about the law of nature. I have a pain in my stomach and it's your fault."

In his ire and distress, Sieracki's resemblance to Count Dracula sharpened. At this moment, watching the store owner, it occurred to Kowalski that the man looked somehow strange: he was oddly a different person. Sieracki fished a roll of antacid tablets from his vest pocket and fed them one by one into his mouth, biting down on each with long, dangerous incisors.

"I'll tell Sergeant Brock to send another officer next time, sir."

"Never mind Sergeant Brock. He's on your side. I'll call Chief Williams myself."

Mr. Bulgari picked up the dump-truck as they were leaving, apparently with the feeling that paying the law's price for stealing entitled him to keep what he stole. Sieracki shouted at Mr. Bulgari, his mouth spraying powdery bits of antacid, and Kowalski had to help the store owner wrestle the toy out of Mr. Bulgari's tiny hands. Mr. Bulgari then screamed at both Sieracki and Kowalski, unpleasant Italian invective by the sound of it.

It was a normal event in Constable Joseph Kowalski's day, normal anger, pettiness and rancour. Some bewilderment in there too, Kowalski told himself. Drab. Not at all an unusual occurrence.

2

Harbour Street was one way, with parking meters down both sides, almost always full. Kowalski had double-parked the old Plymouth cruiser outside a Camaro, red with a black racing stripe. Now a nervous youth was sitting at the wheel of the Camaro, blocked in.

"Got you surrounded, eh, kid," said Kowalski to the youth. "Have you out of there in a tick."

"That's all right, officer," said the youth, in a voice with a crack in it. "Take your time."

Wonder if he's been up to anything, Kowalski asked himself, driving away. Next time Sieracki calls, Kowalski thought, Sergeant Brock will send young Ryan down. He'll be all right with grandfathers, Ryan. Ryan would arrest his own grandfather.

There was still snow along the curbs, with channels cut through it by gutter water. Kowalski turned left on to Pinnacle, one way in the other direction, rolling down the window of the cruiser to let out the must of winter and to taste the winy air. He drove along the bank of the Black River, which was swollen by the spring run-off, thunderously a rapid, white-capped torrent, an awesome act of nature barely contained. In the summer the torrent became a pleasant stream. When Kowalski was a boy, children swam across it in summer and played on the sandy river bed.

Kowalski's cruiser was not equipped with a radio. He had just a walkie-talkie. The provincials, whose jurisdiction was outside the city limits, were equipped with forty-band radios, breathalizer kits, tear-gas canisters, shotguns, loud hailers and resuscitating machines. The Ontario Provincial Police had lots of things to play with, and they got new cars every year. But the Bradfarrow City Police worked to a tight budget.

What Kowalski had in mind was an hour's drive in the country. The weather offered a kiss of springtime from sun and breeze after the interminable winter. The day was a court day, and if he called himself in free to Central Kowalski knew he would be sent to the City Hall parking lot to ticket cars. People with business in the East Hastings Court, beside the City Hall, often parked in the spaces reserved for the higher ranking municipal employees.

It was too good a day to spend exacting small revenge for municipal bureaucrats, as Joe Kowalski saw it.

Kowalski was a man of fifty-nine, due for retirement from duty at sixty. He was big, over six feet in height, and ran somewhat to fatty bulges at stomach and hips from riding in a cruiser, eating doughnuts, and watching TV at night. His grey hair looked like glinting silver fur on his head, with a patch of pink skin in the middle. His face was large and wide-featured, and amiable most of the time.

He meandered along side roads, down into valleys, up rocky hills and across the farmland plains. This was old country north of Bradfarrow, shaking off the snow. Granite came up through the ground in cliffs, looking like icebergs at sea, as they had looked for fifty million years. Where the ploughs had been in fall the earth was black and rich. The pastureland was already a delicate green patched with ice. Some of the farmhouses were built of dressed limestone, reminders of the area's former prosperity, the wealth from mixed farming and hard work as a creed. The large specialized dairy producers and the marketing boards had put an end to that era. The family roadside cheese factories, each with its own formula and distinct taste of cheddar, were closing down one by one. The old homestead sheep farms had gone long since.

Even the deserted appearance of the countryside's sweep hid a change, as Kowalski well knew. Farther north were the lakes, with new cottages owned by city people springing up around the Bradfarrow summer shacks. The public beaches were shrinking everywhere, and had disappeared on the more picturesque lakes.

And lately the city people had moved south, to become weekend farmers. The first wave had bought failing homesteads and large acreage cheaply. More waves from the cities drove the prices higher and higher. Nearly every rock and field Kowalski's eye rested on was part of a hobby farm, a dream of an ancestor by a well-heeled city person.

Nevertheless it was rapturous country and good to see again visited by spring. The regained majesty all around made Kowalski feel like a happy child. He would have accepted and believed the sight of a knight in armour cantering across the marshy fields on his way to a joust in defence of chivalry and honour and suchlike dead principles. Or of Dorothy with her dog Toto and Tin Woodman and Cowardly Lion tripping along one of the twisty roads on their way to Oz.

" . . . morning. Oh what a beautiful day," sang Constable Joseph Kowalski, the truant. "I've got a beautiful feeling. Everything's coming my . . ."

Up 37 and ten miles or so west would bring him to the Cormac turn-off, and so south again to Bradfarrow. Ticket a few cars at the City Hall lot for appearances' sake, write his report, and the day was done.

On 7 going west he would be out of walkie-talkie range so Kowalski switched it on to check Central. He was just south of the small town of Hornblende on Moira Lake. He pulled off the road and parked in front of a cedarwood log fence surrounding the parking lot of a tourist motel, tuning the walkie-talkie with his right hand.

" . . . haven't got a licence number," Central squawked. "It's Seamus Riordan, a red Camaro, white-letter tires, black racing stripes. Briefing sheet twenty-seven twenty-eight and the provincials are moving at emergency speed, but that unit's got forty miles to make . . ."

Kowalski thumbed through the briefing sheets and found twenty-seven twenty-eight. "Oh jeez," he said discontentedly.

He was looking at a photograph of the youth whose Camaro he had blocked in outside The Magic World. The youth, Seamus Riordan, according to the sheet, was the last man at large of the famous bazooka gang that had taken ten million dollars from a Brinks armoured car in Montreal.

The armoured car had been in an alley making a pick-up at the side entrance of the Bank of Montreal's main branch. Four guards with revolvers in their hands had loaded ten million dollars and were inside the bank again when a van backed into the alley. The two Brinks guards in the driving cab were also armed and locked into the armoured car. So they had no worries, not until the van's rear doors swung open and they found themselves staring down the mouth of an anti-tank rocket gun, a bazooka, not more than eight feet from their windshield. The windshield was bullet-proof but not rocket-proof. Because of the wings of the van's opened doors the hold-up men were fairly well hidden from passers-by. The guards sensibly got out of the armoured car.

Two hold-up men then drove the armoured car away. Next day it was found in a gravel-pit, empty, with the van. The bazooka had been abandoned in the van, with four rockets. The bazooka was in excellent condition, and capable of firing the rockets, a lethal item of ordnance in all respects.

A month after the robbery the first man was picked up by the FBI while eating dinner in Cinderella's Castle in the Magic Kingdom at Disney World, an obvious place of refuge for a Canadian in wintertime. Two other members of the bazooka gang were arrested soon afterward in Maui, Hawaii, again not a subtle northerner's hide-out. An army corporal was taken in charge at a training base in eastern Manitoba. At about the same time the Buffalo police raided a rub-club downtown and removed a particular naked man from there, considerately wrapping him in a blanket for the walk to the cruiser through slushy snow.

Clearly the police forces knew exactly where to find those

five members of the bazooka gang. However they did not know where to find the sixth man, the leader, and neither had they found the ten million dollars.

What they had was a name, Seamus Riordan, his age, about twenty, his fingerprints, and a head and shoulders photo of a fuzzy, skinny kid, Riordan, grinning at the camera with a sunlit beach in the background.

"All right, road blocks in place at Marmora and the Cormac turn-off on the west. They're hustling to Dalakar on seven east. Bancroft has him covered if he moves north, but we're in a hell of a lot of trouble if he breaks south and gets into the concession roads because we can't cover all of 'em."

This meant that Kowalski would have to pass through the Cormac road block and explain himself on his way home from his nice drive in the country.

Strange, though, Kowalski thought, it's as if the guys are trying to surround me here.

"Could we have your response, please," Central said. "Let's hear you, eh. We have a report, Seamus Riordan is now inside the Ventura Motel, near Hornblende, that's your briefing sheet twenty-seven twenty-eight. He's dangerous. He's a dangerous villain, fellows."

As he heard this message Kowalski was looking at the poker-work on a cedar motel sign facing the highway just in front of his cruiser. It said: VENTURA MOTEL. There was only one car in the parking lot, the Camaro.

Without zeal or any kind of enthusiasm he pressed the send button and said: "Car 11, Kowalski. I'm at the Ventura, Central. What would you like me to do?"

". . . all set up now at Dalakar, fingers crossed you guys — you're where, Kowalski?"

"At the Ventura Motel, Central."

"Oh God."

"Should I bring him in, Central?"

"Yes, we'd like that a lot, Kowalski," Central said. Some background static followed, and a scrap of consultation aside. "We've got a man right on top of Riordan, sir, but it's Kowalski. God almighty. This is some kind of a day."

"Kowalski. Kowalski, eh."

"Central."

"Look, no, don't try to bring Riordan in. Just hold him for the provincials, okay? We think he's the leader of the bazooka gang, stole ten million dollars in Montreal."

"I know, Central."

"Good, well listen, our idea here is that he'd like to keep the money. He stole the money and we don't believe he's ready to give it back. He might decide to use a firearm. Do you understand that?"

"I understand, Central," Kowalski said. He was somewhat offended.

". . . violent hoodlum, Kowalski, so for God's sake don't start feeling sorry for him, okay?"

"He's a human being."

". . . says he's a human being," Central said aside. Another man took over, anger pitching the squawking voice into heavier static. ". . . is not a human being, dummy, he's . . . and a murdering psycho, an animal . . . too complicated for you just remember that you're a cop and he's a robber. Had some lousy breaks before, but shit we've done nothing to deserve this . . ."

"He's coming out now, Central."

Riordan stood outside the restaurant doorway, a harmless-looking kid, a school kid, skinny and no more than five feet in height. He wore blue jeans and a jean jacket over a tee-shirt with the message LOVE — TRY IT YOU'LL LIKE IT. He had a likeable face, a blunt-nosed Irish face and untidy brown hair. He breathed the fresh air with pleasure and strolled toward the Camaro.

Kowalski stepped out of the cruiser. He approached Riordan with an upraised hand, a big friendly cop.

"Hold up a minute, sir," Kowalski said pleasantly to Riordan. "Like a word with you."

Kowalski had never seen anybody move so fast in all his life. Riordan seemed to flicker across the fifty feet or so from the restaurant door to the Camaro. He was inside the car in a jiffy. I should have blocked the exit with the cruiser, Kowalski realized, amazed by Riordan's speed.

But then the Camaro would not start. The starter whined,

and thankfully Kowalski reached the car door and opened it, and put his meaty hand on Riordan's fragile shoulder. "Like a word with you, Mr. Riordan," Joe Kowalski said, letting out his breath in relief.

Two

Kowalski's Last Chance

1

"Useless pile of junk," Seamus Riordan said. "I paid six thousand dollars for that auto. Cash."

"Yes?" said Kowalski. Naturally Kowalski wasn't taking any chances with Riordan, now that he had seen his moves. They were cuffed together and Kowalski had the car keys. He opened the Camaro's hood with his left hand. "This is a good car as a matter of fact," he said. "A cousin of mine has one, bought it second-hand, never had any trouble in six years. Carburetor gets sticky sometimes when you have a change of humidity overnight." Kowalski lifted the air filter housing out, a car man. "Yes, there's your problem," he said. "What you do, you give it a squirt of silicone lubricant whenever you have a tune-up. No more than a drop, though." He reassembled the parts one-handed and closed the hood. "Did you buy this out of the ten million, Riordan?"

"How do you mean, ten million?"

"Is your name Seamus Riordan?"

"No."

"All right. We're going in the cruiser."

"The mechanical age spells doom for leprechauns," said

Riordan, a very strange remark Kowalski thought. "If we were both on foot I'd be a free man now. A person can truly rely on a faithful horse-coper too. But Detroit will be the death of us all."

Maybe the weeks on the run had deranged Riordan. They sat in the back seat of the cruiser linked by the handcuffs. Kowalski took the twenty-seven twenty-eight from the front seat and held it for Riordan to see.

"Tell me this isn't you, eh. Sit there, Riordan, and tell me this isn't your photograph."

Riordan studied the sheet. With theatrical Irish amazement he looked at it closely, then at arm's length. He held it sideways to catch the low light of the sun. He handed it back to Kowalski wonderingly.

"Oh dear oh dear, this is a very shocking situation," Riordan said. "This man looks exactly like me! That's an astonishing resemblance! Oh dear, now I understand how you came to make the mistake. At first you see, officer," Riordan said in friendly explanation, "at first when you put the arm on me, I thought to myself, well it's a dumb cop, making a dumb cop error." He smiled at Kowalski quite charmingly. "But of course I understand now that you were acting in perfectly good faith."

Kowalski said, exasperated: "I mean, this is your photo for God's sake, Riordan. So why don't we just wait for the provincials. A bunch of OPP cars are going to come screaming in here in fifteen minutes. You can argue with them."

Riordan peered with worry at the photo again. "Oh dear. I know they'll say this is me, and if our fingerprints are alike too what chance do I have? The science isn't perfect you know. Here, let me show you my identification. These tell the truth."

A fat deck of credit cards was thrust into Kowalski's unwilling hand. He wasn't interested in looking at them. He wanted to hold Riordan for the provincials and then try to forget him. An armed robbery convict would do his time at Millhaven, the maximum security penitentiary in Kingston, and at Millhaven time changed every human being for the worse. Pride and character were leached out over the hard years. This skimpy kid, Riordan, the terrible bazooka bandit, more pathetic than Mr. Bulgari in his effort to talk himself free, he would be perfect meat for the long old limestone misery grinder.

It was only three o'clock and the new sun of spring still shone but Joe Kowalski's magic part of the day was done now.

Riordan's identification was in the name of Timothy Hanrahan. Not a bad name, suited to his Irish cast of features.

"You were going to use that bazooka," Kowalski said to Riordan. Kowalski's feelings of sympathy were involuntary, as part of his nature, but his experience was tough enough and simple enough. Places like Millhaven would probably always be around. Somehow the terrible vengeance of the civilized society was not understood, no more than a criminal like Riordan understood his own easy violation of humanity. Innocence played a part in the business too often, according to Joe Kowalski. On the other hand Kowalski's opinion of innocence wasn't the best in the world. "Do you have any idea how much damage a rocket like that could do at close range? Jeez, the armoured car would've exploded, did you understand that?" He said harshly: "You could've taken the lives of twenty people, maybe more, just to get the stupid money."

Riordan shook his head, looking confused.

"Jeez sake," said Joe Kowalski with the same form of anger a father might use to chastize a son. "Then you don't understand the money when you have it, do you? Buy a brand-new Camaro and call it useless junk." He nodded at Riordan's auto, with some envy even. "That's a good auto. None of 'em's perfect, and that one's better than most."

"A bazooka?" said Riordan. "What's a bazooka? I've never even heard of a bazooka. You've got the wrong man!"

"Okay in that case the provincials will apologize to you, give you a ride back here."

"Well. I'm done. No sense pretending I'm not caught. I'll tell the truth now," Riordan said. "I'm disgraced. Oh dear the disgrace. This hasn't happened to one of us for more than two hundred years. The last one in my family was Miles Hanrahan on June 8, 1776, in Wexford, at the Saturday fair in Enniscorthy. Lost his gold and his good name and never recovered, the poor fellow."

"What are you talking about, Riordan?"

"Not Riordan. Timothy Hanrahan. You have the wrong man

but you've caught a leprechaun. I am, as it happens," said Riordan, his sad youthful eyes meeting Kowalski's, "a leprechaun. You've heard of leprechauns?"

"Sure," said Kowalski and looked away embarrassed. "Little Irish elves. They sit on mushrooms and make shoes." The kid was starting work on his insanity defence Kowalski supposed. He said jovially: "Hey, you know something, Riordan? You're a big leprechaun, aren't you? I mean for a regular human being you're sort of short, no offence. But for a leprechaun you've got to be a giant. Leprechauns are about what, six inches tall, aren't they? A very big leprechaun," said Joe Kowalski, giving the subject serious thought, "would go to nine inches. Twelve inches has to be top height for leprechauns, say for their basketball players."

"Those are the ancient mythologies about the sensitive people. Some of the greybeard leprechauns tell stories like that, how we were so small we could hide under buttercups. There's a scientific explanation. Their diet was at fault, they lived on hazel-nuts and water-cresses. But those of us who came to America ate balanced meals. We took our vitamins every day. The average American leprechaun now is about five feet tall. I'm about average height myself. I am Timothy Hanrahan of the Enniscorthy Hanrahans. We're very powerful in the new world now, we leprechauns. There are," said Riordan with a faint threat in his voice, ignoring Kowalski's sceptical eye, "leprechauns in high places, my own family among them. We graduated from hand-crafts long ago, making shoes and the like, and now we have companies and corporations you wouldn't believe. We control a lot of institutions—universities, banks, a few governments. We're a sort of a benign Mafia. Well maybe not so benign sometimes at that."

"Oh yes?" said Kowalski. He had not resented Mr. Bulgari's attempt to free himself but he hated this one. "What do you take me for, Riordan? What the hell kind of dummy do you think I am? You're a leprechaun, are you. Well this is Kowalski the cop you're talking to. I've been on the force for thirty-seven years and I've seen everything. I don't want to hear any more about leprechauns from you, kid."

The sudden hopelessness in the kid's face touched Kowalski

then. This God damn job, he thought. "Thirty-seven mean years, that's my experience of humanity, going through my hands. You know the word drab? That's the word for how I found it. Not as hard as life in Millhaven, Riordan, but not much worth living all the same."

"A man needs some magic in his life," Riordan said.

This understanding startled Kowalski. He shrugged it away.

"Well you're right enough there. A man does need some magic. It doesn't matter to me now. One more year to go and I'm retired. I'd like to retire to the country. Problem's I have to stay in town, I have two aunts to look after. They can't be too far away from a hospital, old ladies. I wouldn't mind raising sheep. That's a very relaxing thing to do, you know, Riordan, raising sheep. Jeez but to own a farm these days you have to be earning fifty thousand a year in Toronto."

"Well listen, here's the leprechaun law. If you catch a leprechaun. . ."

"I don't want to hear about leprechauns."

". . . and don't let go, he'll give you a crock of gold to set him free. Of course it never happens nowadays. Nobody believes in us so we're safe. I mean I walked into something here that won't happen again in a thousand years."

The walkie-talkie on the front seat crackled. "Car 11, respond. Kowalski, what's the word on Riordan?"

"He's right here, Central," Kowalski said, putting the walkie-talkie to his ear and watching his captive. The kid was white-faced with fear at this stage.

"You have him in custody?"

"That's my report, Central."

"Hey, was he armed?"

Kowalski guiltily held the walkie-talkie on receive. "Are you armed, Riordan?"

"No."

"Not armed, Central."

"And I'm not Riordan."

Aside Central conferred again. ". . . your fingers crossed, we could be okay . . ." Then to Kowalski: "All right, hold the bugger at all costs. Now this is important, I have an order for you. Are you receiving me?"

"Yes, Central."

"Shoot him if he tries to escape. That's an order."

"But that doesn't make any sense! Shoot him? How are you going to find the money if I shoot him?"

"Kowalski."

"Yes, Central."

"Leave the brainwork to us, okay?"

"I don't understand the order."

"Shoot the suspect if he attempts to escape custody. Got that?"

"Yes."

"And Kowalski, listen. Congratulations."

Kowalski opened his holster and turned his body so that Riordan could see what was in it. "Kleenex," Kowalski explained. "We're supposed to carry our revolvers at all times on duty. They pick up dust, and what's more handguns are dangerous. I keep mine in a plastic bag at home. Kleenex is more useful than a gun during a regular police day. Also you can't blow your foot off by accident with a wad of Kleenex."

"We don't carry crocks of gold around with us any more either, of course."

"Sure. I understand."

"But you will have your leprechaun's reward."

"Leprechauns. I've never given them much thought, leprechauns. You know something, Riordan, I'd give my right arm to believe in a leprechaun. A leprechaun, something like that, a dragon even." A faint tempting feeling, a good idea, moved in Kowalski's senses. "Nothing is impossible, is it? I've never understood myself what makes people so certain of everything. We're not that smart."

Tears stood out desperately in Riordan's eyes. But he said with dignity: "This is probably your last chance to believe in a leprechaun."

"Yes," Kowalski said and gave Riordan a Kleenex for his tears and then casually got his keys out and unlocked the handcuffs.

Shoot him if he tries to escape. He said: "Take off, leprechaun."
Again Kowalski was astonished by the kid's speed of movement.
In an instant he was out of the cruiser and into the Camaro. But
there he was baulked. The starter motor turned over, *rowl rowl*,
and hopelessly Kowalski went to help.

"Not a very organized leprechaun, are you, eh," he said, a
finger probing the carburetor. "All right, leprechaun, give her
some gas, now." The engine started.

"Hanrahan," the kid said.

"Goodbye, Mr. Hanrahan," Joe Kowalski said.

On his way back to the cruiser Kowalski was of a sudden
almost mowed down by gunfire. The provincial autos, four of
them, swerved rocking into the parking lot and screeched to a
stop, with an immediate firework outbreak of shots. The last car
blocked the exit. The Camaro ignored the exit and drove straight
at the Ventura's cedarwood log fence. It was uncertain for a
moment whether the Camaro would win or the fence. The car
shuddered and stopped after the crash, headlights shattered. A
door panel was sheared almost off, crumpled like paper by the
wood logs. Then a dozen or more policemen emptied their handguns into the wrecked auto. Patterns of bullet holes jumped out all
over the near side. The engine roared, however, and the Camaro
bucked through, slamming down into the ditch and rearing up the
other side before righting itself after a crazy fishtail and heading
south. The metal scraping the tires shrieked and glass shards
tinkled along the roadway. Quite as recklessly as the Camaro, the
police cars spun out backward and rocketed off in pursuit.

Kowalski scratched his chest and belly where sweat had
broken out. "Oh jeez," he said.

One of the provincial police cars had not joined the chase.
A corporal climbed out of this unhurriedly and walked over to
Kowalski. He had his gun in his hand, a chunky, muscular man,
but Kowalski could not see much of the face under the peak of the
cap and behind the wire-rim sunglasses.

"You're Constable Kowalski," said the provincial. "A few of
us were wondering how the suspect escaped, if you'd like to tell
me about that." He put the gun in his holster and buttoned it
down without shifting his eyes from Kowalski's face.

That curious madness could be a sense of magic, Kowalski thought, something lost. Or maybe it was what made men at war charge with weak flesh against impossible firepower, a sickness. A simple disease of the spirit.

"He said he was a leprechaun. That isn't impossible, you know."

The provincial nodded. "Get in your car," he said. "Drive ahead of me to Bradfarrow. Don't turn off the highway. Don't drive too fast, please, constable."

2

"Riordan got clean away. We lost him and we lost the money too. I'll tell you where the ten million from the robbery was," Sergeant Brock said. "The ten million dollars cash from the robbery was in the trunk of the Camaro. Montreal had the information on that. What we would have liked best, then, you see, was Riordan alive and the car. Riordan dead or wounded and the car had to be our next best choice. Like not a lot of villains escape from a police cruiser on foot. He wouldn't want to anyway, not with the car there and all that money in it. What we didn't like at all, what really worried Montreal as a matter of fact, was the idea of Riordan escaping *in the car*."

Sergeant Brock dipped a match into the bowl of his pipe. The flame was good and steady.

"We had reliable identification of Riordan at the Ventura," he said. "Then you made the arrest, Joe. Montreal asked if you were a tough police officer. I said no. So they saw the worst situation, Riordan taking off in the car. That was where we gave you the order to shoot him if he tried to escape."

"How come you didn't tell me the money was in the car?"

"We were trying to keep it simple for you, Joe. That was our best judgement, make it neat. Anyway now he's away again," Sergeant Brock said, his manner quite composed, "with the money. Maybe we'll nail him again too, who knows. But if we do, will he have the money? Could be, but I say it's a lot to expect. I know plenty of people who'd feel we've had more than our share of blind luck on this one already. Two months now, and guys in

Whitehorse watching for him, down in Mexico the same, and all the US in between. An officer of the BCP drops on him, though. Then the officer was persuaded," the sergeant said letting some querulousness show, "how I will never know until the day I die, that the man wasn't Seamus Riordan after all but a leprechaun. An elf. I checked the TV Guide and they weren't running *Finian's Rainbow* or anything last night."

"They're running those late repeats of *Highway Patrol*, sergeant. Broderick Crawford. That's what I watch if I'm up."

"Yes. You see even the Dogans don't see leprechauns any more. St. Patrick's Day they see flying saucers like everybody else."

The main Bradfarrow police station was one of the old stone buildings in the city centre. Grimy, ugly, massive, it was an eyesore that would stand for ever if no city administration took the courage to tear it down over the objections of the Bradfarrow Historical Society. Square in shape and four stories high it had a roof of Welsh slate that leaked from dozens of places into the top floor, where the cells were. Welsh slate was no longer obtainable but the roof as such was protected by the antiquarians. The station evoked a sense of a London police barracks in the foggy era of Sherlock Holmes, and conceivably the builder had used such a model. The entrance was at the top of a set of granite steps flanked by ornamented iron railings. Two boot-scrapers outside the doorway had been boxed in by the historical society to protect them from policemen with snow-caked boots.

The East Hastings Court House had once been conveniently near. Now it was gone, replaced by a comfortable, low-slung modern building near the City Hall because the legal profession was more powerful than the police force and moreover was not on the city budget. Some day a new police station would be built too, it was often said. Meanwhile the old stone one stood beside an abandoned railway branch line, where worthless wooden rolling stock decayed on rusted rails, overgrown with weeds. On the other side was the farmers' market, busy on Saturday mornings only, another dying landmark.

Sergeant Brock had a small partitioned office on the first floor. Lath showed through holes in the mouldering plaster walls. The floor sloped to the centre, like a bed that has seen its day. He had a wooden desk and a captain's chair with a cushion tied to it, and four ancient filing cabinets. Kowalski occupied the visitor's or culprit's chair.

Sergeant Brock was a man in his late forties with blue-black jowls. His dark eyes were pouched underneath and heavy-lidded, and overhung by threatening eyebrows. His upper lip was small, sitting on top of a somewhat fat underlip, which gave his mouth the shape of a spoiled tyrant's, say an emperor during Rome's long decay. These aspects of face, though, had come to Sergeant Brock from nature, as other faces have merriness or honesty, and did not express any truths of character. The sergeant had developed mannerisms based on his face that helped him in his work some-times. A steady stare from underneath the uncombed growth of eyebrows carried useful menace and when his lower lip came up like Mussolini's it could inspire lots of productive fear in suspects as a rule. He had a weight problem. His shirt became untucked from his belt now and then in the course of the day.

He was a worrier by temperament. He worried about his teenage daughter, Sally, since the reports that came across his desk were routinely about car wrecks, drugs, violence and teen-age girls. And Sergeant Brock worried about his superior, Chief Williams, who was a most difficult man to work for. He worried about Joe Kowalski.

It was a well-known fact at the station that Sergeant Brock believed Kowalski to be a principled, worthy police officer, a good cop, maybe not the smartest mind on the force but by no means as inept as the record showed.

Brock was not presently in good humour. He was incred-ulous and somewhat numbed by shock. He felt betrayed by Kowalski.

"All right," said Kowalski miserably. "That's easy enough to say, nobody sees leprechauns. I'm fifty-nine years old. I need . . ."

"You need what, Joe?"

"Sergeant, he was just a kid. He had innocence written all over him. He was convincing, sergeant."

"Now that I do believe," said Sergeant Brock. "You've put

your finger on something. Your kid Seamus Riordan recruited the bazooka gang. That was a heavy crew, two Millhaven men, both killers, one illegally at large, a Vietnam veteran to handle the bazooka. He was . . . tough. To *get* the bazooka Riordan recruited a different type of guy, a corporal from a training base in Manitoba. A good family man, good soldier, no record, Presbyterian. The next thing Riordan did was to convince this gang to trust him to take care of the money after the job. They did. They trusted him. He took the money. They split up. He turned them all in."

"That's hard to imagine, sergeant."

"No, that's not so hard," said Sergeant Brock, sitting as still as a lizard with his pipe between his teeth, and beads of perspiration popped out on his brow, watching Kowalski through the smoke. "What's hard to imagine is the way he handled you. Joe, he told you he was a leprechaun and you let him go. Farrah Fawcett, say he told you he was Farrah Fawcett, I could get a grip on that. A leprechaun is beyond me."

"Well he didn't convince me he was a leprechaun, put it that way. Mostly I convinced myself."

"Yes yes. Don't tell me how a con job works, please. You aren't even Irish. I don't know. I'm all out of my depth. I keep trying to think of some excuse. Do they have elves in Poland?"

"That I don't know. I'm third generation. Baba never mentioned elves."

" . . . would be some sort of excuse you see, if Riordan conned you into thinking he was a *Polish elf*, not anything I could tell the chief, but some . . . On the other hand if you were a Dogan, say you had a hangover, you're an Irishman with a hangover. And you're an Irishman in a sentimental mood, thinking about the old country, head a little soggy, you're riding the cruiser humming Mother Machree and dreaming of the Mountains of Mourne. And you spot a tiny little man *dressed all in green*, little beard, rosy cheeks, smoking a clay pipe . . ." Sergeant Brock nodded to himself, concentrating. " . . .and he conned you into believing he was a leprechaun, this tiny elf—say for the sake of argument he was also carrying a pot of gold—an elf who didn't look anything like Seamus Riordan. That," the sergeant said, "would still be a con job, you see, Joe, and I'll tell you why. *Because there are no such things as leprechauns.*"

"Maybe not. I don't see why everybody is so sure of that, though. Anything is possible."

"No it isn't. Probably the world has many wonderful secrets. But it doesn't have leprechauns. What burns my ass is that we had *Riordan*. We're not a great city, Bradfarrow. But I do believe, even counting in Chief Williams and guys like Ryan, that we have a good police force as we stand. There's no mob here — now and then some small-time organizers try to move in and we always know, *I* always know, and we close them down. We're not on top of marijuana but then neither is anybody else. We're on top of hard drugs, most of the time on the streets, all the time in the schools. We have just one politician taking bribes at the moment and we're about ready to stamp on him. That's normal. We're an expanding community. Plenty of sharks in the water. They can swim around all they like so long as they obey the law."

"Well I'm sorry to spoil everything."

"But we've never been big time. We're not on the map, you see. I don't know why I want that. It must be a sign of immaturity. Last year I was down in California, in a little town called Grabe Pass, population eight thousand. We had an exchange for traffic study. I'd say there isn't an FBI agent over forty years old who hasn't heard of Grabe Pass. Express office hold-up, January 17, 1950, Joe, you remember it, Boston. Eight masked villains got away with three million. Not much over a million in cash, though. The FBI solved the case in 1956 but they got the break because the sheriff's office in Grabe Pass made the first arrest. While I was down there," Sergeant Brock said, closing an eye to the pipe smoke as he remembered recent insult, "I hardly heard any other question except *Where's Bradfarrow?* Where's Bradfarrow, down there in what's basically a pissy little desert *camp*, Joe. You could throw a rope around the place. Because twenty-one years ago they arrested a villain who stole one million. That is, in other words, compared to the Montreal hold-up, petty cash, that's shoe money, Joe. At Malton off the flight home I met a friend of mine on duty at the airport, Bill Baker, we trained together. He's horse now. We had a beer in the airport lounge, chatting there, I told him I'd been down in Grabe Pass, on my way back to Bradfarrow. Guess what he said then, Joe."

"I don't know what he said, sergeant."

"He said, I've heard of Grabe Pass. Then he said, but where's Bradfarrow?"

"Those horsemen are all full of, you know, shit, sergeant. We arrested one of the people in that spy case here, Fabbro. I saw them bringing him in myself. We had him in the cells upstairs for a couple of days."

"Sure we did, but that was just manning a road block. He was coming west from Ottawa on 7 so they said stop him and arrest him, and we did that."

"Well, we arrested him."

"Thirty years ago."

"Jeez sergeant, if you're going to argue about nine years. That Grabe Pass arrest was twenty-one years ago you said."

"The other thing about Fabbro was that he was acquitted. He wasn't a big villain in the first place and he was probably the wrong man anyway."

"That's right," Kowalski said.

"There you go," Sergeant Brock said. "Fabbro isn't anything like what I'm talking about. I'm talking about somebody like James Earl Ray the assassin, who spent two nights here, or August Amundsen the Swedish nurse killer, who was seen here a month ago."

"Amundsen's been seen everywhere."

"All right. But most of all I'm talking about Seamus Riordan the bazooka gang leader because we had the bugger. We had him and we had his car with ten million dollars in it. We had the villain in the car and the cash in the trunk."

"Not," said Joe Kowalski who felt inexpressibly sorry for his friend Sergeant Brock but who nevertheless wanted their talk to be fair, "if he wasn't Riordan. We didn't have him if he wasn't Riordan and there wasn't any money in the car if his name was really Timothy Hanrahan."

"I'm going to bury your leprechaun story, but that's just about all I can do for you on this, Joe."

"If leprechauns are powerful now, it could explain something's always interested me," Joe Kowalski said sincerely. "Look, he said they're five feet tall on average. Hasn't this ever happened to you, there's somebody famous, a president or somebody, everybody recognizes his face, then maybe you get a shot of him on TV, head to toe, talking to other people. He's small, you know. He's a little fellow. It doesn't show until you see him with some regular-sized people around. The same thing happens with movie stars, they look big in the movies but in real life they're short. How do you explain that, eh? How come so many short people do so well, sergeant?"

. Sergeant Brock ignored this and put his pipe away in a drawer and drew out a file. "That provincial who brought you down from Hornblende, he's on my curling team. He won't say anything about leprechauns in his report. I told him you had some shock, getting in the way when they were shooting up the Camaro. Problem's you're probably off the force as of now, and you can kiss the pension goodbye. I haven't heard from the chief. Here." He passed a paper across the desk.

Joe Kowalski read:

TO: Chief of Police Frank Williams
FROM: Commander L. Erskine Ridgeway, Chairman,
        Bradfarrow Police Commission
RE: Budget

Council has been in touch with me again about the
overall costs of running the force.
    Two categories of runaway expenditure are of
particular concern.

(1) Council feels that we are maintaining an
unnecessarily large body of probationers and constables
who seem to do nothing much on the various shifts
except sit in their cruisers and drink coffee.
(2) The pension plan is non-contributory, and was
never intended to be awarded automatically and in full
to everybody upon retirement.

As to (1), when I myself, Frank, wore the blue uniform
of a cadet on the streets of Bradfarrow, we always
understood that it was a case of produce or perish. Cops

who didn't produce got fired, Frank. The tight times are
back again, and now the city fathers would like to see
manpower reduced by 15% at the very least. It's a
question of cutting the fat away and toning up the
muscle.

In the matter of the pension plan, (2), the free ride
is over. What's needed here is close scrutiny of the
pensions awarded upon retirement. You have the
discretion to award a reduced pension, half-pension, or,
in the case of the free riders and the coffee-drinkers, no
pension. Let me see reports on your progress as soon as
you can, Frank. I want you to start compiling a list of
redundant personnel for submission to Council by the
Police Commission.

"I need the pension," Kowalski said in a practical tone without self-pity. "It's a question of the aunts. But that's the city for
you, isn't it, sergeant? A great place to live but the buck rules."

"I can keep you out of sight, so that nobody sees you riding
around in the cruiser drinking coffee. I'm putting you on the foot
patrol in Regency Gate. But don't get your hopes up." Sergeant
Brock wiped the back of his hand across his sweaty brow. "I wish
I could do something."

Kowalski handed the sergeant a Kleenex. Sergeant Brock
dried his forehead and looked at the tissue in his hand.

"You carry Kleenex."

"Yes."

"You always carry Kleenex. There's a thing right there, Joe,
a man who always carries Kleenex is showing forethought. It's
like string or a jack-knife, anticipation of contingencies. Those
are good qualities in a policeman."

"Lots of people who aren't policemen carry Kleenex,
sergeant."

"Yes, and they'd make good policemen, wouldn't they? I
don't know, though. I'm always finding reasons to think you're
a good policeman. I wonder why I do that."

"I don't know either, sergeant," Joe Kowalski said, worried
about his pension, buttoning down his empty holster.

Three

The Aunts

1

"It's spring singing in my veins," said Kowalski's Aunt Caroline some days later. She was eighty-three. "I feel as if I've been buried in a dungeon for six months, Joseph. But I don't know what I want. I enjoy going to church of course. Perhaps we should go to church more often than once a week. What do you think, Myrtle?"

"Once a week is enough."

Aunt Myrtle was seventy-five, and fond of reminding Aunt Caroline of the difference in their ages, not as an unrealistic claim of youthfulness but so that Aunt Caroline should be aware always that they were not journeying to the grave on an equal footing. Whatever time was left, Aunt Myrtle had, Aunt Myrtle felt, eight more years of it than Aunt Caroline. Aunt Caroline, though, was a sinewy, spare woman, leathery even, the active housekeeper and shopper of the pair. In winter she was the one who cleared the walks of snow every day, and shovelled the driveway too when Kowalski was not around to forbid it. In summer she cultivated a thriving flower garden at the front of the house and bushels of nourishing vegetables at the back. Aunt Myrtle was larger, stout and indolent. She spent much of her time dozing in her armchair. Kowalski thought Aunt Myrtle would be the first to go.

He had lived with them since he was a child, except while he was in Italy for the war and while he was married.

Joe Kowalski's second marriage hardly counted. In his forties and settling in his habits he met Angela, who was from Georgia and known to her friends as the Georgia Peach. He changed a tire for her on 62. Kowalski was captivated by the vividness the Georgia Peach brought from the big outside world. She was a traveller and a lover of the exotic. She needed roots at the time but they did not go down deeply enough for her in Bradfarrow, where the exotic was not encouraged anyway. The marriage lasted three weeks, a mistake by both of them but the kind of mistake anybody can make.

Kowalski was twenty-seven when the war ended and he arrived home from Italy to marry Heather, who was six years younger. They had been friends as children and loved each other. Heather was a planner, though. At the age of twenty-three she showed him a brochure of a community development down south and said: "That's the place I'd like to live in when we retire."

She planned to work at each one of her father's small chain of clothing stores so that she could take over the business when she was thirty-five. She wanted two or three children, depending on their sex: a boy and a girl, or two boys and a girl, or even three boys, but not three girls which in Heather's view would be a minefield of worry laid in their future.

This was before science produced the birth control pill and Kowalski would often tumble Heather into bed at unplanned times. It troubled Joe Kowalski to have his lifespan cut and laid out ahead with no room for surprises. The thought of a strange, unexpected future filled Heather with real panic. Also Kowalski was not able to co-ordinate his own progress in life with Heather's arrangements. He was still a second-class constable when he should have been a sergeant according to the plan.

After the divorce Joe Kowalski knew accurately what Heather would be doing at any period of her life. When he was depressed after the Georgia Peach mistake he called Heather at the clothing store office in Peterborough where she was supposed to be. They had an affectionate talk. She and her husband were content. She had only one child, though, a girl, having had trouble with the birth.

And right up to date, with Kowalski aged fifty-nine, he knew that Heather at fifty-three, if alive, was living down south in the warmer climate she had made plans for at twenty-three, with very little taming of the future left to do, just as his own life had hardly any room left for surprises.

Aunt Myrtle had been married too, with several children now middle-aged and living in far away parts, and perhaps it was the experience and duties of marriage that had slowed her down, compared to Aunt Caroline who was a maiden aunt. Aunt Myrtle, the stout and dozy, had a hearing problem. Aunt Caroline, the snow shoveller and gardener, could hear everything. In particular she could hear criticisms of herself, from unbelievable distances.

"Yes. I know I'll die in the winter. In the autumn my spirits sink right down to my toes. After Christmas I don't care whether I live or die. Now that winter's over I have time again. I'd like to do something."

"That's wonderful. I feel exactly the same way," said Aunt Myrtle. "I surely would like to do something new. My back isn't too bad these days. We're a nuisance to Joseph, of course, two cranky old women. Still I suppose he wouldn't mind taking us out just for one night."

Kowalski, having finished dinner and cleared dishes into the dishwasher, was reading the Bradfarrow *Times*, pleasantly relaxed in the cushions of his wicker chair, contoured to his body by long use, with his feet stretched out and shoes off. After the paper he wanted to enjoy a glass of ale or two and watch the police dramas on TV. Mellowed by ale, Kowalski would imagine himself in the role of lieutenant Kojak, say, *street-wise* utterances issuing from the side of his mouth like bullets, saying *cootchy-coo* to criminals and closing ruthless Greek lips on lollipop sticks. Then too sipping plastic cups of black machine coffee without wincing and treating the captain like an office-boy. Best of all, shouting for his assistants from behind his desk when an idea hit him: *Crocker! Sapperstein! Get in here!*

"Does he have *Kojak* tonight?"

"No, *Baretta*, I think, and *Honk*. There isn't much on TV so maybe he wouldn't mind."

"Oh jeez, Aunt Caroline," Kowalski said. "You know this is *Kojak* night. You do too, Aunt Myrtle, you know this is a good night. *Kojak, Baretta, Bronk*."

"I'll make tea," Aunt Myrtle said.

"Thank you, Myrtle," said Aunt Caroline. She said to Kowalski: "I don't understand why you're being so selfish. We've hardly left the house all winter. You've been out in the fresh air every day. Besides, you can watch all those programs later, on the re-runs," said Aunt Caroline, "after we're dead."

Kowalski kept his eyes stonily on his newspaper. He was thinking the name Kowalski would be a perfect title for a police drama. *Kowalski*. Set in a growing town like Bradfarrow, ringed by highways that linked the major cities. Chases on the highways, arrests. Sergeant friendly but the chief a son of a bitch. But Kowalski treated the chief like an office-boy and called him by his first name. Say for a gimmick Kowalski had a peculiar domestic situation, he was a Mormon married to two women, both grousing, nagging, demanding.

Aunt Myrtle with the tea tray crossed the long width of the polished wood floor from the kitchen, staggering now and then. The house was Bradfarrow aristocratic of the twenties, there having once been money in the family, white frame with large airy rooms lighted by french doors, and soaring windows. The furniture was mixed now, some of it from Aunt Myrtle's old place. It was all good of its time, the tables dark and weighty, the chairs and cushions covered with balding velvet or worn chintz. Some day one of his aunts would fall on the floor and break a hip, Kowalski worried on occasion. Throw rugs and mats and such were scattered around in plenty like traps for brittle bones.

Sliding his paper down, Kowalski suspiciously watched his Aunt Myrtle. She handed a tea-cup to Aunt Caroline, who added milk from the silver pourer and one sugar lump with the sugar tongs. Aunt Myrtle sipped from her own tea-cup without adding anything to it. Ice tinkled in the cup.

"All right," Kowalski said, reaching for his shoes. "I'd rather miss my programs, Aunt Myrtle, than sit around here watching you boozing it up. Where would you like to go?"

An hour later with his aunts Kowalski pushed his way through the bingo crowd at the Loyal Orange Lodge hall. He found a table for six with just one wispy man sitting at it.

"Okay if we sit here?"

"No. Nobody sits here except me. This is my lucky table. All reserved."

"We'll sit here," Kowalski said to his aunts. The man immediately stood up as if they were disease carriers. "You've spoilt it," he said angrily. "You've ruined my table. It'll take me weeks to find another."

The aunts were not anticipating an evening of bingo with pleasure.

"But these people are so pathetic," Aunt Caroline said, looking around her. "Poor lonely people. Don't they have anything better to do?"

Kowalski did not reply to this. "Chances are you'll like bingo," he told her, "when you get the hang of it."

"Do we have to play at the Orange Hall?" Aunt Myrtle asked. "Herbie would have a fit." Herbie had been her husband, a Catholic bigot. Kowalski explained the ecumenics and economics of bingo to his aunts, that it was a floating game, with Catholics and the Orange Lodge, Lions and Kinsmen and Kiwanis sharing the week so that each could have a full house of what was substantially the same crowd of bingo regulars. Get them involved right away, he thought, ease them into the gambling excitement and innocent fun.

The wispy man he had displaced stopped by Kowalski's table on the way back from the snack bar with a bag of potato chips. "I've put my hex on you so watch out for trouble," the man said. "Heart attack."

Most people nearby played twenty cards, the maximum allowed. Aunt Caroline would only take one. Aunt Myrtle was persuaded, with difficulty, to buy a separate card of her own. Kowalski did not play himself. He waited for the bingo fever to grip his aunts. They were, he thought, so ripe for bingo.

"I can't remember when I've played a duller game," Aunt Caroline said.

Aunt Myrtle nodded, blinking with sharp resentment at her card. "This is boring me to death."

"Cover 'em, use those chips!" yelled a woman two tables away at Aunt Caroline. "G sixty-six, honey, what's the matter, are you blind, eh?" The woman was playing twenty cards herself and apparently watching Kowalski's aunts' cards also in her idle time.

Aunt Caroline said austerely: "I wouldn't want anybody here as a friend, Joseph, even if I enjoyed this wretched game."

Kowalski began sketching the face of August Amundsen, the Swedish nurse killer, on a score card. A simple, vicious face, with a quiff of hair lapping the forehead on the right side, then straight hair too falling on both sides of his head, hiding his ears. Then a moustache, a much more ambitious moustache than for instance Hitler's, more like a Mexican bandit's.

"It's the excitement of the game, Aunt Caroline," Kowalski explained. "They're probably very polite people when they're not playing bingo."

Aunt Myrtle said: "What's the use of this? I'd rather be asleep."

It was thinking of Sergeant Brock that brought Amundsen to Kowalski's mind. If a Bradfarrow policeman captured Amundsen, Bradfarrow would become a renowned police town. Sergeant Brock could take a trip to Grabe Pass and swank around down there. What, you arrested who here? Twenty-one years ago, that long? Tell me something, have you done anything much lately? We were lucky enough to put August Amundsen in the birdcage where I come from. Yes, Bradfarrow.

Then something about the sketch of Amundsen seemed familiar to Kowalski. He began another sketch, this time without the moustache and with shorter hair. He gave Amundsen pointy ears.

"Bingo!"

"Home please, Joseph," said Aunt Myrtle.

"Now," said Aunt Caroline.

Kowalski's sketch of Amundsen looked a lot like Count Dracula. Or in other words, like Albert Sieracki of The Magic World toy store.

2

Chief Williams's office had been furnished according to the spirit of the old building's period as understood by his wife, Mavis. He had a high, carved desk. He had sentimental water-colours on his walls: young girls gathering wild flowers, swans with their reflections upside down beneath them crossing millponds, a litter of thoughtful puppies and a group of croquet scenes. However Chief Williams himself was not a sentimental man. He sat on a horsehair couch, with Constable Redmond Ryan sitting opposite him on a brocaded chair, one of a four-piece matched set. An antique oak chest acted as a table, and on this were Kowalski's personnel file, bank statements, and a number of police reports.

"Would he be stupid enough to deposit it in a bank account, though, sir?" said Ryan.

Redmond Ryan was a lean blond man of twenty-five with blue-eyed good looks that suggested a fearless airman of World War I on the German side. The clothes he favoured supported that idea — jackets cut long on the lapels with half-belts at the back, cravat-style neckerchiefs in summer and bulky white silk scarves in winter. He wore Italian boots of fine leather in all seasons. Being attractive, Ryan had grown accustomed to certain attentions in the society. His opinions were listened to with respect, in particular by people who did not know him well. Some girls more or less offered themselves to him from time to time. Children trusted him on sight and told him their secrets. He had been a dim student at school but had made average marks in most subjects because he looked good.

Chief Williams was fifty or so and in just as good physical condition as Ryan. He played tennis in summer and squash in winter and owned a small sailboat too. He had excellent political connections through his wife. His eyes were flat, not given much to enthusiastic expression, and his nose fleshy and thrusting, a satisfactory masculine nose in his own estimation. He thought of himself as an administrator and wore business suits.

"Kowalski would be deficient enough in inspiration to do

that, yes, Ryan," Chief Williams said. "He might not have thought of it, that could be one reason why he didn't do it. We haven't come up with any stupendous deposits, so where is it?"

"Well but I can't even, you know, imagine anybody taking that much money and putting it in a bank. Or just hiding the cash somewhere around the house. Twenties and fifties mostly, we're talking of two big suitcases full of banknotes he's got somewhere. I've been trying to look at this from a crooked officer's point of view," Ryan said carefully. "Trying to figure out how much money we're looking for, and I'd say we're looking for all of it. In Kowalski's position nobody's going to take a hand-out from Riordan and let him go. If I had Riordan in custody and I was the sort of man to take a bribe," said Ryan, shaking his head with distaste at this thought, "I'd make him cough up every penny. How could he argue? Okay, that provincial, he says he had Kowalski in sight all the way down from Hornblende. What if Kowalski paid him to say that? Kowalski could have buried the money in the bush anywhere between here and there."

"No," Chief Williams said. "No, Ryan, you aren't on track, you see you persist in crediting Kowalski with, oh practically with imagination. What we'd better do, you get to know Kowalski, infiltrate his confidence."

"Well, all right, sir."

"Try to come up with the sort of simple answer we need, something that Kowalski could think of. I have," said Chief Williams, "never been accused of naïvete, but I'm wondering now whether Kowalski has the money at all."

Ryan said with an alert attitude: "How's that, chief?"

"What I'm wondering is, did Kowalski get the money? With Kowalski one has to get down on one's hands and knees and see the thing from the point of view of a six-year-old. It's possible that Kowalski let Riordan go for some reason that had nothing to do with money."

"I'm sorry, sir, I don't understand that. When an officer arrests a villain there isn't any reason to let him go, unless the villain offers money and the officer is the kind of man to take it." Ryan could be seen to be bothered by the possibility of any complication of this arrangement. His airman hero's lips were pursed in thought. He clasped his hands together, elbows on his knees, watching the chief. "What else can happen?"

"Well you aren't taking the six-year-old perspective, are you, Ryan?" the chief asked. He probably has three or four girls, thought the chief irritably, whereas I have Mavis at home. "Say Riordan had a Lafleur hockey card. You can't get Lafleurs and you need one for every set."

"I see, sir." Ryan's eyes watching the chief became vague. "I didn't know that. A Lafleur, eh?"

"I have a young nephew. Search Kowalski's house after you make friends with him," Chief Williams said. "Do it intelligently. Don't get caught. We'll let him run free for now until we see what the search turns up."

"You can rely on me, sir. I'll be looking for money, right? Just the large sum of money?"

"Yes," the chief said. He thought: the genetic imperative doesn't seem to have any sense of responsibility. No particular moral direction either of course. Ryan will possibly take hockey cards as well as cash from now on. Chief Williams indicated a change of subject and mood by leaning back comfortably and smiling at Ryan, friendly and confident, sociably but as a social superior at the same time. "You've been in my house, Redmond, haven't you," he said. "That's a pretty pile of stone, that house, eh?"

"Very attractive, chief." However, Ryan did not respond with warmth to the chief's confidence. Indeed his blue eyes showed immediate caution.

"They don't build them any more, not for people like you and me, Redmond, anyway, not nowadays. Fourteen rooms, real old beams in the living room, broadaxe cut, flagstone floor in the kitchen. Six fireplaces, diamond-pane leaded windows in the sun room. You don't see conservatories any more. But you've been at our place, Redmond, don't let me go on enthusing. I wouldn't want to sound like the fellows who talk about their Pontiacs in bars. Mind you, I will say this in my own defence," said Chief Williams to Redmond Ryan with fine democratic amiability, "I don't brag about the Mercedes. My wife had the greatest diffi-culty acquiring that house—political difficulty, everything comes down to politics. The campaign to get on the university's board of governors, then the fight to revive the university's expropriation powers. The people who owned the house kicked up a terrible fuss, their family had always lived there in Cambridge Mews, and so on, an awful fracas. After a woman goes through that kind of agony she likes to share the joys of her treasure, Redmond."

"I understand. Mrs. Williams is giving another party. Sir, I had that duty last time."

"Just shut up, Ryan, would you? Kindly shut your mouth." The chief relaxed on the couch once more then, satisfied by Ryan's fear. "Well, yes, that's the position," he said and smiled at Ryan again man-to-man, almost as an equal, in recognition of the needs of all women, of which Mrs. Mavis Williams was one. "A spring thaw party for the political crowd, very boring people but what can one do. My wife isn't able to give a party without inviting her sister, Mrs. Letresky, that's one of the political realities. The question of Mrs. Letresky's daughter Helen then arises, you see, Redmond."

"I had Christmas, sir. Maybe somebody else could do this, spread the work-load around."

"Work-load, Ryan?"

"I only thought Mrs. Williams might be tired of my face, but you know best. Thanks for the invitation. I had Mrs. Garvey's daughter at Christmas, the statistician. Helen Letresky is the girl who wears the harlequin glasses, is she?"

"Helen is studious, yes. Your face is all we really need you for, well, just the general appearance, Ryan, we simply want to impress people, that's all. Make your arrangements with Helen, then, cater to her whims, except of course in the matter of sex. We have hopes of a suitable husband for her if she can stick to the new diet."

3

The off-duty room had lockers around the walls and some wooden chairs and tables, a coffee machine, a soft-drink machine and a heavily-layered noticeboard. Ryan found Sergeant Brock there changing into his street clothes. They were not friends,

Sergeant Brock and Constable Ryan. Ryan wanted Brock's job. Brock knew a few things about the Ryan beneath the showcase appearance, the booted airman's looks.

"Seen Joe Kowalski?"

"Joe's in my office looking at records. I'm putting you on evening shift for one week next month, the chief's party. Helen Letresky," the sergeant said, "was my daughter Sally's baby-sitter. We like Helen. She comes around to our house when she's home from university. I'd take it badly if she suffered any un-kindness."

"Yes well, that's one girl's safe with me, sergeant."

"He looks more like a policeman than anybody else on the force," one of the young probationers said when Ryan had gone. "Mr. Ideal Policeman. Doesn't he, sergeant, what do you say?"

Sergeant Brock tied his shoelaces and said nothing. Another man said after a silence: "Yes, we should have him mounted and stuffed, stand the shit in the hall."

At the door of Sergeant Brock's office, Ryan heard Kowalski talking to somebody inside. He listened.

"Don't make me laugh about your rights," Kowalski said loudly. "You don't have any more rights now except breathing rights. Also you just blew your chance for citizen of the year. That's the way, baby, pray for your soul, your body's going in the iron room. What am I," Kowalski asked, "a dodo, do I look like a dodo to you, is that how come we're not communicating? *Cootchy-coo, doll.*"

Kowalski shouted then: "Ryan, get in here!"

Ryan hit the door with his shoulder, drawing his revolver in the same athletic lunge, and went down on one knee inside. Kowalski, sitting behind Sergeant Brock's desk alone, looked at Ryan in surprise. Kowalski had a pencil in his mouth and was rolling it between his lips. "Jeez, I'm sorry, Redmond," Kowalski said, having removed the pencil. "I didn't know you were really out there."

Ryan put away his gun, watching Kowalski with uncom-prehending curiosity.

"Kojak, hey do you watch him on TV, the bald detective? I was trying it out, the way he does it."

Ryan dusted the knees of his trousers.

"I watch him all the time," Kowalski said. Ryan waited.

"Come and take a look at these," Kowalski said, to break the ice. He had several of his sketches of August Amundsen spread out on Sergeant Brock's desk, with the alterations that made them look like Albert Sieracki.

Ryan took his eyes reluctantly away from Kowalski's face — he didn't understand what had been happening — to look at the sketches. Ryan could not understand either why Kowalski was a policeman or how he had managed to be a policeman for thirty-seven years. "Is he on TV now too, Dracula? Like you have these drawings for when you finish playing Kojak, you're going to *colour* them, is that the idea?"

"It's Albert Sieracki, the man who owns The Magic World toy store. See how he looks like August Amundsen."

"Well anybody would, wouldn't they, the way you're doing it." Ryan compared the Stockholm police photo of Amundsen and Kowalski's sketches of Albert Sieracki. "You're just taking a blank face and drawing on it. Al Sieracki's been operating a store on Harbour for years, Amundsen only started killing nurses in January. I see Al a lot now, since you went on foot patrol. He's a good client, he's okay, Al. Always prosecutes shoplifters. I like him. I do good business with him. We see eye to eye."

Kowalski replaced Sergeant Brock's records in the filing cabinet. "Maybe you're right," he said. "I'll check some more. How about dropping me out to Regency Gate if you're not busy, Redmond?"

"Sure will, no trouble," Ryan said cordially. Get to know the big Polack. "Yes, I heard they stuck you on patrol in the Gate. Tough luck. Could be a lot worse, though, could be the north end, pool halls, arcades, all kinds of ethnic shit. Do you know how much a house costs in Regency Gate, eh? Two hundred thousand is the cheapest. I bet Chief Williams's house costs more like five. Where," Ryan asked, putting a disingenuously friendly arm on Kowalski's broad shoulder as they walked down the corridor together, "would ordinary cops like you and me, Joe, ever in our lifetimes get a chance at big money like that? We never ever see any big money, do we, Joe, like really big money?" Redmond Ryan asked, those sky-blue eyes watching the big Polack's face, scouring the slab face for any cloud of guilt or tic of knowledge.

Four

The Voice of the Leprechaun

1

Regency Gate began at Teagarden Street. The lawns on that proud and winding street were green as golf greens, the maple and oak trees a hundred years old, walls and wrought-iron gateways enclosing them. Eastward, Talleyrand Avenue, the Hunt Road, Belleville Crescent and numerous other crescents and culs-de-sac breathed the same discreet magnificence. Chief Williams's house stood on the protected sweep called Cambridge Mews. Northward the wealth was still unarguable, but taste fell away somewhat — some fake Tudor here, a flashy Cadillac in the garage there. Huddled around the Regency Gate district were other expensive but inferior apartment buildings and houses, crowding as near as the moats of privilege would allow in order to participate in the address.

It was a pleasant shift for Kowalski. How did you do, Sergeant Brock asked Kowalski after his first day on the new duty. Well, I strolled down Teagarden Street —. You *patrolled* Teagarden, Sergeant Brock interrupted, upset. So for Kowalski it was a stroll, an agreeable walk through the abodes and gardens of the wealthy, but he had to call it a patrol in his report.

A friend and a good man, Sergeant Brock, and he will certainly be glad he kept his trust in me when I bring Amundsen in, Kowalski told himself, making his way along Trafalgar at patrol pace, hands clasped behind his back. Gardeners were burning winter's leaves or forking the flower beds, and nannies walked children. A maid in uniform polished the brasswork on a door.

Kowalski was greeted with friendship by every child he met and responded as a friend too, though the children saw a policeman. Out north the children threw things at policemen and ran, and they twisted the antennas off the cruisers and knifed the tires when they got a chance. Different children, different lessons.

Around a curve in the pavement Kowalski came upon a demolition job on Trafalgar. One side of the house was already gone. The wrecker's vehicles and debris, wheelbarrows, a bulldozer and a crane were parked on the former lawn. Up on the scaffolding the hard-hats plied wrecking bars and drills and saws, a noisily destructive crew. The house was, had been, an ivied brick. A Georgian door was still intact, with a pretty stained glass transom-window above it.

PALMIERI WRECKING a sign fixed on the scaffolding read. This pleased Kowalski, Alex Palmieri getting what looked like a good wrecking contract in Regency Gate. Somehow the Italian businessmen never seemed to win contracts outside their own territory in Bradfarrow. Not because of any conspiracy against Italians certainly, it was simply that the people of influence in the city were Anglo-Saxons themselves, and inclined to value Anglo-Saxon virtues and other Anglo-Saxons. With these values went a reluctance to entrust important work to people who might sit around on the job drinking *vino* and singing opera and whistling at passing girls.

Alex Palmieri, a bear-like man of thirty, climbed out of a loader cab and came across, flashing a smile at Kowalski. Alex's tartan shirt was open to the navel and his yellow hard-hat was perched on top of a huge mass of black hair. His face and hairy chest ran with sweat. "Eh, Joe," he said. "Hold up there a minute. See what we got going?"

"Good work, Alex," Kowalski said. "When did you start here?"

"Eight o'clock this morning." Alex, standing beside Kowalski, plucked a cigarette from a sweat-soaked package and lit it, surveying the disappearing house with pride. "Bastard'll be all gone tomorrow. Sure, good work, it's work you wouldn't believe. That's a perfect house. All inside, perfect. Old, but perfect. Like, the stairways, antique. Floors the same, two-inch black cherry, Joe. Would you believe that? No veneer inside there. You try to get some of that black cherry, they'll sell it to you by the pound. But you can't get it. See that door? That'll go for five hundred bucks. The glass above the door, another thousand. Come on inside, let me show you."

"Thanks but I'm on duty. How do you happen to be wrecking a good house?"

"Business," Alex said, shrugging. He waved his arm along Trafalgar, vaguely indicating a long stretch of the street. "We're wrecking all that, some more too maybe, for Equity Mortgage and Trust. Families along there don't even know we're coming. Complaints, you know? These rich people, they don't understand not having some place to live. I'm going to make a fortune, Joe. Tell you what to do, come and work for me, Alex Palmieri. I'll give you a job in the office. All you got to do is pretend to be Italian. Here." Alex as if by magic produced a bottle without a label and pulled the cork with his teeth. "Have some *vino*."

Kowalski readily took a swig of the wine, which was mellow. "Is there a highway coming through here?"

"No. Here is going to be a park. With a zoo, I think, some animals, my brother Dominic has the contract from Equity Mortgage and Trust for landscaping, building work. A pond right there," Alex said, wiping his mouth and passing Kowalski the bottle again, pointing at an unsuspecting stucco residence with a swimming pool and a sparkling emerald tennis court at the rear. "For the rest, I don't know. A nice park here, though, Joe. Lots of these rich people," said Alex, who was not in awe of the splendour he was levelling, "they have development investments all over, in places they don't live themselves. One day you got a park for the kids, you know, Joe, and the old people. This is especially in Little Italy. Next day you have a couple apartment buildings, and no more park."

"Yes, that happens. That's a shame."

"Ha, except now we're doing the bastard the other way around, you see. We're pulling the buildings down, putting *in* a park."

The men lining the scaffolding suddenly stopped work, looking down over their shoulders at the sidewalk where a long-legged nursemaid with red hair to her waist was walking past, or more accurately swaying past, pushing a stroller. Palmieri's men broke into a chorus of admiring whistles. The pretty girl looked up and blew the men a kiss, continuing on her way with a pleased smile. Some of the men drew workmates into their arms exultantly, some held their hearts and bayed at the sky, some bent over from the hips as if to ease a tenderness in the groin. Alex's whistle was the most accomplished, a blast with three modulations around a thumb and forefinger. He hit his forehead with the heel of his hand, saying: "Let me die now, God, while I'm a happy man." He took a long swallow of wine and so did Kowalski, celebrating joy.

The wreckers went back to work jubilantly, as if renewed by the thought of fair limbs and by the gift of the smile. Alex climbed into his loader singing the aria *La donn'è mobile*, and Kowalski continued his patrol. A car turned into Cambridge Mews ahead of him and stopped. It was Chief Williams's Mercedes sedan with Mrs. Mavis Williams at the wheel. Mrs. Williams rolled down the window and called to Kowalski: "Oh, officer, would you come here a moment, please?"

Kowalski had met Mrs. Williams three or four times at police social functions but he had not talked to her. She was a handsome woman of large build, and certainly in her earlier days she must have had a showgirl's figure. Now her body was somewhat overnourished and her face had taken on commanding lines. Her snow-white hair was set in tiny clusters of curls.

"Yes, ma'am?"

"Good, good, this is lucky. Billy isn't able to come today, and I planned to start him on the outside work. There's the deck furniture to be brought from the sun room, and the sun-room furniture must come up from the basement. The parasol table for the deck and the sun-room chaise longue are the only heavy pieces. You'll have to take those apart because I don't want the walls scratched. If you would just clean the gardening tools in the shed, you'll find rags there and whatever Billy uses, that will be enough—I should ask you to rake the back lawn too, it's a dreadful mess, but I expect your shift finishes at four. This is perfect. How lucky. If you would just come with me up to the house, please."

As she spoke, Mrs. Williams's eyes moved from Kowalski's face to one side of him and then the other, as if she were talking to three men. She had a loud voice too, being a politician. Kowalski did not particularly want to do the chores but neither did he have any strong objections to an hour's work, and anyway there was no escape. I just walked into this, Joe Kowalski told himself. From now on I go by Cambridge Mews carefully on the Regency Gate patrol.

But as he walked round the rear of the Mercedes to reach the passenger seat Mrs. Williams drove off up the driveway. It was a long driveway, a foot-slog. Come with me had been her way of saying follow me. Probably she doesn't want Kowalski germs on the upholstery, Kowalski thought. He then thought: I feel small now. I wish people like Mrs. Williams wouldn't do that. What's the point of treating somebody like a dog?

When Kowalski did not follow, Mrs Williams's car slowed and stopped. She reversed furiously and when she came abreast of Kowalski again she said: "Why are you standing there? Don't stand there like a fool, I want you up at the house." An understanding occurred to her. "Don't you know who I am?"

"What you're trying to do here, Mrs. Williams, is use a policeman for private work. That's the same as stealing."

Her face became blank for a moment. Now Kowalski indeed met Mrs. Williams's eyes, and it was an angry scrutiny. "Oh but you poor shit, then you must complain to the police," she said. "If that doesn't work, tell your story to the Police Commission. Write to me if you like. I'm a commissioner. Mr. Kowlski," said Mrs. Williams, although she had not seemed to know his name before, "this was a good town, Bradfarrow, before you and your kind started moving in, with your empty pockets and your stupidity and your . . . *restaurants*. You're going to regret this day before I'm finished with you," Mrs. Williams said.

Jeez, I'm fifty-nine years old, Joe Kowalski said to himself. I was a child and wanted to be a policeman. I wanted to be a good guy. I should be down on Harbour Street arresting August Amundsen, murderer, not standing around in Regency Gate listening to this woman.

"I'm on patrol here to keep people honest, lots of money in this district," Joe Kowalski said to Mrs. Williams quite sharply. "I'm not particularly on anybody's side, you see, a villain is a villain here or anywhere." It could be that he was still brave from Alex's mellow wine. "This time it's a warning, but I don't want to hear you tried this on any other policeman."

He skirted the Mercedes and continued his patrol, with his hands clasped behind his back. Strong words of abuse followed him from the woman in the car, strange words for a lady who was active in the councils of charities and churches. Kowalski felt good, though, all the way down to his toes.

2

The light was failing and the city shadows were violet by the time Kowalski got from Regency Gate down to Harbour Street by bus. The Magic World and its proprietor must have had a good day of business. Albert Sieracki was singing "April Showers" as he fixed the shutter grill in place outside the store.

". . . so keep on looking for the bluebird. And listening for his song . . ."

When he saw Kowalski, Sieracki stopped singing and sighed heavily. He jingled a ring of keys in his hand and gave his attention to Kowalski impatiently.

That's Amundsen all right, Kowalski thought.

"May I help you, officer?"

"Just finish locking the store, sir."

"Yes, but then I must count cash and make up the bank. Come inside, come inside. We're going to draw a crowd standing out in the street like this, it's bad for business."

Some idle people began to dally in fact. A group of children stopped and gazed at the policeman and the toy store man.

"Forget about business, that won't worry you from now on." Kowalski was angered by Amundsen's contempt for the law.

Catch an old man pilfering a toy truck and call the police, indeed make a habit of calling the police, with the blood of young girls on his hands, six nurses. He doesn't respect the intelligence of policemen, Kowalski thought angrily. "What you've got to worry about," he said to the toy store man, "is that you're a killer and your time is up. Now lock the store and come with me."

An audience of curious passers-by was now standing on both sides of Harbour. Autos slowed. Kowalski took out his handcuffs and the watchers exhaled a breath of interest and waited for more.

Sieracki in some confusion locked the door grill.

"This is impossible, what you're doing. You're arresting me? You have handcuffs, why do you need handcuffs? Look at all these people. They think I've done something against the law. This is a big mistake, Mr. Kowalski."

"I don't think so," Kowalski said, still with a good tingle in his toes. "What I think is, I'm beginning to do things right for a change. You're going in the birdcage, Amundsen."

3

Within the reference room of the Bradfarrow Public Library, blue denim jeans were slumped and perched on the chairs, or rode them like horses. Young upper bodies were asprawl over the tables in postures that expressed the endurance of severe pain. Sounds of books being slammed on the tables — crashing down with the exaggerated force of grievance — echoed from the shelves, and gasping yawns of boredom rose to the tiled ceiling. Examinations were imminent and the students were at work.

Sergeant Brock, in civilian clothes, sat at a table in a corner. He felt self-conscious as the only adult in the reference room and also because of the nature of his business. It was four o'clock. About this same time Joe Kowalski was making his way from Regency Gate to Harbour Street to arrest Albert Sieracki.

"Leprechauns," said Abe West, the librarian. He was a man of clerical demeanour with grey wings of hair and a trim salt-and-pepper goatee beard. West placed a stack of books on the table. They were ancient volumes, some with cracked bindings and missing spines. "Not many scholars are interested in leprechauns and their like nowadays. They make a fascinating study, leprechauns, alhodes, clabbernappers, bogles, gringes, sprets, nacks, dobbys, fetches, boggy-bos, lianhanshees and dogles. Marmos, clatcars and nick-nevins. Time was when every farmer knew them. Live in an apartment building, though, and you can go through a whole life without giving them a thought, cradle to the grave. Now the farmers are disappearing too."

Sergeant Brock noted that most of the books brought to him by the librarian were not in English. "Well look, Abe, it's like this," he said. "I don't exactly want to *study* leprechauns. I'll tell you what's on my mind, a friend I have got himself into a whole bunch of trouble last week, I can't say who or how or what kind of trouble, but there was, well, a leprechaun connection. A leprechaun technicality, you might say, in his version of events. I'm seeking technical advice. No fooling, this is a technical enquiry. I thought if I knew something about leprechauns I might be able to come up with some kind of a technical defence. What's the, you know, Abe, story on these Dogan elves, leprechauns?"

"Well the little fellows have devolved from literary reality to legend, and from legend to a sort of inaccurate logo," said West, tenderly unstacking his books. "Like harps and shamrocks. The reality is all in these books, or most of it. It's just as valid as scientific reality, in my opinion. Indeed some of our very respectable sciences have only literature to support them. I don't suppose, though, that you can read Rus or Middle Irish? Norse?"

"You're right," Sergeant Brock said.

"You would have to learn the Irish at least, I'm afraid. There aren't translations of these. They wouldn't be great sellers."

"Yes, well, you see," Sergeant Brock said as if truly regretful of not being able to follow the librarian's advice, "I'd love to study Irish, and get into leprechauns and the rest of them, but I'm up against the wall on this problem I have. Can you give me a quick run-down, Abe?"

Abe West said: "Well, all right, but that's how inaccuracies creep in, when you start abridging and simplifying. The word leprechaun comes from the Irish *deamhain an leath-brogain*, lahbro-gawn, and means the One-Shoemaker elf. The leprechaun was always seen working on one shoe. From the leprechaun's point of view it was a sensible way of working outdoors on dangerous ground — he needed to be able to escape quickly if a human chanced by, and he wouldn't have time to gather lots of shoes. When humans did get close to leprechauns it was because the leprechaun's working-place was betrayed by the sound of his hammer." West opened a book that looked to be in better shape than the others. "This is a poem of William Allingham's, about eighty or ninety years old, collected by W.B. Yeats, an Irishman."

> Lay your ear close to the hill.
> Do you not catch the tiny clamour,
> Busy click of an elfin hammer,
> Voice of the Leprechaun singing shrill
> As he merrily plies his trade?
> He's a span
> And a quarter in height.
> Get him in sight, hold him tight,
> And you're a made
> Man!
>
> Nine and ninety treasure-crocks
> This keen miser-fairy hath,
> Hid in mountains, woods, and rocks,
> Ruin and round-tower, cave and rath,
> And where cormorants build;
> From times of old
> Guarded by him;
> Each of them filled
> Full to the brim
> With gold!

"The word *merrily* is wrong, of course," said Abe West, "and clearly it's part of the modern reduction of the leprechaun to a jolly little man, but look at the previous line, *Voice of the Leprechaun singing shrill*, that's a better picture. The leprechaun was an alien being, after all, alien to humans, and not a merry friend."

"These are facts, are they?" Sergeant Brock said politely.

"The leprechaun isn't necessarily good, that's a fact. Saying leprechauns are good would be like saying men are good. A span and a quarter gives you something like ten inches, up from earlier accounts which say six inches and, going back farther, four inches. That's a curious fact, the leprechauns growing larger. The more recent the literature, the larger the leprechauns are. Leprechauns were artisans in the fairy lore, and of course they were what we would now call the tribal treasurers. It isn't a fact to say that the gold belonged to them, or that they grew so rich just from mending shoes . . . they were makers of shoes . . . or that they were misers, as Allingham has it. That's an easy assumption, that custodians of gold are misers. In some fairy tales there are other mistakes, like drawings of leprechauns working on human shoes: a little man sitting at a human-sized last, with a human shoe on it. How could that be? Sheer fantasy," West said, smiling at the things people will believe. "But we have to ask ourselves why the fairies needed the gold, since that has human value but no fairy value."

"To buy leather?" Sergeant Brock suggested with a straight face. He thought: Good God, Abe is crazier than Kowalski. "The leprechaun would need leather to make shoes, right, Abe?"

"No, he tanned his own leather, fairy leather. That was why he often chose to work in the open air. If you've ever been in a tannery you'll understand why. The stink is terrible. According to this book," West said, reverently opening a particularly decrepit and mouldy volume, "O'Kavanagh's *Na Daoine Sidhe*, or *The Fairy People*, the One-Shoemaker was the only member of the fairy tribe allowed to have a material body. So the accounts of him as a hermit fairy were wrong. He was simply the visible fairy. That makes sense too. He had to be connected to a society. Where else would he find customers for his merchandise?"

"Good thinking, Abe. You make fairy shoes, you need fairy customers, stands to reason." Sergeant Brock was beginning to recognize practical answers to these fairy questions. "Now the One-Shoemaker was allowed to have a material body, and to be the guardian of the gold. Why would you say that was? Sounds to me like the fairies traded with humans."

"That's my belief too," Abe West said. "I mean it's the only answer. But there isn't any proof. Why would they do that anyway?"

"All right, say you're a fairy," Sergeant Brock said—without self-consciousness now, massaging his forehead while he considered possibilities, based on his policeman's experience. "You're a fairy in Ireland in the old days, minding your own business, fairy wife and kids, you're doing okay. But you have the problem that these *giants* are in and out of the neighbourhood all the time. They're digging up your house to plant crops. They're starting floods and fires. *They're stepping on your kids.* They're too big to fight, so what you do is, you study them, see what makes them tick. What makes them tick is mostly gold. That gives you a handle on the problem. Okay so far?" He shot a look of shrewdness at Abe West, to check that these human deductions could be validly applied to elfland.

"That's fair enough," West said. "The fairies lived in fairy forts, or raths. That's *raw*, a circular vallium, enclosing a garth, called a *lios*. Liss. They were often disturbed by humans, these fairy dwellings. You're right so far."

"Take it a step farther then."

"Well in the scholarly understanding —"

"Never mind about scholarly," Sergeant Brock said. "Or, sorry, sure by all means give me the scholarly, but the situation we're talking about now has to do with money and violence. You get a standard pattern there. Correct me if I'm wrong on the scholarship, Abe, I mean what do I know about elves and leprechauns. I'm a cop. All right, say you have some way of getting gold, some fairy know-how, and you can give the One-Shoemaker a body. What you do is this, you make the leprechaun the pay-off man, he's the cashier. So some particular giants get on the payroll, people who can see to it that the fairies are left in peace. As a fairy that gives you a temporary solution to your problem. Wait, though, you'd also need enforcers in that situation, to make sure nobody takes the money and leaves town. Also for the welshers, who'd take the money and wouldn't deliver the protection."

"But there were, of course there were," West said. "Leaving town wouldn't be wise. The phantoms of travel are well documented. The *bean-sidhe*, banshee, she covered the roads and wild country. The Dallahan was a headless phantom — it stood at crossroads on dark nights and counted coaches as they went by.

Whenever the Dallahan stopped a coach, that coach was never seen again. The Black Dog haunted ships at harbour, and sometimes went to sea with one, and any ship the black Dog went to sea with . . ."

". . . was never seen again. It didn't," said Sergeant Brock as if admiringly, "make any kind of sense at all to double-cross those little bastards, did it?"

"The Puca too, of course, for the welshers. The Puca had no form usually, but you knew when it was close because fear came into your mind. It lived in the world of nightmares, the Puca. You were dragged into that world by it if you earned the Puca's displeasure. You were condemned to live your worst nightmare forever."

"Very nice, a very charming fellow, that Puca," Sergeant Brock said, nodding as he thought the matter through. "Their size was always one of their problems, I guess. A leprechaun couldn't pretend to be human. He couldn't travel, either, could he. He didn't have some magic way of getting from place to place. The leprechaun," the sergeant said, "couldn't get out of Ireland, could he?"

"Well they stayed in their own regions according to all the records. The Puca sometimes took the form of an eagle, though. Sure, if the fairies wanted to travel they could do it that way, ride on the Puca's back. Don't ask me how many fairies could ride an eagle, or how far the eagle could take them. There's one report here, in Thomas Keightley's *The Fairy Mythology*, of an elf in England in Elizabethan times, called a *lubberkin*. That's close, right? Leprechaun, lubberkin. The lubberkin was like a brownie."

"Let's not get into brownies."

"Oh? They're a rewarding read, brownies. I have good up-to-date information on clurichans, and on the *fear dearg*, the Red Man, and the Hungry Man, the *fear gorta*. Ever hear of the Water Horse, or the Lake Dragon? We don't close until eight o'clock, now we're on the summer schedule."

"No thank you," Sergeant Brock said to the librarian. "It was just the leprechauns." He got to his feet and laid an enjoining hand on Abe West's shoulder. "Do something for me. Don't ever tell anybody we had this conversation, this leprechaun talk. I have a reputation as a smart cop that took me fifteen years to build in this city. Word gets around that I'm some kind of an elf-fancier and down the drain it goes."

One of the students, a lad of sixteen wearing a moustache of baby hair, crashed his book closed and said with stricken eyes to a sympathetic girl sitting opposite him: "This is garbage! It doesn't make sense, it's stupid, Leonora, it isn't *meaningful*, all it is," said the hounded student, flinging the book away from him, "is pure crap, C-R-A-P-P, and there's no way that any of it is going to help me break into the big time heavy metal."

Five

The Watergate Dimension

1

Aunt Myrtle was asleep in her armchair, mouth agape and her sewing on her lap. She would stay that way for the evening if nobody disturbed her. Kowalski tiptoed to the TV and tuned down the roar of surf from *Hawaii Five-O*. He poured himself a cooling ale. Aunt Caroline, who had been planting Dutch onion sets in the back, came in just then stripping off her gloves.

"Oh but it's a glorious evening for little green things," she said. "I'll just have a wash and tidy my room. Such a clutter in there. Then we'll all go somewhere, Joseph. Think of somewhere we can go." Aunt Caroline toddled across to Aunt Myrtle and shook her awake. "Wake up, Myrtle. Sleep is death and we'll have enough rest when we're dead. Right now we're alive, and I'm restless."

"I told you before, Aunt Caroline," Kowalski said. "There's nowhere to go. There isn't anything to do. Very well, you two and me, we can share the TV shows, and that's my best offer. Or how about this, I'll see what I can do about getting another TV set for my den and you can watch this one here. I'll see what I can do tomorrow. You didn't like bingo and you didn't like the movie."

Awakened, Aunt Myrtle focussed her sleepy eyes on Kowalski.

"You're despicable, Joseph," Aunt Myrtle said.

Aunt Caroline looked at Kowalski also, and coldly.

"I didn't like the movie because I had seen it before. I saw it in the twenties. I saw it in the thirties too, when they added sound and Cary Grant. The only difference in this new one was that instead of kissing at the end of a reel they went to bed together. If you think that man with the hair is more attractive than Cary Grant, Joseph, then you have a very poor understanding of women, very poor. Anyway," asked Aunt Caroline, quite decidedly hostile, "how can a wedding be a happy ending for them when they've already spent most of the movie in bed? That was just silly. When she put the wedding gown on it was practically the first time she put on any clothes at all."

"Well it was a regular movie," Kowalski said. "I picked out a sentimental love story. The other shows on in town right now are sex movies." He said to Aunt Myrtle: "You've been having a nightmare, Aunt Myrtle. Go back to sleep. We're staying in tonight."

"No, we're going out, please, Joseph, just as soon as I tidy my room," Aunt Caroline said. "I can't imagine how it got in such a mess. While I'm doing that, try to think of something interesting for us to do."

"Joseph has thought of something for us to do," said Aunt Myrtle. "Talking of lust and so on, he has a surprise for us, although it's in bad taste if you ask me. I'm far too old, Caroline, myself, even if I'm eight years younger than you are."

"Oh do shush about that eight years. I'll live to cry at your funeral and you know it."

". . . probably got the idea from one of those movies. I never said, Joseph, that I was restless for beaus and companionship," Aunt Myrtle said crossly. "I merely agreed with Caroline that we needed some new occupation or hobby. What would Herbie say? And Caroline's had no experience of men, she's a spinster. Now it's too late for her. Now she has her arthritis. It's a despicable idea."

"I can bear my arthritis very well thank you, Myrtle. At any rate there's no fear it will carry me off, like your heart will one of these days if you don't get some exercise. Or your liver with your sousing. Herbie was more of a breadwinner than a man. I mean he wasn't in the least interesting, was he. Having Herbie for a husband for thirty years isn't having experience of men. Not in the least the same, Myrtle, what you had was experience of *Herbie*, that was all."

"But I was married. A man chose me, to be his for life. I wasn't left on the shelf to become an old maid. I'm saying that I've never known rejection. That is why I'm contented now in body and soul, Caroline, you see. I feel no need to rush around digging and vacuuming, because my psychology doesn't call for fuss. I have the memory of a husband to sustain me."

". . . don't know how many times I must remind you that leading poor Herbie to the altar did not amount to anything as fancy as being *chosen*. There were always Herbies around as you know very well. Herbies were always possible, for those who were willing to settle for a Herbie."

"Break," Kowalski said. "All right, there's something you have to tell us, Aunt Myrtle. What's this about despicable?"

"As if you didn't know."

"Well?"

"I'll show you. But you understand very well what I'm talking about."

Both aunts' bedrooms were on the ground floor because of the difficulty of the steep old mahogany staircase. Aunt Myrtle led the way past her room to Aunt Caroline's and pointed at the cedar linen chest in the corner. Lace-edged pillow cases, sheets and tablecloths and other linens had been piled on Aunt Caroline's bed. "There," said Aunt Myrtle.

"Yes, somebody's taken the linen out of the chest," Aunt Caroline said. "I don't mind either of you coming in here if you need anything, but you should tidy up afterward."

Kowalski lifted the lid of the cedar chest and stared down at Redmond Ryan who was crouched in there with his knees drawn up under his chin, a sweaty and uncomfortable-looking police constable in uniform.

"Redmond, eh," Kowalski said. "Come out."

2

"God damn old pussycats," Redmond Ryan said. "Who needs them. What use are old women like those, for God's sake? When women are too old to be mothers they should become grand-mothers. After they finish that we should get rid of them. Same goes for old men."

The aunts were not present to hear this young opinion. Kowalski and Ryan were in Kowalski's den and workroom, a place of retreat in the basement which had a bench and tools and several retired easy chairs. Kowalski kept his ale in a beat-up refrigerator down here.

"They're my aunts," Kowalski said.

"That's all right for you," Ryan said. He was sitting on the arm of a broken sofa, clenching his bottle of ale. "You have them as aunts but what good are they to anybody else? This is gospel truth, Joe, I wanted to talk to you. I saw the old lady was out planting so I thought I wouldn't bother her, I'd just step in the back door and wait for you. That's the whole story. They look under their beds every night, I suppose, check on the bogeymen."

"How did you happen to be in Aunt Caroline's linen chest, Red?"

"Well is that important, for God's sake? I suppose I lost my head when I noticed, God, that there was *another* old lady. God, *two*. They scream their heads off, don't they, old women, I didn't want to start that."

Kowalski was troubled about finding Ryan in his Aunt Caroline's linen chest. There had been a breach of an important rule. He stood leaning against the workbench, drinking from his bottle. Had he found a stranger in the linen chest Kowalski would of course have arrested him. Ryan had been a stranger in Kowalski's life until recent days.

"What was it you wanted to talk to me about?"

"Oh talk, a beer, pass the time. God, two old ladies. What a way to live."

"Aunt Myrtle sometimes does her snoozing with one eye open," Kowalski explained. "When you know her well you can tell when she's doing that, her eyes flutter. It's her way of keeping a watch on Aunt Caroline and me. She likes to keep an eye on how we act when we think she's asleep. Problem's now and then Aunt Myrtle does fall asleep while she's doing it. So Aunt Caroline and I get accused of stuff that happens in Aunt Myrtle's dreams. This time she says she saw you dodging in the back door. She says you sneaked in, Red, and you searched Aunt Caroline's room, the drawers, closets, under the bed, and then you searched the linen chest. You dumped all the linen on the bed."

"That's a lie," Ryan said. "There's no reason for it, why should I search your aunt's bedroom?"

"Then she says you took all your clothes off and put on pyjamas."

"*What!*"

". . . and you said: 'I'm not in love with these ladies but this is something I must do for Joseph Kowalski.' After that you heard Aunt Caroline coming and you hid in the linen chest in your pyjamas."

"Wait a minute," Ryan said angrily. "Now look, hold up a God damn minute, Kowalski, that aunt of yours fell asleep and dreamed that story. She's an ancient old lady, who's going to believe her?"

"You were *in* the box, Red. You were in there, scrunched in there hiding, there's no question on that account."

"Well am I wearing pyjamas too, does this uniform look like pyjamas?"

"See we went to a movie the other day, and a man did that, because of love. He was a good-looking fellow like yourself. I don't need to go into all the story, but he hid himself in a woman's bedroom. He was doing a favour for another girl, the one he really loved. He looked at himself in a mirror and he said, This is something I have to do for Veronica, God help me. Well he didn't put on pyjamas either, he was naked as a jay as a matter of fact, but Aunt Myrtle is old-fashioned. Anyway it was the same idea, and the same words more or less. I'd go along with saying Aunt Myrtle dreamt the whole thing. . ."

"Well, obviously."

". . . except for finding you in the box, Red."

But there had been no search done in the movie, and so there was no particular reason why Aunt Myrtle should have dreamt that Ryan searched Aunt Caroline's room. She could have, however, in near-sleep, seen Ryan searching the room and hiding in the chest. Kowalski understood then what had happened. It clicked into place in his mind like an understanding of a twist of the plot in *Kojak*. Had he been smart, admittedly, he would have seen the thing earlier.

Kowalski said: "This doesn't look too good for you, Red, talking honestly here. I don't have any friends who feel free to come in the house and wait for me, never mind about hiding in my aunt's bedroom. I don't know," Joe Kowalski said, as if advancing a far-fetched idea, "what could've been going on just now, unless you were conducting a police search, one of the chief's unofficial jobs, bending the rules to wrap it up fast. Say you thought Riordan paid me off and you figured you might take a look around my house here, see if you could come up with a large amount of cash, that could be an explanation. Otherwise this looks awful, Red."

"I can look after myself," Ryan said.

"What worries me is this covert stuff," Kowalski said. "If anybody thinks I took money from Riordan I should be suspended and investigated. I should be hauled up before the Police Commission if they can make out a case. So the thing to do now is, we'll call in and have some guys down here to turn the house over. Any other way, I don't have any guarantee you won't be back, scaring my aunts. Jeez," Kowalski said, "we might find you in the chandelier next time, eh Red?"

"But nobody is accusing you of anything. Word of honour," Ryan said, with a sinking feeling that the big dummy was outsmarting him. "Those old ladies you're keeping here, that could give them hysterics too, cops trampling around their house and groping in their private possessions."

"Well, don't trouble yourself about that, eh," Kowalski said. "They're seeking a new experience, now it's spring. Watching a police search, that's new, no reason why they shouldn't enjoy themselves. Before this came up what I had in mind was to take them to the wrestling match at the Armories."

3

The six policemen who searched Joe Kowalski's house did a professional job but of course they found no dollar loot. They all knew Joe Kowalski. Two of them knew Redmond Ryan. At first they worked silently, hiding embarrassment.

As soon as they realized they would find nothing they relaxed, and accepted coffee from Aunt Caroline, and made conversation, wondering aloud in Ryan's hearing for instance what kind of asshole had come up with the idea that bribe money might be turned up in Joe Kowalski's place.

The aunts took advantage of the occasion of having strong and friendly men in the house. They had the search squad rearrange some of the heavy furniture, with the usual pauses for consideration and changes of mind. How does that look, Myrtle? No, I think I liked it better over there. Try it where it was before. And so on. Since the police business was a search, the aunts also asked them to keep an eye out for articles that had been lost around the house. And so Aunt Myrtle recovered her second-best scissors, a number of letters, a full bottle of Glenlivet single malt and a ruby pin, while Aunt Caroline got back a pair of gloves, a cache of Harlequin Romances, and the stuffed tiger, Rusty, she had had from childhood. Aunt Caroline helped the search squad to replace everything neatly. Indeed she persuaded the men to search messy and neglected areas of the house, and saw to it that everything was replaced in better order.

Redmond Ryan was an energetic presence, hurrying from room to room. He thought it possible, not being a trusting person, that somebody might find evidence and not tell him. Ryan was beginning to wonder how Joe Kowalski had come by his reputation for being dumb. There's that dopy Polack slab face, Ryan thought, and sure, a long career as a loser, but there's something else in that thick bone head. Not a smart brain maybe, but something else for certain.

Afterward Kowalski settled down to watch *Highway Patrol* on the late show. The aunts drank their bedtime Ovaltine. Aunt Caroline was irritated.

"Cheer up, Caroline," Aunt Myrtle said. "Joseph isn't in trouble. This was a blunder. We knew he would never accept a bribe."

"It isn't that, Myrtle."

"Then why are you grouchy?"

"It's you, Myrtle. You're such a chatterbox."

"But," said Aunt Myrtle, "I hardly opened my mouth all evening. I told Joseph about that young man hiding in your linen chest, and what else? Oh yes, we had one of our little arguments."

"I'm not talking about the argument."

"Well I didn't chatter to the policemen. You did."

"I know. I'm going to bed now," Aunt Caroline announced. "Goodnight, Joseph. Goodnight, Myrtle. Myrtle, I wish you weren't such a chatterbox."

Six

Dallahan

1

Sergeant Brock usually ate his lunch from a paper bag. Every now and then, though, he took a walk across the old town to Mossy's Diner on Ferry Lane in the clothing district. Kowalski was often Brock's companion for these lunches before Kowalski got the Regency Gate foot patrol. Out there amid the leafy mansions there was no boisterous deli crowded with cloth workers for Kowalski, no munchy potato salad or the fragrant pastrami Kowalski could eat until he yielded a notch of his belt, paper-thin slices heaped three inches thick and steaming between the bitter rye.

"How it goes on this new thing for Joe depends on Sieracki," Sergeant Brock said to Constable Dave Cardozo, angling his knife on a kreplach to collect just the right amount of noodle and spicy filling on his fork. The sergeant had tucked two paper napkins into his collar, which with his menacing cast of face gave him the appearance of a power-weary Cromwellian churchman. He used a third napkin to dab at his mouth. Sergeant Brock was worried about what Chief Williams might do now. "Maybe Sieracki has a sense of humour. He wasn't in the cells more than four hours, we were lucky Gino was officer in charge. Some bugger in the Crown Attorney's office got back to Chief Williams I think, that's what worries me. Like they have all these little smooth twits working in the CA office now. Twenty-five years old and what they want is their pictures in the paper, switch to politics when they're thirty. Maybe Sieracki will just laugh it off."

"Joe didn't have any kind of case on Sieracki then?"

Dave Cardozo was the kind of probationer Sergeant Brock preferred, a policeman with ideals, with almost a dewy outlook on life it sometimes seemed. The way Sergeant Brock saw police training, humane feelings went through the fire of experience and in due course produced the best kind of officer, a policeman tempered by both experience and sympathy. This combination was impossible when you started by looking for worldly smartness and toughness. According to Sergeant Brock's belief, sympathy could be refined to a practical shape by experience. It did not gradually grow, or appear overnight, in some smart tough who had lacked it before.

Inconveniently, the sergeant's idea in the short term took the form of youngsters like Cardozo, who was twenty-three, earnest, interested in everything, quickly delighted and as quickly crushed, exceptionally intelligent and gullible. Cardozo's face was long, bright, and eager. His fingernails were bitten down and sandy hair fell into his eyes. He had plenty of talent for police work but Sergeant Brock knew that the kid was nowhere close to a realistic understanding of his fellow man as yet.

"Well he had a case but it was like something in a storybook, very nice if you believed it. Amundsen was seen a month ago out in Creek Pond, so the story goes. Sieracki lives in Creek Pond. You can make a sketch of Amundsen look like Sieracki if you take the hair away and give him pointy ears and fangy teeth. Well there you go, you have to be a believer. I'll tell you what I think. I think Joe went for one of those TV hunches. Joe never liked Sieracki in the first place. Do you watch those police dramas on TV, Dave, *Kojak* and *Baretta* and the rest?"

"Yes, they're very real, aren't they," Dave Cardozo said. "I watch them all the time."

"That's what I thought," Sergeant Brock said, somewhat

depressed. "Shows like that, they're a bad influence on impressionable cops. Nobody collects evidence. You have a chase and a shoot-out, hardly ever a court case. Joe got a TV hunch Sieracki was Amundsen."

"Instinct. He got an instinct. I believe in instinct myself."

"Sure you do. We can't take it into court, though. Joe's what you call instinct goes like this. Amundsen arrived in Bradfarrow a month ago. On the run, he wanted a way to take on a new identity. That meant Amundsen was looking for a man about his own age, single, no family. The man had to be a sort of a son of a bitch, because somebody with friends wouldn't do. The man had to live alone and work alone."

"Sieracki doesn't work alone. People are in and out of the store."

"Right, Dave. But they aren't the same people every day. Joe says Amundsen needed somebody with the kind of face Sieracki has. If you see a man who looks like Dracula, chances are you won't notice if somebody else who looks like Dracula takes his place, that's how Joe had it worked out."

"What does Joe say happened to Sieracki when Amundsen took his place?"

"Well naturally Amundsen killed Sieracki, buried his body in the basement or somewhere in the bush. It's the way it happens on TV, you see. I think I saw something like that on *Ironside*."

"Could be, though, sergeant," Dave Cardozo said, munching steak-on-a-bun with his sandy hair in his eyes. A zealous light showed in one of the eyes, fixed on the sergeant through the curtain of hair. "Find Sieracki's body and you have a case. Our next move is to look for that body, isn't it?"

Funny, he reminds me of my daughter Sally every now and then, Sergeant Brock thought, there's the same unkempt appearance left over from childhood and the struggle to make sense of the world and look cool doing it. "Or we could panic our impostor into making a run for it," the sergeant said to the constable. "Chase him at ninety miles an hour, wreck a bunch of cars, kill a dozen pedestrians, he climbs the clock on the East Hastings Court House, we climb up after him and shoot it out with him up there on the clock face. Do you know how many times a month your

Swedish killer is on the phone to us, asking for a policeman down at his store? Six or eight times a month."

"He would, though, Amundsen. He'd have to. He'd have to follow through on Sieracki's habits, sergeant. And look, one foreign accent can sound like any other if you aren't listening for a difference. Why don't we take a chance and search for a body?"

"We might send a squad down there with jack-hammers and wrecking bars," said Sergeant Brock, mopping up the last juicy sauce of kreplach with a crust of bread, his thoughts of dessert hesitating pleasurably between apple strudel and Mossy's thick cherry cheesecake. "Tear his house apart, comb the bush, helicopters, dogs, if we lived in TV-land. What Gino did instead was, he compared Sieracki's fingerprints with Amundsen's. They're not the same. Is Sieracki Sieracki, Gino asked himself then, and by this time he was just looking for some way out for Joe Kowalski. Well, Christmas is the time of year for toy stores, right, and last Christmas, that's *before* Amundsen started killing nurses over there in Sweden, which happened in January, Mr. Sieracki got pulled in for impaired driving, he was celebrating a good Christmas season. Impaired's a criminal charge, so he was fingerprinted. First offence, fifty dollar fine. Gino had those prints, and the prints that were taken when Joe made the arrest. Same prints, Dave. Another part of the story was that Sieracki's handwriting changed a little, he had an accident and cut his fingers with a chainsaw. We checked it out, and that happened even longer ago, last summer."

Cardozo nodded at that, yielding the argument. He said: "Well I guess Joe gets thrown off the force. We're seeing it more and more lately. Nearly every day in the off-duty room some-body's cleaning out his locker."

"I'll have the strudel," Sergeant Brock said to the waitress. He said to Constable Cardozo, more as an order than a suggestion: "You have the cheesecake. We'll split them. You're right, that new budget is killing us, Dave. The trouble there the way I see it is the chief is getting rid of all the policemen and keeping the assholes."

"He wants a police force in his own image," Cardozo said, to which Sergeant Brock did not respond. "Joe Kowalski right now should get smart and start sucking up to Mrs. Williams," the young constable said, and rested one elbow on the back of his chair, with the thumb of the other hand hooked in his trousers pocket. The sergeant recognized this as the sitting posture of an illusionless man, with bleak answers to every human problem. "He could do it very well on the Regency Gate foot patrol. Call in at Mrs. Williams's house, is everything okay, ma'am? I'm just patrolling, ma'am, give her the big smiles. We stand on guard for thee, ma'am. Suck up to her. Smile, make her feel good, offer to cut the grass. She's the chief's wife and she's Mrs. Police Commissioner, so how can he go wrong?" Constable Cardozo asked with a shrug, a cynic tired by knowledge of the world.

"I'll pass the idea along to him," Sergeant Brock said, even more depressed. His daughter had been christened Sally but wanted to be called Sarah now. Sally was just as fascinated by postures of bored sophistication as Constable Cardozo was. She was only sixteen, though. "But it doesn't sound to me like the kind of thing that Joe Kowalski could handle with any, you know, finesse."

The time being then around one, Mossy's was doing heavy business. Incoming customers were backed up behind the cash register, tough women from the sewing-machine lines on forty-minute breaks fixing hostile eyes on any lunchers who were toying with coffee. Chief Williams eased himself to the front of this mill, chin lifted to survey the restaurant. "Ahoy there, fellows," he said pleasantly.

The chief was dressed for leisure in tan slacks and a white sports shirt and a light blue blazer with dark blue piping on the cuffs and collar. The crest on his shirt's left breast depicted a knight slaying a dragon. The motto *Sans argent l'honneur n'est qu'une maladie* ran beneath the crest. Above it was the message: *Bradfarrow Lawn Bowling Club*. A similar shirt could be bought for forty dollars but the crest was not to be had for cash.

"Booked yourself out to this address, but I had a devil of a job finding the place," Chief Williams said. "Sergeant, my afternoon is one appointment after another. I need a quick word with you."

"All the chairs are taken, sir," said Constable Cardozo, looking around the room with an attitude of reluctant helpfulness for a free one.

At sixteen my kid Sally is more grown up in lots of ways than this young cop is at twenty-three, Sergeant Brock told himself, in his depression. Truth to tell, Cardozo could turn out to be another Kowalski, Brock thought, as if one is needed in every generation.

The chief noticed Cardozo. "Nonsense, constable, you're sitting on a perfectly good chair," he said. "Get the hell off it." He took the chair from Cardozo and then looked up at him. "Cardozo, right? I'm afraid you're on the cut-back list, Cardozo. We're letting you go. It's an immediate budget requirement," the chief said with a grimace although his manner was cheerful. "If we get a better budget at any time we'll be in touch with you, you can be sure of that. See Sergeant Pulthorpe when you report at the station. Good luck."

The constable's face reddened and his hand moved to his mouth as if to bite the fingernails. Then he straightened his shoulders, made a sort of composed bow to Sergeant Brock and walked away with dignity, indeed showing fair nonchalance. Good steel in that backbone already, the sergeant thought.

"I made a mistake there."

"Well Cardozo would've made a good policeman, chief. He's a little green right now."

"No, I mean I should have told him to take a turn of duty guarding my car, walking papers later today. I suppose they vandalize cars, scratch the paintwork, in this part of town, do they?"

"No," Sergeant Brock said.

"I think you're wrong. I noticed coming in, this is a terrible neighbourhood. Children playing in the streets and no trees. You keep a close eye on your auto in this kind of high crime district, sergeant. You don't leave your car unattended unless you want a big bill for bodywork and new tires." But Chief Williams seemed in no hurry now. He sat back and looked around Mossy's Diner with the curiosity of a tourist from a far country. "Yes, the ethnics, they've brought a lot of colour to our city. I hear we should be grateful. I don't," said Chief Williams, "go along with the general run of opinion that most of these people are on welfare and living off prostitutes. If indeed they are on welfare that's what social legislation is for, after all. That's the problem with it."

Chief Williams added cream and sugar to Cardozo's coffee. He forked the two halves of strudel on to his own plate and gave Sergeant Brock the cheesecake.

"You can have that junk, I'll have the pie. Rotten-looking apple pie it is too. What kind of Europeans are they anyway, in this part of town?"

"Well they aren't Europeans, not immigrants I mean, it's a Jewish area," Sergeant Brock said. "This is the old town, they were here first, after the French. Immigrants now, you get some Greek and Ukrainian as you go down Ferry toward West Harbour. . ."

The chief put down his fork and pushed the plate away. "I can't say I care much for kosher food. That fellow Kowalski, sergeant. My wife says he abused and insulted her. She's wretchedly upset."

"What? Oh God."

"He's on foot patrol near our place apparently, in Regency Gate. She asked him to move some deck chairs or something. Naughty of her, of course. Then the obscenities, shouting, lost control of himself completely by all accounts."

"What, Joe Kowalski?"

"Mavis feared he would attack her."

"Joe doesn't know any obscenities, chief."

"I'm just going on my wife's word, sergeant."

"Yes, I understand that, chief, but is she sure she has the right policeman?"

"I think so. The Polish friend of yours. Same man who let Riordan go, same man who arrested one of our downtown merchants without authority and without a warrant. He's been abusing my wife."

"I'm going to have to ease up on the spicy food. I'm getting an ulcer, I think." Sergeant Brock, worried, began stuffing his pipe, drawing looks of hatred from the customers backed up behind the cash register. "I imagine this will mean his job."

Chief Williams looked at Sergeant Brock, very much surprised. He said: "Dear me, no. We can't possibly let it go at that. Kowalski released Riordan from custody. Why? What we have there is reasonable suspicion of a felony. We investigate felonies, don't we? I'd like you to handle our investigation, sergeant. You put together our bribery case against Kowalski for the Police Commission. We're officers of the law, you see, friendships not-withstanding. The harassment of Mr. Sieracki isn't so serious comparatively. Some private spite, I suppose, breach of the police articles, well a gross misdemeanour let's say. We have what happened down on paper and witnesses and so on. You won't have any trouble with the Sieracki end of your presentation to the commission."

"You're arresting Joe?"

"No. I want to stick him for taking the money. On the felony, you see. We don't have any evidence he took the money yet, that's why I want you to work on it. I could suspend him for the mis-demeanour until the hearing but he'd be on full pay, reporting once a day. He reports in every two hours now. He won't have more than a two-hour start if he runs with the money."

"He doesn't have the money."

"Don't worry, we'll give him a fair hearing. Naturally my wife and I won't let our personal feelings about Kowalski influence our judgement when we hear the bribery case."

"No."

"Call on me if you need any help, sergeant. Build a good strong chain of evidence and you'll earn my gratitude. I think you understand what I want."

"Yes," Sergeant Brock said. "You want me to help send Joe Kowalski to jail for five years because he insulted your wife."

Chief Williams stood up, having finished Cardozo's coffee. "Yes, you or somebody who takes your place," he said. "I'd better go see about my car."

Sergeant Brock submitted to a particularly gloomy mood of worry then, sitting there with a bleak eye while the pipe between his teeth lost its consolation and went cold. A very tall bony woman wearing a knitted beret and flapping knitted clothes took the seat opposite him. "Is it nap-time now, sport, or are you waiting for the floor show?" she asked angrily after a moment. "Why don't you haul your fat ass out of here and let a working girl eat a sandwich?"

2

The Bradfarrow Lawn Bowling Club, in the way of such institutions, was more a social than a sporting club. Only a modest amount of lawn bowling went on. The members to be found on the bowling green were always outnumbered by members in the bar, the restaurant, the lounges, and even the reading room. The clubhouse was a palladian, rubble-stone structure with modern additions, situated ten miles outside Bradfarrow.

Chief Williams, whose first afternoon appointment was for two o'clock with his lawyer, Enoch Nesmith, of Nesmith, Buchanan and Grant, made his way toward one of the smaller lounges through the aroma of fine food and tobacco and liquors. He heard the murmur of agreeable talk.

"American socialism is the worst kind. If we traded on the New York Exchange the Securities and Exchange Commission could force us to publish the salary figures for all officers and directors earning over forty thousand a year."

"Good heavens, that's everybody, Henry."

". . . a plumber, *a plumber*, makes more money than. . ."

". . . plenty of jobs around for anybody who wants them . . ."

". . . no incentive to go out to work, you see, with a government cheque in the mail regular as clockwork . . ."

". . . what you don't see any more? You don't see any pride of craft any more . . ."

". . . bitching about unemployment but just try to get somebody to work on your . . ."

". . . immigrants will take any kind of work, it's the finicky God damn *natives* who . . ."

". . . never spent a penny in my life I didn't earn but these people . . ."

"Here we give them just the aggregate salary figures and they're as happy as clams."

Enoch Nesmith was a plump man, a rumpled person with straggling white hair and dandruff on his shoulders. His sun tan bespoke generous stretches of winter holiday time. He wore a dark three-piece suit with the two bottom buttons of the waistcoat

undone over the swell of a small rounded stomach. His manner
conveyed an impression of fidget and rush, as of one who carries
an unfair burden of work. He was perched in a corner armchair,
paging through old, yellow papers, his glasses up on his forehead
and a briefcase at his feet.

"How are you, Frank?" he asked with a seriously enquiring
stare, like a doctor beginning an examination. "Here, sit down. I
had to leave Myrtle Beach a week early this year, pressure of
work. I caught that last snow storm. I hate this time of year, no
heat in the sun and too early for golf. How's Mavis?"

They exchanged remarks as to the well-being of their wives
and talked of them briefly. Chief Williams said: "Enoch, do you
happen to know anything about this demolition in Regency
Gate?"

"Yes indeed. We're hearing a good deal about that these
days. The victims are all up in arms and litigious, not that anything can be done for them. Company called Equity Mortgage
and Trust is responsible, so I understand. A fifth-rate little operation up to now, it's very surprising." Enoch Nesmith added
peevishly: "They're causing all kinds of work. That's what
brought me back from Myrtle Beach too early."

"They're knocking people's houses down, Enoch."

"Yes. It would be interesting to know where their financing
comes from because they're not getting sound advice. Whatever
they have in mind, they're making a mistake. Regency Gate is
zoned for single-dwelling housing. That's permanent as to any
development in the area. That's a provincial mandate now, Frank,
with the city zoning coming under the county plan, administered
by the province. No apartments. Demolishing housing property
in Regency Gate is like pulling down casinos in Las Vegas. I don't
know what the hell they're up to. Nobody does."

"Yes well I'm not particularly interested in what they're up
to . . ." the police chief said, showing some peevishness on his
own account. To Chief Williams's knowledge Enoch Nesmith
worked for five weeks in the year and his senior partner Percy
Grant, a more ardent golfer, put in about the same or less. Their
fees were enormous, though, as one of the oldest Bradfarrow law
firms, inheritors of unlimited goodwill and respect.

". . . and they seem to be able to send Italians into my neighbourhood to tear down perfectly good houses. Splendid houses, Enoch. Enoch," the chief explained to the fidgety plump man, "look, they're doing that *against the wishes of the owners*. The owners are being thrown into the street with their furniture by bailiffs."

"Well, perhaps, but Equity Mortgage and Trust are acting quite within their legal rights," Enoch Nesmith said, abruptly since Chief Williams seemed to be expressing something less than utter confidence in Nesmith, Buchanan and Grant. "We have our eye on this, of course. The problem goes back, oh more than a hundred years to a conveyance of fifty acres of unimproved land in what's now Regency Gate. Our old legal rivals Corcoran and Craddock were responsible, a very unfortunate blunder, Frank. That was in Tiny Craddock's time, Busby's grandfather. I have a copy of the old document here. A beautiful old paper, historically valuable of course, but these Equity Mortgage and Trust people somehow came up with an order that it's legal also." Enoch Nesmith spread copies of antique papers on the table in front of him, with others on his lap, and burrowed into the briefcase as he spoke, as if racing against time. "Astonishingly quick work," he said disapprovingly. "You get much the same sort of legal argument in Indian treaty litigation, what you end up arguing is old English law. As a general rule it takes years."

"What about my house, Enoch?"

"I have a map of the fifty acres, if you're interested . . ."

"Yes."

". . . at the office. It doesn't show houses, just the land. Ponds, streams, trees, the old roads, they're all gone now. We nearly merged with Corcoran and Craddock in 1897, imagine that. Old Percy Grant, grandfather of our present Percy, he and Tiny Craddock were the best of friends. Midge, they called old Percy, Midge Grant, tough little bantam of the old school. Man with a wicked temper, Midge, but he was the best lawyer this town's ever seen. Our Percy has a photo of them in his office, Midge Grant and Tiny Craddock, standing beside a Graham Paige dual-cowl phaeton. You could be robbed of your house now, you know, Frank," the lawyer remarked inconsequently, pointing out an unimportant oddity, "if that merger had taken place. Midge Grant was twice the lawyer Tiny Craddock was, but Midge was a man of his time, a modern man. The Graham Paige was Midge's. An extraordinary machine, pure work of art. Nothing like it exists nowadays. Ah yes. Midge Grant drove the first auto on the streets of Bradfarrow at seventy-seven years of age."

"Company history is always good to chat about," Chief Williams said savagely. "But didn't you say that one of these old-timers, didn't you say that one of these smart old lawyers of yours made the mistake that's already cost nearly a million dollars in Regency Gate?"

"That's so. It was Tiny Craddock's oversight, but it could have been worse. It could have been a hundred acres. The other fifty was conveyed by us."

"That means my house is okay, Enoch, does it?"

"Well, certainly," Enoch Nesmith said, a little hurt by the question. "You have ironclad title, Frank. You're with us."

Chief Williams recovered his ease of manner. "Good," he said. "You'll understand my nervousness. The Italians have knocked down six houses already. They're working very fast, for Italians."

"The Italians are ruining the neighbourhood, eh?" Enoch Nesmith said, looking up from his busy papers and winking at Chief Williams who returned an uncomprehending stare. "Corcoran and Craddock weren't able to get a restraining order in the matter of the evictions and demolition. But they've started proceedings for compensation of course. They have an excellent chance of success too in my view."

"Good Lord. You mean the people losing their houses in the Gate aren't even being compensated?"

Enoch Nesmith extracted one of the yellow copies.

"This will amuse you. The clause at fault stipulated that the fifty acres *and any buildings put upon it* could be bought back at any time by a women's organization called the Little Sisters, nuns or some sect or other I imagine. The Little Sisters were disbanded in 1850. Only that original organization had the right to buy back the fifty acres. Unfortunately it comes to light now that some tatty branch of the order did survive somewhere, in an Irish bog I believe. Equity Mortgage and Trust are acting for them, on the record. Actually that Regency Gate operation must have respectable financial backing, Frank."

"Who's behind it?"

"Hard to tell. But a corporation, I'd say. The way we are, a corporation can protect its anonymity far better than an individual. Yes, here's the amusing part, the buy-back price. The fifty acres and buildings, it says, may be bought back at any time and instantly upon the payment of *two hundred strong oxen, no more than four years old, one thousand rails of straight cedar, not less than twenty feet in length and not less than eighteen inches around at their thinnest part, split and barked, twenty-five gold sovereigns, fifty hundredweights of wheat flour, milled fine, and forty hogsheads of prime Newport rum.* Beautiful, some of those old documents, pure works of art."

Enoch Nesmith shuffled the paper back into the others hurriedly. He fished a pocket watch from his waistcoat and blinked at it. "Did you know, Frank, that the acreage Regency Gate stands on used to be called 'the Rath'? There's a reference to it somewhere in here. 'A pleasant prospect of country known to the common farmers as *the Rath*.'"

"The other fifty acres," Chief Williams asked. "The land your firm conveyed back then, Enoch, is my house on that?"

"That's right."

"No old documents around to surprise me, are there, Enoch?"

"As a matter of fact, yes," the lawyer said, smiling. "The Good Neighbours of the Rath, ever hear of them?"

"No."

"Neither has anybody else in Bradfarrow. We're neglecting our past, Frank. We don't know our own history. Who were the Good Neighbours of the Rath? It's a mystery. They yielded their land to us and vanished into oblivion."

"Very accommodating of them," Chief Williams said coldly. "What old document, Enoch?"

"Well, something like the other one. Longer, though. Earlier in my opinion. When I joined the firm in '52, we didn't work under constant pressure, as we do now," Enoch Nesmith complained, and lost himself for a moment in reflection on those idle days. "Our evenings were free as a rule, and we had all of Saturday afternoon off every month. Many's the happy hour I spent in the dust of the filing room, reliving our past. Oh, the joy! I found that Good Neighbours document, Frank. Now obviously I had no idea that Corcoran and Craddock had the Little Sisters one in their old tin deed boxes. I could see, though, that our Good Neighbours paper—by the wildest bad luck, you understand, the form is improper and challengeable in a dozen different ways, but I could see it might be taken for a valid contract. I just thought the thing could be a nuisance if it got out of our hands."

"So you destroyed it, did you, Enoch. Good man."

Chief Williams spoke in a quiet, hopeful voice. Enoch Nesmith's face lost colour. His chubby fingers trembled on the pile of papers. "Of course I didn't damn well destroy it," he managed to say, frowning unbelievingly at the police chief. "What in God's name do you mean, destroy it?" he asked loudly, a wounded shout. This was not heard in the small lounge, however. Three middle-aged men, quite drunk, had seated themselves at the far side, guffawing and rowdily shrieking. ". . . other little drink to celebrate Chuck's divorce. When your wife begins to look as old as your mother it's time, eh Chuckie?" one of them said. All three fell forward on the table with shrieks and streaming eyes, made helpless by mirth.

". . . kind of a barbarian do you take me for, Frank? I'm a founding member of the Bradfarrow Historical Society. I've been chairman four times. Destroy it? I took it to Percy and we went over it together . . ." Here mist appeared in Enoch Nesmith's eyes. "I was only an employee," he said apologetically. "I wasn't a partner then. I didn't have any power or any money you see. Still, I was able to save most of it—the description of the land, that's all saved. Those lovely old phrases. 'From Forty Sheep Meadow to the Stream of the Fat Fish.' 'The Path that Goes by the Mud House where Lives the Lonely Fiddler.' The buy-back clause was on a separate sheet, just that one troublsome clause, Frank. Oh eminently disputable. Even an Indian would think twice before wasting his time on it. Hardly any historical value," Enoch Nesmith said firmly with misty eyes, "one paragraph on old paper. Percy put a match to it in his ashtray."

Chief Williams said in ill temper: "I don't feel in the least sentimental about this. You do understand that we're talking about my house, don't you? Dressed stone, Enoch, nobody dresses stone nowadays, I'm still waiting for the garage to take off my winter tires. It's a favour they do for you at the garage now, for money. The day of the working man is gone. Five fireplaces. I had a nightmare last night, I arrived home and I found the Opera Circle swarming all over my house dislodging it stone by stone."

"Yes, well Nesmith, Buchanan and Grant searched your title," Enoch Nesmith said, making himself heard above the hubbub from the divorce celebrants, in fact shouting somewhat again. "However, if you feel jittery we can go over it for you, back to neolithic times if necessary. We'll see if there are any clay tablets, Frank. I'll talk to Percy, but probably we can waive a fee in this case," the lawyer said reluctantly, "in view of that dreadful business, the Corcoran and Craddock scandal. Have somebody drop your deed by at the office."

"Right here." Chief Williams drew a thick envelope from the inside pocket of his blazer. Chief Williams was unimpressed by conjury of lineage and error-free tradition from a lawyer who spent winter days within the sound of the surf and summer days hitting golf balls. He pressed the envelope into Enoch Nesmith's unwilling hands. "Check everything. Check everything twice. Enoch, see to it yourself. Use whatever help you need. Charge whatever fee you like. The wreckers are in the Gate. It's home and hearth, Enoch. How soon can you get this back to me?"

Enoch Nesmith considered the question against his will. "Well we can give it priority, put a rush on it, say September."

"No no no. Days, Enoch, please."

They haggled and settled on three weeks. The chief went on to his next appointment satisfied, leaving the lawyer grumpy, and resentful of pressure so severe that his brief year had to be divided down into the fineness of days. He ordered a brandy to cheer himself up. 'From the Mohawk Camp to the Syrup-bearing Trees of Thadd Auslan,' he read, browsing in his papers, 'and next in a Straight Line to the Spring Well of the Good Neighbours, All of that Land Enclosed.' He loved the effortful spartan beauty in toil and the magic past that nature had cheated him of by putting him in the world a hundred years too late. Up at first light, he dreamed, in the grief of his loss, crack the ice and wash, build the fire, attend to the Forty Sheep, whatever had to be done, draw water from the Spring Well and brew the coffee, a breakfast of milk and oatmeal sweetened by some of the Syrup from Thadd Auslan's maple grove. Then the honest work, the lawyer told himself, vague about its nature, until dusk came on the land. Homeward with a Fat Fish on a string for a simple supper. When the sun went down sweet music would come to him with the wind from the Lonely Fiddler.

'. . . but that the same Land within the Rath together with any Fences, Bridges or Roads or any Barns or any Other Buildings put upon the Land may be Bought by the Good Neighbours . . ." Enoch Nesmith read wistfully now, patting his pockets for his cigar case. His hand stopped and he read it again. First he was surprised by joy, that a copy of the Good Neighbours paper that he had seen aflame in Percy Grant's ashtray as a young man of twenty-seven had survived. In a while however he became uneasy. The practical ruin of Corcoran and Craddock had been the subject of complacent talk at Nesmith, Buchanan and Grant since his return from Myrtle Beach. It could never happen to us, could it, Mr. Nesmith, somebody had said. At the time he had taken the words to be an expression of confidence and not a question.

He cancelled the brandy.

The lawyer was in an agitated state, almost trotting, as he made his way toward the far end of the club parking-lot near the attendant's box. Enoch Nesmith was always able to choose his parking spot in the empty lot as an early arriver and to drive comfortably away from an empty lot as a late departer. Now, though, cars were lined up and filtering through the exit one by one.

"Enoch. Look at this."

It was Chief Williams, standing beside an unmarked BCP Oldsmobile. The two side tires were flat.

"Only club members and guests are allowed in the lot, Enoch."

Somebody had also cut gouges in the door panels on the same side of the Olds, a dozen or so criss-crossing slashes that exposed streaks of metal under the paintwork.

"How could this happen, Enoch?"

Chief Williams looked from Enoch Nesmith to his damaged auto, waiting for an extraordinary answer.

"Frank, I have to get to the office. I can give you a ride in."

"Thank you. I've radioed for a car. I don't understand this."

The three men celebrating the divorce were climbing into a taxi near the exit. They were arguing. One broke free and produced a pocket knife with a red handle, a Swiss Army knife. "Kill the Olds," shouted this man, the divorcee, Chuck. "An Olds a year for eleven years, but now it's Maserati time, Mona." He worked a knife blade into the tire of a car. The cab driver rolled his window down and shouted a protest.

Enoch Nesmith waited. There was a wild man with a knife, but on the other hand the Oldsmobile being vandalized was his. He looked around for Chief Williams and saw a police cruiser passing through the exit with the chief, a perplexed man, in the back seat. By this time Chuck the new bachelor had been shoved into the cab by his companions. The driver swung out to the head of the line and the cab was gone when Enoch Nesmith reached his car. One wheel sat forlornly on its rim.

"Trouble, Enoch?"

The lawyer with an effort recognised the woman who asked this question, leaning from the driver's window of a Lincoln. A portly woman dressed in pink — a name like Preston, somebody in Grumach-Erdly the pharmaceutical company.

"Get in. Have that picked up later."

Enoch Nesmith climbed into the front seat of the limousine, a somewhat funereal black car. "Thanks. I'm very much obliged."

"No bother, Enoch. I'll get some free legal advice from you on the way in," the woman said, and laughed. But then she said: "There's an easement runs through the back of my place at the lake and the bastard puts gravel on it when I'm not there." She courteously allowed two converging cars into the line ahead.

"I have to get to my office without delay."

"Ah yes, it's always the same, isn't it. The first two hours or so for lunch are always okay, but that last fifteen minutes makes you feel guilty as sin."

The parking-lot attendant rested his elbows somnolently on the sill of his box watching the cars go by. Opposite the box stood a strange, tall man, shadowed by the afternoon sun from the south. The man wore a greatcoat that reached to his shins. The greatcoat collar was turned up and stood as high as the man's head so that two wings of cloth in silhouette framed the face, invisibly recessed. As the autos rolled out, this man pointed at each one and waved it by.

Now Enoch Nesmith took notice of the greatcoated stranger on a mild day, and felt menaced.

When the man pointed at the Lincoln he did not wave it by. He took a pair of black gloves from his pocket and flexed them on hands and fingers, walking around to the driver's side.

"Who is he?"

"Grumach-Erdly chauffeur. Lazy buggers, never around when you need them."

"I'll take over now, madam," said the man in the greatcoat. He did not bend down to the driver's window. He opened the door. The woman got out, grumbling, and she and Enoch Nesmith occupied the back seat.

". . . never understand what makes some of you guys think we run a limousine fleet for your convenience. Where were you at eleven-thirty? *Dr. Warwick* was looking for a driver. *I* was looking for a driver. How did you get yourself stranded out here without a car?"

The man did not reply. Seen from behind, his great collar enclosed his head like a monk's cowl. The big car rolled smoothly along the highway.

"Well, answer me, please," said the Preston woman, who had become irately managerial. "Your name's Fogarty, isn't it?"

"Dallahan, madam."

"Yes, Irish. We're up to our ears in Fogartys, Callaghans, Dallahans."

There was a pause while the woman and Enoch Nesmith watched the back of their driver's collar.

"No, madam, I am the only Dallahan," the man said. "There is only one Dallahan, madam."

Seven

Watchman, What of the Night?

1

"Getting caught in Kowalski's house was a big mistake, Ryan," said Chief Williams. "Talk about donkey stupidity. Why should I have to put up with it?"

"I had the worst luck, chief."

"Why do I have to do everything myself? Why can't I have people working for me who'll do what I tell them to do? Maybe you think the president of General Motors has to run down to the factory every day to tighten all the little nuts and bolts."

"I didn't count on two old ladies, chief."

"Well, what do you think now, did the bazooka villain pay Kowalski off?"

"Sure he did. He paid Kowalski, Kowalski let him go. That's the only explanation for Kowalski letting him go."

"So where's the money, eh, donkey?"

Redmond Ryan knew that he could lose his job at any moment during this conversation. He was sweating but his face was a wholesome, good-looking mask. "He's got the money, chief, buried, safe deposit, a locker somewhere, at the house of an accomplice. I'll find it."

"No, forget Kowalski."

"Give me a week. He has it."

"I'll handle Kowalski myself from now on. I'll attend to him personally. I don't need you, Ryan," Chief Williams said, staring at the constable with bland hatred. "I'll tighten all the nuts and bolts myself. I'll do the dishes and take the dog for a walk. I've always had the feeling at the back of my mind," he added thoughtfully, "that you made a mistake when you joined the police force, Ryan. You didn't do yourself justice, choosing a career. Look at you, you have amazing charm. Look what Robert Redford made of himself. People can't get enough of Robert Redford. Of course he has acting talent," the chief said and shook his head, "which calls for intelligence I understand, remembering lines and instructions, and outsmarting tough competition. I daresay the route is blocked off for a man who comes out a loser matching wits with Kowalski's aunts. Have you ever thought about selling? Not sophisticated selling, not selling deodorant on TV, I see you as doing something more basic," Chief Williams said in the manner of somebody offering useful advice, "more like selling encyclopedias door to door."

However, Ryan had a card to play here. He grinned down at his hands, kneading the fine-boned fingers. "Funny the way people take an interest in my career, chief," he said. "Even in your own family, just on that personal level, I was talking to your niece Helen yesterday. We've made the arrangements for your party tonight. She's very happy."

"I imagine I can pick out another warm body for her."

"Well, Helen said me, chief. She said she was happy about having me. For some reason Helen likes me personally," Ryan said innocently, glancing up from his fingers at Chief Williams, whose look of hatred was now a little curious too. "She says her mother thinks I should have Sergeant Brock's job. Of course that's just silly."

"Yes."

"Mrs. Letresky doesn't run the force."

"That's right, Ryan."

"But she's very seriously interested in me, Helen says. Helen says she's going to speak to Mrs. Williams, I thought you should know, sir, to see what can be done. Naturally I don't expect to be popped into the sergeant's job on that account," said Redmond Ryan with another bashful grin downward. "Sergeant Brock does great work. But anyway Mrs. Letresky is watching my career on the force. She's a very kind person. I honestly appreciate it when nice folk like Mrs. Letresky take an interest in me."

"Folk?" Chief Williams said. "What strange ideas you have, Ryan. We are not folk. *You* are folk." The chief had become a shade mellower, however. "You're a thorough shit, though, Ryan, aren't you," he said approvingly. "I keep forgetting that. I suppose I lump you in with the boy scout riff-raff because of your appearance. Very well, we'll allow you one more little run. Just the one."

Chief Williams consulted his day journal.

"A question of finding out who's behind the demolition work going on in Regency Gate. The case is alive with insurance investigators, and it isn't a police matter. I want you to get the whole story, find out who's putting the money up and what they're planning to build. That will affect the value of my house, you see. We don't like changes in the Gate."

"As good as done, chief." Ryan wrote in his notebook. He looked fresh, clear-eyed and heroic but the sweat was standing out on his blond airman's face in drops.

"Yes. You have a decent suit for tonight, do you?"

"There's a dark grey and I have a new russet brown. The brown looks best outdoors but with my light colouring I prefer the grey for evenings . . ."

"Shut up, Ryan. Remember the rules. Pay attention to Helen. Nothing less than affection, and in particular nothing more. You don't touch strap or button, hem or zipper. I'll be angry if you do any more sucking up to Mrs. Letresky. Nothing alcoholic to drink for you at the party. I don't want you brave. We'll have a prospect for Helen to look at, a lad named Chilton. He doesn't have your salesman's charm but they tell me his family fought for the king against George Washington."

The phone rang then and Ryan was able to escape. It was Percy Grant, senior partner of Nesmith, Buchanan and Grant. Percy Grant had that breeziness of manner with which many lawyers get through a day of human greed, hope, misery, violence, crime and punishment.

"Question of your title to property in Regency Gate, to wit your house and lot," said Percy Grant. "Thought I'd give you a buzz. We have it all locked up tight for you. Set your mind at rest."

"I was expecting a call from Enoch."

"Unfortunately Enoch's been taken away."

"He's been . . .?"

"Taken away suddenly, can't be helped, but the work's all done now. So I'll shove your deed in the mail to you right this minute, terribly sorry you were upset, how's that?"

"I'll stop by the office and pick it up."

"Shutting her down, though, in fifteen minutes, rites of spring," said the lawyer cheerfully. "Fertility rituals, blessing of the seed, sacrifice of kings and virgins, worship of balls." He added: "A drift of snow still in the caves, they tell me, but the high ridges are dry. I hear the song of the hills, Mr. Williams, the gentle green hills and dangerous water, the glorious wood and the passionate iron. Golf is calling."

2

While Mrs. Mavis Williams worked the levers of political power in Bradfarrow, her sister Mrs. Alisha Letresky knew many ways of finding business capital. They were not loving sisters exactly but on a material footing they did need each other. When they put politics and business together they needed other people too. Every party Mrs. Williams gave was purposeful and she did not judge its success on whether or not the crowd had had a good time.

The spring thaw party had been a failure in this sense. Chairman of the Bradfarrow Police Commission L. Erskine Ridgeway had phoned in an apology. Mrs. Williams had planned an informal talk with the commander about Constable Kowalski. Through the evening a man from the Black River Conservation Authority who Mrs. Williams had been told was an alcoholic and careless in his cups had remained sober, businesslike and unwilling to yield an inch of river to development. On the other hand the deputy mayor, whom Mrs. Williams needed with all his wits about him to report to her on the work of a number of municipal committees, was tipsy when he arrived, and pawed every woman he saw, and had to be taken home by his wife. Then too the suitable young man for Helen Letresky, Chilton, who was shy and likeable, brought an unforeseen girl friend. The girl was extremely attractive. A secretary or something Mrs. Williams guessed, moving in on them to split them up, which she failed to do; the girl deflected all Mrs. Williams's gracious efforts to take Chilton away, giggling while her eyes remained calm, and during the whole evening she maintained that same combined role, of an enchanting guileless person and a trained guard dog.

At ten when in fact everybody was merry Mrs. Williams found herself recognizing her party as noisily useless. Her one source of satisfaction was Redmond Ryan. He looked quite beautiful. He was in every particular deferential. He sipped soda water. He made cavalier efforts to unstick the intelligent secretary from Chilton.

Mrs. Williams pleaded a headache to the more important guests and went to her room, having ordered the caterers to take the bar away at eleven. She showered, put on a Holt Renfrew robe of crimson silk, and sitting at her desk near the window began to go through the guest-list, together with her address book, making new plans. Autos started up and were driven away outside.

Chief Williams came in and sat in one of the boudoir chairs, dejected. "How did it go?" he asked. "Waste of time, right? I've just seen the last of them off, except for Helen and that God damn Adonis, Ryan. They're having coffee in the kitchen."

"It was a disappointing party," Mrs. Williams said. "I've been wondering about drinking parties, Frank. Now that we're doing more, we should be thinking of small dinners. Maybe even two or three every week. The Ryan boy behaved very well tonight. I practically promised Alisha that we would let him be a sergeant."

"Trouble is, he's not as useful as he looks," the chief said. "I nearly fired the son of a bitch today to tell you the truth. He looks good, but that's it with him. He looks like a Hitler Youth and everything, so you think you have somebody who can handle himself, but he makes dumb moves." Chief Williams said: "Well, I'll go and send the Polish wonder home."

Chief Williams had put Kowalski on overtime for the evening as parking supervisor. These days the chief liked to know where Kowalski was.

Mrs. Williams returned to her work. She heard the front door close and looked out. Chief Williams was seeing Helen and Ryan off. The chief kissed Helen, growled at Ryan, and went to look for Kowalski.

The young couple had arrived early, so Ryan's zippy little Triumph was parked near the door, and Mrs. Williams waited at the window to see them drive away. However, they seemed to be arguing, Ryan trying to move toward the car while Helen held him back.

The moon was full and the night bright as day except under the big oak tree which overhung the garage. Moonlight flashed on Helen's glasses. That little sex maniac, Mrs. Williams thought. I wonder. Then Helen released Ryan, who went to the car and started it. He backed toward the garage instead of driving forward, and parked in the darkness under the oak. This puzzled Mrs. Williams, who asked herself why they should *hide the car*, until Helen skipped across to Ryan and took his hand, and together they disappeared into the bushes.

Mrs. Williams paused only to push her feet into flat-heeled shoes and then, whimpering, she rushed out and down the stairs and through the front door, following the pair into the hedge without hesitation. This hedge bordered the Williams's lawn. It was clear to Mrs. Williams that a seduction was on Helen's mind and Mrs. Williams had specifically promised her sister that Helen would be protected from seduction.

There was nothing to be seen on the lawn except the dappled carpet of day-bright moonlight.

"Helen, come here at once!" Mrs. Williams called. "Constable Ryan, bring Helen out of there and be quick about it."

Redmond Ryan wanted to obey this call. His jaw muscles ached from civil smiling through the long evening. What he had forgotten about Helen was her interest in his body. She was an anthropology major. Up to home-going time he had resisted suggestions of moonlight walks with the argument that duty forbade it. This excuse had now expired.

". . . and the men were slaves, while the women were queens and goddesses," Helen said. "The soil was female . . ."

They were stepping along a dark pathway with night-dark trees on one side and rose-beds branching out at right angles on the other. The rose bushes made a magnificent show in summer, set in crescent beds and separated by lawn and gravel walks. In the light of the moon they were gaunt and thorny like barbed wire on a battlefield.

". . . and so under that system the woman was all-important. Pay no attention to Aunt Mavis."

"Are you out of your mind? She saw us coming in here. She's just Aunt Mavis to you but to me that's Commissioner Mrs. Williams and Chief Williams, and you don't fool around with those two."

Helen seized Ryan's ears and kissed him on the mouth. "God, you're beautiful," she said. "Trust me, honey. Would I do anything to hurt you? They'll go off to bed if we keep quiet."

"I'm going back, Helen."

"No, I won't let you be a coward. Young men should be young bulls. I want you to know," Helen Letresky said, her hands resting on Redmond Ryan's shoulders while she gazed honestly into his troubled blue eyes, "that I care for you. *God*, you're beautiful."

She was a butty, bulky girl with gifts of leadership. Behind the harlequin glasses her face had a predatory character with a round mouth, wet and full-lipped at the moment. She wore a simple shift dress that left her shoulders bare. "Let's move on, honey. If we stay in the shadows and work down to the back lawn we can reach the Graveleys' without crossing a road."

"God damn it, Helen, we've gone too far already."

"Ryan! Bring that girl out of those bushes right now. That's an order, Ryan!" It was Chief Williams's voice.

But Ryan was following Helen. He judged that having Helen on his side later when the time came to explain would be better than having all three against him immediately. Like ditch-running night animals they trotted along in the shadow of bush and tree; stepping sometimes on squashy flowerbeds, and halting twice to look around with care before darting across the lighted driveways. Ryan did not know where they were. But the moon's lamp and their progress through unfenced stretches of forest and ravine gave him a strange feeling of travelling in some alien country with different rules and inhabitants.

"The Graveleys'. Why look there. The house has been torn down."

They emerged at the rear of the devastated property in an orchard, looking across a swimming pool and patio at a house's shell. It had been of medieval design, with turrets and lancet windows and stone facings. Now the roof was gone and the starry sky could be seen through the windows' empty arches. Great slabs of the walls were down too and piles of brick rose against the foundations underneath.

"That is positively weird. I was here last week," Helen said, looking in wonderment at the ruin. "The Graveleys didn't say anything about moving. Phoebe and I are old friends, you see, honey. She was going to assist me in the ceremony. But it doesn't matter, no reason why we shouldn't go ahead without her."

"Ceremony?" Ryan asked.

"The rite." She took his hand. "Come with me, bull. First we must find wine and bread."

They went into the darkness of the orchard, and soon reached a clearing with picnic tables on the perimeter and a massive stone structure in the centre. The monolith, as it seemed, was chest high, long and narrow, and had iron grilles set into its sides.

"Altar," Helen said.

"What do you mean, altar? It's a fieldstone barbecue, Helen."

Ryan followed her across the clearing. A short distance along they came to a footbridge spanning a busy little stream. Helen swung herself down under the bridge and began groping in the water. She brought out a bulging plastic bag.

"I cached this here last week."

"What is it?"

"Not yet, darling. Don't worry your pretty head and don't be alarmed."

"Why should I be alarmed?"

But Helen took his tingling ears again and kissed him on the mouth. "Man, oh lovely *man*," she whispered. "God, women knew how to enjoy themselves in those days. Now we go to the altar."

On the barbecue's slab top, dark itself although the moon lighted the clearing, she opened the bag and reverently took out a bottle of wine, President red, two silver baby mugs and a loaf of Wonder Bread. Being the substance of a meagre picnic these had no effect on Ryan, who was trying to guess what his role in the game might be. He was uneasy when he saw the knife. It caught the light on its blade, a carving knife, quality German cutlery with a needle point. Out of the bag also came a coil of rope, and finally several heavy bunches of grapes, quite a lot of grapes.

"The king, the man, was nothing," she said. "He was sacrificed every spring, since the ground needs new seed every year. His body was ploughed into the ground. They made no distinction between the seed of crops and a man's seed. Of course they didn't distinguish either between a man and his seed, both were quite useless in themselves. On the other hand you can understand the supreme value of the female. When she took the useless seed into her body she became the creator of her people, both male and female. The soil took the seed and produced the food for the people, bread and wine, and so the soil was the all-important female-creator too. It was a fantastically simple and innocent system, don't you feel, honey?" said Helen, uncapping the bottle of wine and filling the mugs.

In fact Ryan thought it was the worst system he had ever heard of. "What's the knife for?" he asked directly.

"Well for the sowing rite, the knife can be symbolic, like the grapes and bread," Helen said with abstracted petulance, as to somebody in a classroom who was jumping ahead of the lesson. "See, this is what we'll do, it will be glorious here in the moonlight. You are tied down on the altar. It's just a question of cutting the rope to length and knotting you tight to the grilles on either side. The bread and grapes are placed at your feet, to show the Goddess what we would like to have from her in return for the sacrifice, after you're ploughed into the ground. Oh yes, and you're naked of course—the fertility rite comes first, then the rite of sowing. But don't worry," Helen said, "you don't have to do anything except lie there, I'll take care of the details. And it will be just me. Back then there were as many as twenty women and they became terribly angry if the man's seed failed. Failure of seed was an omen."

"Forget it," said Ryan.

Helen shrugged off her shoulder ribbons and wriggled out of her dress, sipping from the little silver baby mug now and then while undressing. "We drink wine from cups of precious metal but I couldn't find gold," she explained, and hummed a dreamy chant to herself, a pagan hymn perhaps, as she unhooked her bra with one hand.

"Chilly," she confided. "But fortunately I'm warm-blooded."

The display did not entice Ryan, though it was not bad. A low-to-the-ground person, Helen had her own integrity of proportion, as if a potter's hand had come down heavily on the head of one of Ryan's willowy girls, depressing her to a shorter, wider symmetry. She danced with the rope and, waltzing, began to cut it into lengths with the knife.

"The part I didn't tell you," said Helen, "is that they always drugged the man. I put something in your wine. I'm sure the king wanted an anaesthetic, knowing what was going to happen, the poor darling. But I thought you might object to taking your clothes off, and lying down on the altar, and being tied, and so on. How do you feel?"

"Fine and dandy," Ryan said. He felt refreshed and happy. He thought now he might go along with her, to be polite; she was only a girl after all.

"Are you ready to lie down?"

"All right."

"Great. Feet here. Head there. That's perfect."

Still humming to herself Helen stripped Ryan of jacket and tie and shirt and unbuckled his belt.

"Can I keep my pants?"

"What? Of course not."

"I've changed my mind. Let me up."

The trouble here was that Ryan had only taken one gulp of the wine. But Helen had the quick wit to assure him that she respected his modesty, and thought more highly of modest men than of the racier kinds, and wanted him to keep his pants. Meanwhile she trussed his upper body to the grilles as tightly as a turkey to a spit. Removing his shoes, she tied his ankles down too on either side. She picked up the knife.

"Men are so selfish and cruel," she told him. "A woman must be a plaything or he won't look at her. Unless he has some other way to use her. When I think of the unfairness of it . . ." She made a careless gesture over Ryan's body with the steel blade. "The trouble I went to arranging all this, and you my proud selfish bull, you'd like your clothes left on, you think there's nothing to pay. Is a woman allowed to keep her clothes on when she doesn't feel like taking them off? Oh no, she's begged and forced, she's bought and sold. She must have generosity and compassion. She must have a sense of guilt. She must have hips that look good in jeans and a mother's bosom."

With these words of complaint Helen cut away the pants of Ryan's best grey suit. She wielded the knife with loose ill-tempered strokes in long rips down each leg. Ryan closed his eyes and hoped that any gashing that occurred would be just of his legs. When Helen cut his shorts away he heard her whisper: "Gee, thank you, Goddess. Your servant thanks you."

"I want to go home now," Ryan said. "I can't afford these kind of games. That suit was expensive. I suppose you know I have to drive home without pants."

"I wasn't planning on letting you go home," Helen said, peering with short-sighted tenderness into his eyes. She took his mug in her left hand then pinched his nostrils closed with her right, her forearm immobilizing Ryan's head. He had to choke down the wine to get air. She filled him another mug.

"There, drink up the wine, you handsome king. The wine deadens your vocal chords, we don't want a lot of shouting out here. You get very thirsty, that's all."

As he swallowed the last drop of wine Ryan's throat dried up suddenly. His tongue seemed to get larger. He said in a cracked voice: "That's an illegal drug, isn't it." However then he began to feel like a lion as promised. He felt on top of the world. Strength rushed along his limbs to the very tips of toes and fingers.

"We'll have a rehearsal, okay? Just the fertility part, practice never hurts. Alley oop."

For some reason Ryan did not understand, being somewhat fuzzy in the head, Helen sat astride him, lightly on his thighs, her elbows resting on the slab on both sides of his chest. She lowered her face to his and their breaths misted her glasses.

Now Ryan felt helpless and indignant beneath the good wine strength. An outraged thought struggled in his fuzzy consciousness. My mind and personality are not important here, Ryan thought. I'm only a carcass. I could be any kind of person in the world and it wouldn't make a difference.

"You're absolutely splendid. What a man."

"You're hurting me."

"Do you have to talk?"

Ryan in his daze looked up at the tendons of Helen's neck as with face clenched her head reared to the stars. He felt the long trembles of her body.

"Wow, Goddess, that wasn't at all bad."

Helen gave Ryan a practical kiss on the forehead, a little absent-mindedly, and slipped to the ground, ignoring his feline shriek of pain.

"We're going to have to do that again for the rite proper," she told him, looking around searchingly at the trees. "I mean it's not supposed to be so personal. I have to find a thyrsus. These branches aren't any good, they're too twisty. Tell you what, you wait here and I'll go inside and see if I can find a slat or something in the house. A thyrsus," Helen said to Ryan kindly, seeing his misgiving, "is just a ceremonial staff the bacchantes carried. Well, mostly ceremonial, but don't sweat for goodness sake, it's just a long spear with an acorn point. The acorn was symbolic for them of course. We really don't need an acorn. If I find some kind of stick or pole I can just whittle a point on it with the knife."

"Why does it need a point?" Ryan asked at once.

"Just don't think about it for now, your majesty. I'll be right back."

Helen Letresky found it quite easy to believe herself one of the bacchantes, tripping naked across the orchard. She kept to the shadows as usual and skirted pool and yard. Avoiding the edged rubble she entered through an open side door what might have been a ruined temple of her ancient sisters. But the moon shone on prosaic modern vehicles, four or five trucks parked inside the walls with cabs lettered ALEX PALMIERI WRECKING. These were filled with salvageable material, copper pipe and bathroom fixtures for the most part.

Helen looked for a thyrsus. Right away she saw dozens of them on a truck partly in shadow: beautiful scrolled wands, gallery rails tied in bundles with twine. The truck said DOMINIC PALMIERI BUILDING.

She had to wade through ankle-high cold water to reach the truck, where one of the water pipes from outside dripped on the floor. When she pulled on the nearest bundle of rails the load shifted. Something heavy toppled toward Helen, who leaped aside in time. The object hit the water with a loud, bursting splash and powder exploded around, cement or dry plaster of some kind.

A voice outside said sharply: "What was that?"

Watchman, Helen thought, these wreckers probably have a watchman to guard the salvage. She opened the cab door and hopped in. Staying well back in the dark, she looked through the driver's window on the opposite side. Chief Williams came cautiously through the gap where the front door had been, followed by Mrs. Williams more confidently, hands in the pockets of her dressing gown.

Helen groaned in disappointment, for she would have preferred a watchman. Dreary questions if they find me naked, Helen grumbled to herself, and worse trouble if they come upon that lovely boy in the orchard. I suppose the first thing they would want to do would be to untie him. Middle-aged people like Uncle Frank and Aunt Mavis, Helen bitched innerly, should go to bed at a proper hour and leave the pleasures of night and moon to the young.

"Over there," Chief Williams said. "Something fell from the truck." He shouted: "Anybody in here?"

"But what has happened to the Graveleys' *house*?"

Chief Williams, approaching Helen's hiding place, read the Palmieri name on the truck and hissed to his wife: "*It's the Italians!*" At the same moment his foot slipped on the wet floor. Helen saw her uncle's arms flailing as he strove to keep his balance but then the other foot shot from under him also and he crashed into the water.

"Frank! Are you all right, Frank?"

" . . . damn silly question, any fool can see I'm soaked in mud. Italian sons of bitches left a tap running or something," said Chief Williams. "Let's go home, Mavis, we're doing no good here."

"Ryan's car is still in the driveway, Frank. I'm sure Alisha will call and ask where Helen is. What should I tell her?"

And Helen sighed, oh for goodness sake go home to bed and let me honour the goddess and the past, blood and loins, earth and bread.

"Tell her the truth, tell her we searched every bush . . . Mavis, this revolting muck is going stiff on me."

Chief Williams's favourite charcoal suit had turned a white colour. He stood with his arms straight out from his sides, looking down at himself. Mrs. Williams, though not unsympathetic, kept some distance away from her muddy husband. The chief then awkwardly removed his jacket, which cracked loudly. It looked much like the upper part of a scarecrow without a head.

"Weighs a ton." Chief Williams let the solidified jacket fall and it thudded on the floor and remained upright and entire. "This is concrete, Mavis, some kind of filthy Italian instant cement, my clothes are turning to stone."

The chief had difficulty getting his tie and shirt off. By working the tie up and down like a pump handle he was able to break the cement and tear the material, but the shirt had to be prised off in layers. Chief Williams worked on the sleeves and front while his wife broke shards from the rear.

It became evident that the lower clothing would be much more of a problem when Chief Williams tried to take a step forward and toppled over on his face like a tree.

"Would you turn me on my back, Mavis, please. See if you can find a chisel or something."

Helen could not escape unseen from the truck cab, which smelled of oil and the male. But while she waited she did not consider the chipping of her uncle free of concrete to be an entertainment worth watching. The vinyl was sticky on her bottom. She drew her knees up to her breasts, hands linked around her shins, staring in sullen spirits at the black windshield. I could forget the thyrsus and the sowing part of the ceremony, she thought, maybe it's too much and it might be awkward to manage without Phoebe's help. But that would make the fertility rite less authentic. In any case, Helen decided, I must rehearse several more times, he should be properly warmed up again and so should I.

"There's a loose piece there, Mavis."

"My fingernails are ruined."

At last Chief Williams said: "That will do. I can walk."

"Poor Frank. Are you sure?"

"Yes, but you'd better fetch the car around here and bring me some clothes too. I can't be seen walking across people's lawns at night stark naked."

Who *cares*, Helen screamed in her mind, exasperated to the limit of her patience, who on earth would want to look at an old uncle jiggling his way home, *go*.

"Oh I think you're being silly and prudish. I have just this dressing-gown. See. I don't feel in the least self-conscious."

"Mavis, you are completely clothed in the dressing-gown. A naked man on somebody's lawn at night is a different matter."

"Frank. Have you noticed the moonlight?"

"What do you mean?"

"Isn't the moonlight mysterious? I feel giddy, somehow."

These subtle words from her aunt horrified Helen. She knew she could not endure a vigil in the man-smelling truck while some form of middle-aged or practically geriatric coupling went forward outside.

But Chief Williams said: "Don't be foolish. I'm freezing, there's a wind rising, and this is absolutely not the time for moonlight and getting giddy. Fetch the car."

Still Mrs. Williams did feel that there had been missed pleasure for that moment in the ruined Graveley house with the stars for a roof. By now a wind had risen, and as Mrs. Williams under the giddy moonlight set out on her errand, she thought she heard words on the wind from the Graveley orchard and went to investigate, sure that she had located her niece and Redmond Ryan.

Soon after Helen left him Ryan found that he could call for help, though from his dry mouth his cries were alternately high-pitched, like a child's, and a gargled bass. A fresh wind was sweeping through the orchard by then. He was desperately thirsty. As Ryan cried out he moved his head from side to side. His cheek touched the grapes. Straining all his body sideways, he began to devour the juicy bunch with grunts of need.

He did think for a moment that a woman whose face was familiar, wearing a crimson dressing-gown, was on her way toward him across the moonlit grass. However he did not believe that oddity of vision momentarily, knowing himself to be drugged. When the dressing-gown was thrown across Ryan's face he continued his ravenous chewing and swallowing in darkness, just one tiny part of his mind recording the new occurrence. He could almost abstractly feel the heft and gasps of a woman who was heavier than Helen, fumbly, and apparently in something of a hurry. Ryan very deeply resented what was happening even as he kept feeding his thirst, crushing grapes between his teeth and uttering little screams of pain. His need of drink was increasing. Then his lolling head could find no more grapes in the dark under the dressing-gown, nothing except the bare stone.

"If you were just passing by, lady," Ryan said, muffled and squeaky, hurt in body and with his male sense of himself much depleted, "at least you could set me free before you take off. I'm going to die of thirst out here."

His opportunistic visitor did not reply to this. The dressing-gown swirled away from Ryan. All he could see after it went, though, was its square shape and flying feet beneath, since Mrs. Williams was holding two corners above her head to make a screen behind. Ryan was conscious only of his raging thirst, the chill wind, and the injustice of his circumstances.

While he watched in this discomfort the flying feet slowed and the woman seemed to peer into the trees toward the Graveley house. She threw her hands in the air and the dressing-gown snapped free. She turned and ran back to Ryan, knees pumping, heedless of nudity and recognition.

"Save them, get up and save them, there's a *horrible thing* over there," Mrs. Williams shouted, throwing herself on Ryan. "You must get up at once and help. Hurry." Casting looks of terror behind, Mrs. Williams found the knife and cut the ropes. "A monster's chasing Helen and my husband." Strange keening howls rolled through the Regency Gate parkland as though from a wolf-king stating his possession of territory in an old country; in any case sound more bloodchilling than could come from ordinary wind.

Redmond Ryan rubbed his wrists and stretched his racked body, vaulted to the ground, groaned, seized a bunch of grapes from the foot of the stone and pushed his face into it greedily.

"Save them! Do your duty!"

"Yes well, Mrs. Williams," Ryan said, noisily spitting out skin and seeds and chomping to get more juice down his gullet, "that's not easy for me to know, my duty. Seems to me, though, for the last hour or so I've been doing duty as a salt-lick if you see what I mean. Well sure you'd like me to switch back to being a policeman when you happen to need a cop, but I'm human, you see, Mrs. Williams. I'm a person. I have feelings, just like everybody else."

Mrs. Williams was looking into the night. She squealed suddenly. "Well, look at him, the asshole dummy, the pompous yellow-belly, he's leading it this way," Mrs. Williams said.

Leaping over the grass toward Redmond Ryan and Mrs. Williams came the naked Helen Letresky, and the naked Chief Williams whose body was chalked white.

Not long after Mrs. Williams left to fetch the car a face had appeared in the truck windshield in front of Helen's terrified eyes. This was a drawn woman's face with a toucan's nose and a low-slung stubbled chin, the mouth open to show teeth like a dog's, the upper lip on one side curled back in a snarl. The apparition's skin was greenish, the inside of the mouth bright red, the eyes also as red as rubies. This sudden phantom from the dark was the most unnerving thing Helen had ever seen in her life. She wailed. She jumped from the truck cab. Chief Williams hardly looked at Helen in his dread of what he saw pursuing her. He hopped nimbly through a window, breaking for open country and home. Helen followed her uncle, screaming, her instinct being for company. Her thought was that she stood a chance of escape if her uncle fell to the clutches of the fearsome hag, whereas alone she might be chosen and run down as the sole victim.

With his niece running strongly abreast of him, Chief Williams regained some sense of what was happening. He, a policeman with a reputation for toughness, was running like a scared child from some old crone of the streets who had been sheltering in the ruin. The chief glanced back to confirm this idea of the pursuer. What he saw did not do so. The ghastly woman seemed to be more than seven feet tall, covering the ground with speedy strides, shawl and skirts black and blowing in the wind. One hand brandished a club while the taloned fingers of the other were outstretched to reach him. Moreover she was quite close behind. Her mouth opened and a sound came from the red-toothed cavern, that chilling howl also heard by Mrs. Williams and Redmond Ryan. Chief Williams ran faster then, on melting knee joints.

3

It was the matter of not owning a car that put Joe Kowalski in position at the Graveley house site to see the naked running people and their pursuer. Sergeant Brock was to pick Kowalski up at the Williams's house to drive him home. Then Mrs. Williams closed down her party early and Chief Williams dismissed Kowalski at eleven.

So Joe Kowalski took a stroll through his Regency Gate beat to pass the hour, not expecting to come upon anything of interest so late, with the last bus gone and window lights blinking off along the privileged streets. A dog-walker or two to say hello to maybe, he thought. Kowalski was in low spirits after his drab evening of car-parking duty. He wanted to be at home with an ale in his hand and the aunts in bed, watching something violent and soothing on TV.

He reached the Graveley site on his way back to the Williams's house to meet Brock.

Kowalski thought at first that the cry he heard came from a wakeful dog. But what size of brute would be responsible for such a howl, he asked himself then. He made his way unhurriedly up the Graveley driveway, an officer investigating an unusual noise. He saw, flashing from the orchard and running across the back lawn, the naked moonlit figures of Redmond Ryan, Chief Williams, Helen Letresky and Mrs. Williams. Moreover Ryan was eating a bunch of grapes on the run and Chief Williams seemed to have daubed his body with white pigment.

Though ale and doughnuts had taken their toll Joe Kowalski was not in bad shape. He broke into pursuit at once, at an intersecting angle. He was angry, especially when he recognized Helen Letresky running with the others, against her will very likely, Kowalski thought. He had met Helen Letresky a few times at Sergeant Brock's and he had liked the girl.

The runners swerved to the right as Kowalski ran to cut across their path. He had a glimpse of the other figure then, the woman, fleet and black. She also went right so Kowalski lost his angle and found himself running behind and to the left of the naked people, with the black pursuer closer up and to their right. The chase was taking everybody on a line that ran somewhere between the Graveley site and the Williams's house, away from both places, in fact northward out of Regency Gate.

Kowalski was hurdling the back lawn fences when he could. Sometimes he had to crash through bushes. He sought the short cuts, while the naked people followed the lie of open country. Watching the terrain, Kowalski noticed a privet hedge coming up which blocked their run. They ran along the hedge, through a gate, and were deflected again by a swimming-pool fence. They broke back along the privet on the other side. Kowalski put his head down and tried to bull through the stiff privet hedge.

He made a lot of noise. The black tireless figure was at the gate. She turned and saw Kowalski. He was busy fighting the whippy branches, his hands protecting his eyes. He heard the howl, though. It rose and fell weirdly like a primitive song, a chant on a high pitch. The terrible sound stopped Joe Kowalski.

He lost his momentum and the branches snapped in around him. The naked runners went past his angry eyes left to right, beginning to string out, Ryan, Helen, Chief Williams gasping, Mrs. Williams puffing fatly.

The black-clad woman went by at speed too just as Kowalski got free of the hedge. Who the heck is that anyway, Kowalski asked himself. Regency Gate parties, he thought angrily.

He had lost ground. He saw the people next on a rise ahead in full moonlight, the plateau of a small ravine. The open ground was to their left now and as they followed it they were roughly on the route Helen Letresky had taken with Redmond Ryan. They were making for the Williams's house. In fact Kowalski saw that the black woman in pursuit was chivvying them. She veered left and right like a dog herding cattle toward a pen.

By the time Kowalski topped the rise the people were in Cambridge Mews sprinting for the Williams property. Now it was all open lawn, road and driveways, with no obstructions. Joe Kowalski slowed to a jog. They would go in the house. Then it would be a simple matter of ringing the doorbell, he decided. He was looking down at the Williams's rose garden and he saw the four jumping over the rose bushes and then moving in the direction of the lawn hedge and the front door.

However, they appeared to change their minds all at once. Instead of quitting at the Williams's door they dodged sideways and around the house.

"Hell and amnation," Joe Kowalski breathed, really angry now.

A light flashed in the rose garden as the runners dashed toward it from their circuit of the house. While they were jumping the rose bushes for the second time bright flashes lit the scene a dozen times or so.

Joe Kowalski jogged up to the garden. He saw Sergeant Brock standing behind the lawn hedge. Only the sergeant's head showed above the hedge. He was watching the house on the right side where the naked running group was due to reappear.

"Jeez, what are you doing, sergeant?" Kowalski asked, panting and utterly exasperated. "What the hell, eh."

"Joe, some people are running around out here in the nude."

"I *know* they are. What are you doing standing watching it, sergeant? Ryan is eating grapes and the chief has himself all painted up. What the hell, eh?"

Sergeant Brock resented this. He said, over the hedge: "I only just got here. I got here about one minute ago. I thought I'd pull them in the next time round."

"Who has the flashlight? Were you using a flashlight? Somebody was shining a flashlight or taking pictures."

Kowalski drew deep breaths, of exertion and fury. His wide face was hard as stone.

"I didn't see anything. I just got here, Joe."

". . . old is Helen Letresky? Had to chase them halfway across Regency Gate. Sort of nonsense might be regular for their parties. Not in public on my beat . . . "

"Watch behind. Here they come now."

The four runners broke from the trees in line and cleared the first rose bush abreast and in step, as if performing a disciplined ballet leap. The toes of the leading legs were pointed and the arches on the following legs extended, over the reaching thorns. They hurdled the bushes in series, Helen Letresky followed by Chief Williams, then Ryan and Mrs. Williams, quite evenly spaced but landing with ragged timing. Ryan was still gnawing at his bunch of grapes. All four swerved toward the house. A shadow rose there, near the door, and the runners shot off at a tangent, willing to begin another tour apparently although they looked exhausted.

Joe Kowalski stepped into their path holding up a traffic-stopping arm.

"That's enough, now, Chief Williams, please," Joe Kowalski said. "I suggest you take your party inside. Orgy's over now, please, inside everybody, time to get dressed, let's break it up here."

Sergeant Brock was fascinated. He was fixed on the same spot, only his head showing above the hedge. I wouldn't have done that, what Joe's doing, he admitted to himself. I suppose I'm too smart, if that's the name for it.

But the naked people seemed to hang with gratitude on Joe Kowalski's large and solid form. Redmond Ryan collapsed, turning as he fell, and sat down partly on Kowalski's shoes with his back against Kowalski's shins. He pushed grapes into his face automatically. Mrs. Williams wrapped her arms around Kowalski's waist and slid to her knees. Helen Letresky clung to his neck like a lover, with one foot on Ryan's thigh. Chief Williams's back was pressed against Kowalski's as he scanned the darkness around. Indeed they all looked into the night with fearful hunted eyes from the security of Kowalski's body.

"How about giving me a hand here, sergeant," Kowalski said. "I can't move."

Later riding home in the cruiser Joe Kowalski was not speaking to his friend Sergeant Brock. Kowalski stared straight ahead at the road.

"Helen is not a minor. I know that for sure," the sergeant said. "I remember her twenty-first birthday."

A few minutes later Sergeant Brock said: "We have to live with the facts of life, Joe. You can't put the chief's name on a charge-sheet. First the desk-man, any desk-man, would tear it up. Second, the chief's in shock now but he won't stay in shock for ever, will he. God damn it, Joe."

They turned into Kowalski's street.

"Okay, tell you what we'll do," Sergeant Brock said. "Say we get a lot of complaints from people who were looking out their windows. If we get enough heavy complaints you can lay a charge. Okay, Joe?"

Kowalski kept his eyes ahead on the windshield and did not reply.

Eight

Floucing

1

"We got a description says he's small build, green jeans and shirt, doesn't sound like the Slasher to me, lieutenant."

"No? What does he sound like to you, yo-yo, a leprechaun? Look, he's an animal, he's loose in the streets and I want him in a cage, is that asking a lot."

Makes sense, thought Kowalski. All leprechauns are small people but not all small people are leprechauns.

"Joseph."

"Jeez, Aunt Myrtle, this is *Kojak*."

But it was anyway not one of the bald marauder's better nights. Kowalski switched off the TV and looked at the aunts who were sitting together on the couch like two intelligent birds on a perch.

"We are bored. We would like to do something, Joseph."

"All right. Let's talk about the problem." Kowalski swallowed a long draught of ale. He had unkind things to say. "The problem has to do with your age. Old age is the problem. Bingo, bridge club, TV, movies, they're fine. But you aren't interested. You can't afford to be choosy any more, there isn't much choice left. A few other things, yes, baseball now the season's started, just to watch, you're too slow to play. The same goes for bowling, football, tennis, Aunt Myrtle," said Kowalski with a nervous picture in his mind of his sleepy Aunt Myrtle flying down a bowling lane gutter, thumb locked in the ball. "Dances, discos, rock concerts, nothing's suitable. Nothing's been worked out for your age group. Probably it's a money thing. Nothing's been worked out except by the churches because they don't have to show a profit."

"It's a disgrace," said Aunt Myrtle. "At the church they make you cater wedding receptions and knit afghans for draws."

"Myrtle, be fair. The church wants us to feel useful."

"That's no excuse for exploiting us. I don't see why I should have to work to feel useful."

"Raising sheep now," Kowalski remarked, making conversation, "that's a useful thing to do for those with the cash. That's work and recreation in one job. See, you don't have to go to work, doing drab stuff, and then find something else to do to relax. If we raised sheep, we'd be relaxing all the time, even when we were working. That's the life. Makes more sense than a yacht."

"Yes," Aunt Caroline said. "That sounds very worthwhile."

Aunt Myrtle said: "But butchering them must be difficult work."

Both Kowalski and his Aunt Caroline turned to stare at Aunt Myrtle.

"Aunt Myrtle, we'd raise the sheep for wool. I'm surprised at you. Naturally we wouldn't butcher the sheep, that would be sickening. There's lots of work all the same, dipping and shearing. Aunt Caroline and I could handle it."

"Would we make a lot of money selling wool, Joseph?"

"No."

"It's a dream of an idea," Aunt Caroline said. "A pretty green pasture with sheep grazing on it. Think of all the manure for the garden. The lambs would make us feel young again every year, if we wanted to feel that way."

"I could spin fleeces into yarn," Aunt Myrtle said. "What you need is fleece stock that gives long-staple fibre with a good crimp. I haven't spun wool in years."

The other two looked at her again, astonished.

"Spinning is not work. It was taught to me as an occupation for a young lady, a married lady with a husband to be the provider. Then," said Aunt Myrtle, quite animated by the idea, "we could sell the yarn to the church for their damn afghans."

"Splendid. Let's do it."

"Well not so fast, hold up," Kowalski said. "I was just talking. We can't do it. We have to think of costs and finances."

"Oh Joseph, you're so dreary. The first good idea you've had and you're making excuses."

"Please don't think of costs and finances for too long, Joseph," said Aunt Caroline politely. "Myrtle and I will be in our graves soon. We'll be pushing up the grass for the sheep."

Aunt Myrtle agreed with her sister, for once not starting the argument as to which of them might first be pushing up the grass. But she said: "We must have a man in to put my spinning-wheel in order. Caroline's using it as an ornament, all waxed and polished. That's a working machine, Caroline, and no more of an antique than I am."

2

Chief Williams did not like the way Redmond Ryan was sitting in his office. Ryan's general posture was insubordinate. While his long legs were not propped on the chief's desk, neither were they together on the floor respectfully. The set of the shoes was out of line because the knees were slumped. Ryan was resting his shoulders against the chair back, almost lounging, Chief Williams noted, instead of sitting correctly upright in fear.

Drawing some security toward himself, Chief Williams said: "Good lunch at the Lawn Bowling Club today, or not bad anyway. They haven't given us chicken Matignon in a while. The quenelle stuffing was excellent. Quibbler might think there was a pinch too much of thyme. Canned truffles unfortunately."

"That's a coincidence, chief. I had chicken for lunch too."

"Oh yes?" said Chief Williams who did not want to hear about the constable's Thrift-Box. "What do you have on Equity Mortgage and Trust so far?"

"They do nice chicken at Morley's," Ryan said, apparently willing to share his own views on food with his superior. "Stuffed breasts, oysters and artichoke. I thought the artichoke could have been crisper, but my truffle slices were fresh."

"The men don't eat at McDonald's any more then?" Chief Williams asked, eyes brilliant and showing the whites. "McDonald's changed the chef so the fellows talked it over in the off-duty room and decided to switch to Morley's. The reason I don't go to Morley's myself," said the chief, speaking with his nose raised, over his lower teeth, "is because the auditors won't sanction Morley's on an expense sheet. How the hell do you happen to be eating at Morley's, constable?"

"I was taken there by a friend."

"What else are they talking about in the off-duty room?"

"The usual. Sex, crime."

"You're telling me that Brock and Kowalski are keeping their mouths shut?"

"Nobody knows anything about what happened at your place, chief, it's a fact."

"I don't believe it. I don't believe it because of human nature, Ryan. All human nature is basically the same. Look inside yourself to know the world. A man who understands that much can be a mind-reader . . . "

Redmond Ryan listened for a few minutes to Chief Williams's standard little talk on human nature, which paralleled Ryan's own view by and large and was therefore boring. He then reported on his investigation of Equity Mortgage and Trust.

"I haven't tied it back to any individuals yet, chief, but Equity Mortgage and Trust merged in 1965 with Montreal Mutual Insurance. Montreal Mutual is part of O. P. Delaney, that's a conglomerate with a head office in Chicago — their main operations are in meat and dairy products, bicycles, mortuary supplies. It's a subsidiary of Beecham Oil, one of the independent exploration companies. Beecham's been trying to diversify to renewable energy. There's a report in the *Financial Times* file that Beecham picked up O. P. Delaney for the stockyard properties. Beecham was doing methane gas research, it says. That can't have worked out for them — last year Beecham was taken over by

Harrison's Fine Foods. This gets a little tricky," Ryan said, flicking competent notebook pages, "because only four weeks ago the board of Equity Mortgage and Trust submitted a bid to purchase all shares of Harrison's Fine Foods. The directors of Harrison's put the offer to the shareholders and it was accepted. They paid fifty cents over last year's best market performance," Ryan said, shaking his head in wonder at boardroom acquisitiveness.

"Ryan," said Chief Williams.

"Must have wanted it pretty bad."

"Ryan, that goes round in a circle," Chief Williams said. "That's rubbish. That has Equity Mortgage and Trust purchasing its own parent company."

"Well I'm not a businessman. Has it ever occurred to you, chief, that there might be big nickel deposits in Regency Gate?"

Chief Williams put fingers to his temples, pressing on a pulse, curiously feeling his own blood in its flow as it brought oxygen to his brain and returned to the pump of his heart. My heart is sound, he thought, and I have a good head of hair for my age. The minutes of a man's life are golden. "No," he said.

"No? Well I happen to think so. The two largest shareholders in Equity Mortgage and Trust are Deloro Nickel Mines and Mini-People Incorporated. So if you want my opinion, chief, there's nickel in Regency Gate. Lots of it."

"Nickel?" But look here, the nickel industry isn't underhanded, Ryan. It's one of this country's great industries. Forget about nickel. Can't we get anything on the chairman of Equity Mortgage and Trust?"

Chief Williams attentively watched Ryan relaxing deeper into the chair. Ryan crossed his legs.

"We could think about that, but I don't see it," Ryan said curtly. "He's living at the Four Seasons right now. His house in Regency Gate was one of the first to go."

"What about this other company, Mini-People Incorporated?"

"Mini-People don't have any nickel interests, though," Ryan pointed out. He added less confidently: "I'd just as soon not go round that track again, chief. According to the first records I looked at Mini-People owns Beecham Oil. Also Montreal Mutual."

"Mini-People. Mini-People, that's an odd name for a company, wouldn't you say?"

"Not really," Ryan said. "Mini-People started out as a manufacturer of children's clothes. You get lots of companies in children's merchandise with names like that, Tiny Tots Incorporated, Wee Folk Products, Little People Ltd., it's very common. We should be thinking nickel. There are," said Redmond Ryan, addressing the chief courteously but with a didactic slant to his body, "two reasons for acquiring expensive land, one to build on and two to mine. Now in Regency Gate the built-up properties are being demolished at extra cost. That leaves mining. Who does mining? Deloro Nickel. What do they mine? Nickel."

"I've always admired deductive reasoning, the syllogism in particular," Chief Williams said, smiling at Ryan. "Pity it appeals so much to trashy minds. But look here, constable," the chief went on sympathetically, "your chair isn't comfortable, is it? I've been watching you squirming and shifting. That's often a problem with overstuffed brocade. I should warn people who come in here, the comfortable way to sit is to conform to the discipline of the chair itself, an upright posture in other words, but I suppose if I did so," Chief Williams said, so amused at the thought that a merry laugh broke from between his teeth and smiling lips, "it might give the impression that I was soliciting deference—almost like asking visitors to sit to attention in my office, eh, Redmond? What kind of a democracy would that be, eh? No, I should get these Victorian chairs out of here. I want to make people feel at home. What I need is a brighter scheme, a bowl of those marvellous polystyrene roses on a glass coffee table, a recliner for the folk who come in, say olefin upholstery with smart glittery silver threads woven into the fabric . . ."

Ryan's attention wandered. Ryan knew full well that he was being aggressively patronized. He wasn't, though, being intimidated. I guess every dog has his day, Ryan told himself pleasurably, and I'll be a son of a bitch now I have mine.

" . . . and classical wall-hangings to impress people. Van Gogh sunflowers, they're good, Redmond. Don Quixote and

Sancho Panza, by Picasso. Have you seen that? Everybody has one. I could hang it over there in place of my watercolours, my old polychrome James Bourne, or look at that faded Girtin. Or plaster plaques. What do you think, ducks or geese?"

Even more pleasant for Ryan was the understanding that he didn't have to sit around and take it.

"Must be off now, sir. I don't have an eye for interior decoration, chief," Ryan said apologetically, rising to his feet with regret. "A few black leather armchairs, TV and stereo, exercising equipment, couple of old guns on the walls, that's my apartment. Hell, I don't have the sort of mind it 'akes," he said, turning at the door and brushing his hand in a lazy diagonal gesture in front of his forehead, more of a friendly wave than a salute, "to appreciate those things. I guess my taste is too rough and masculine to understand colour schemes, and fabrics, and, you know, flower arrangements, sir," Redmond Ryan admitted humbly and closed the door.

3

Eight hundred miles from Bradfarrow on the twenty-fifth floor of the Exxon Building in Manhattan, Gable Sweeney's new secretary was in his office assembling his conference folder for the security chiefs' meeting, the SCM. Sweeney, the director of Mini-People Incorporated Security, was a man in his late forties with bushy black hair and a full black beard and moustache, an unruly man. He ran ten security divisions for Mini-People Incorporated.

He was a social theorist on occasion and was known to see multi-national corporations, especially MPI, as countries. In this view Sweeney directed espionage and undercover diplomacy for a country, Mini-People. The comparison he liked to make in explaining his thinking was to Ireland, homeland of his ancestors. MPI had larger capital assets than Ireland. Worldwide, MPI's dependents were six million people or more compared to Ireland's population of under four million. To the argument that a country was more than its wealth and its loyal people, that it was a landscape of the soul, Sweeney replied that MPI owned five hundred thousand square miles of real estate, plenty of it scenic, compared to Ireland's overpraised twenty-seven thousand which included many ugly bogland tracts.

Yet Ireland could have a police force and a standing army openly whereas MPI had to use codes and circumspection to protect its interests in the same way. "They can appoint judges and make laws," Gable Sweeney would complain reasonably from time to time. "They can decide what justice is. Mini-People Incorporated is more important globally in every sense you care to name, we're of more benefit to more people and also to the economy of the free world. But if MPI built its own jails and appointed its own judges we'd hear it loud and clear from every darn consumer group in the country."

Sweeney was talking on the phone to the president of Mini-People, Bigg Proudfoot. The president's voice was bone-dry and scholarly. It carried with remote authority on the wire as if from a distant height of command inaccessible to ordinary people. His office was thought to be in Germany or Japan.

Sweeney said: "On the way back I stopped off in Peking, the USSR. Yes, sir, I talked to him. Well Mr. Brezhnev wants the subsidy raised again, nothing's new with him. He has more people in the Secretariat to take care of now and he doesn't get round much himself any more. We had a few hold-outs the last time we passed the hat."

"I was down through the canal. Khalid thinks we're trying to corrupt his council of ministers."

"Well the guy is paranoiac. We do a little lobbying now and then in Saudi, who doesn't."

"He could," said the faraway voice of Bigg Proudfoot, "turn the taps wide open. He could pump ten million barrels of oil a day for the western tankers, if we should ever lose our arrangement with the OPEC folk."

"Well our lobby isn't that loose, sir, we're keeping an eye on what he does," Sweeney said with irritation. He wasn't in the best of tempers. "We have the council of ministers in our pocket is what we have. He can call it corruption, we call it education. If Khalid tries to reach for a tap Heads Aprep have a man ready to put in." Heads Aprep was the Mini-People Security division

Heads of State Appointments and Replacements. "Yesterday I was checking out the next guy for Iran and had to eat sheep stew for lunch in the desert outside Ar Rimal. The stew-pot was ninety per cent grease, the rest bone. What is it, ten o'clock now and the glop's still lying in my stomach like a cannon ball. My host treated me to both of the sheep's eyes. He was able to do me that honour because the sheikh and his family brought Happy Meals. Back here in the office, Mrs. Humacher's retired and I have a new secretary to break in. The way it stands with me this morning, sir, I have a ball of sheep grease on my ulcer and jet lag, this girl to deal with and the SCM," Sweeney said. "It's raining outside and the garbage strike is still on." He asked: "The *Sea-Girt* is pulling well after the refit, is she sir, no trouble balancing the new discodeck?"

"Suppose I call back when you're in a better mood, Sweeney," the MPI president said, thousands of miles away. "Meanwhile you might start the Governor of Louisiana's campaign. On the oil question, I haven't seen a pessimistic projection of Alaskan resources recently and that concerns me. Naples says the propaganda visuals on their US TV monitors are down. And look here, Sweeney, everybody's still wearing denim, when can we expect an end of it?"

"I'll ask around."

"And you might see that our colleagues are in line on the subsidy this time, we'll pay the increase of course. Some firm words with the people who are holding back would help perhaps."

Gable Sweeney's eyes looking out from the bush of face hair were streaky when he put the phone down. He needed a night's sleep. The new secretary was talking to him. She had been moving with an efficient swirl of dress from her own desk outside Sweeney's office to the file cabinets inside, and between the cabinets and his desk, where she was putting the SCM material together. The director's office was large enough for two conference areas, a formal centre with upright chairs for serious talk and a cosily-furnished corner for chats. There was a refrigerator and bar. The carpet was kelly green and the paintings on the walls were of speedy machinery in monochrome. Sweeney had figured out that one was a grey jet on take-off from a grey carrier and another was a pink racing car circling a pink track.

" . . . and the information that's come in on Flouncy I'm putting under new reports, last on the agenda. So far we don't have too much information on Flouncy. Manufactured in Saddler's Springs, Pennsylvania. It's a fabric softener, like Fleecy and Bounce. Flouncy briefs are in the brown file. You have umpteen briefs on leprechaun business, green file."

The new secretary, whose name was Mandy D'Arcy, wore a grey dress that at first glance seemed drab and oversized. But apparently the dress was made of material lighter than air and floated around and in against her with every move she made. She wore numerous long strands of beads around her neck and clinking gold bracelets on both wrists. Her full upper lip rode on rabbity teeth which with doe eyes and hair tied in braids gave her considerable gawky charm. She was twenty-five and did not believe in make-up and would not need to for perhaps another three or four years.

Mandy guessed that Gable Sweeney probably had a lot of drive because of being short in height. Her experience was that short people were compensators.

"Why do we need Flouncy anyway?"

Sweeney said: "It's fabric softener, why does anybody? We're interested in the phenomenon." He began organizing the paper on his desk, putting the notes of his talk with the president on top. "Okay, honey, it's the security chiefs' meeting today. You're familiar with the SCM from the chiefs' level I guess, all you need to remember working in this office is that the chiefs are a heck of a bunch of guys, you couldn't ask for a team with more heart. They're liars and intriguers by nature, though. We're an espionage and deception section here, the career is in the baroque mode. The requirements of the work are Byzantine, put it that way, integrity is only one way of looking at the world, the truth doesn't have a particular value in itself if something else gets the job done better." The damp of sweat was on Sweeney's forehead from the ulcer ache. He dragged a tired hand down his face and through his beard. "All right. I have a few calls to make. I'll fill you in as we go this morning."

Mandy had sat down to listen to him. She happened to rest one arm behind her chair quite innocently which pushed the other shoulder forward and outlined a pear-shaped breast hung with beads. She asked: "What are leprechauns?"

Sweeney, who was kneading his stomach, took time to consider this question, as if choosing among responses. Mandy moved between the folder on Sweeney's desk and the cabinets, her dress floating around her like seaweed on a naked underwater nymph. She said: "I have that background in Corp-Inter and Ecpolcol and EM, besides my clearance for here. It's okay to let me know, Mr. Sweeney. The word keeps coming up. I've always thought it was a bad code. There aren't any leprechauns, so people can see it's a code."

Corp-Inter was the MPI Security division Corporate Interface which dealt with outside corporations and non-government organisations. EM was Electronic Monitors, handling information gathering for all ten divisions. Economic and Political Controls covered much the same ground as a department of the economy in government except that, MPI being a multi-national, Ecpolcol had an overseas as well as a domestic function.

"Well it goes right back, the word leprechaun," Gable Sweeney said with an air of utter frankness. He made himself a Jameson and ice at the bar in the corner. "There was no MPI Security eighty years ago, when MPI started, the company just used the Pinkerton agency. Mini-People sold children's merchandise back then, we had these ads with elves and fairies, dragons and so on. Kodak did the same when they brought out the Brownie camera. Kodak had little brownies climbing all over the camera in their ads. It was a brutal age, sentimental as hell," Sweeney said, a little relieved after a couple of sips of whiskey. "We were spread out more than Kodak, we used a different kind of fairy for each line of goods. The research was primitive. What they had was this ancient fairy book, three hundred years old, written in some Gaelic dialect. The company didn't have anything like an art department. They just lifted the illustrations from the book, translated the captions I suppose, most of those folklore creatures were weird and couldn't be used of course. Well they used some weird ones anyway. The Lake Dragon is more of a monster than a fairy if you ask me, he was a swimwear product. But the leprechaun was the big seller. Leprechauns and Mini-

People have always been good business together."

While he explained the place of the leprechaun in the company's history, to Sweeney's surprise his new secretary went to the bar and helped herself to a vodka and tomato juice.

"I see, it was a tradition, so MPI Securities took over the fairy names for their personnel."

"That's right. A long time ago, the system's been greatly streamlined since naturally."

Mandy made a note in her notebook. The phone rang. The Corp-Inter chief wanted approval for his list of contributors to the Russian subsidy. He was a likeable person, fond of gossip, with a reputation as a top-notch lobbyist in the boardroom world. Had he been less obviously civilized and in another career what the Corp-Inter chief did best might have been called blackmail from time to time.

"I don't remember offhand who held back before, Frank," Sweeney said to the Corp-Inter chief. "I remember US Steel was one. We'd like steel in on the operation, also duPont and Union Carbide and whoever else didn't ante up on the previous collection. We want everybody in line, Frank."

"Their position at US Steel is it's the government's responsibility."

"Right, and if the government was big enough and smart enough we wouldn't need to bother, would we. Like this isn't a pay-off to a political gangster in the Caribbean or somewhere under the name of economic aid," the MPI Security director said. "We're talking in the area of patriotic duty, the subsidy gets into both chambers of the Supreme Soviet and it reaches twenty out of thirty-seven members of the Praesidium. We went to a fair amount of trouble setting this one up."

"A couple of the people would like input. IBM says if they're paying into the subsidy MPI should let them make a few Soviet government decisions once in a while."

"Well forget that. MPI makes the Soviet decisions."

"I know, they're not serious. The steel industry means it, though, Gabe. They won't be sending a cheque."

"Well I'd like you to get back to them, Frank," Sweeney said. He felt pinpoint twinges between his bottom ribs again. "MPI sees a duty here. We're a live-and-let-live corporation but we'll play hardball if needs be. That's the word for every hold-out on your list."

"Okay, I'll go round again. There shouldn't be a problem, except steel. I'll probably have to shout to make myself heard."

"That's fine, you can do that, we'll follow through for you. Tell them we're talking about take-over, Frank. If we don't see co-operation we're prepared to move in on US Steel with the big buck."

Mandy brought Sweeney another Jameson with ice just as he needed it. His drink without desert tribesman sheep's stew in his stomach and on his full quota of sleep was Perrier, gallons per day in six-ounce increments with a twist of lime. She sat in front of his desk demurely and put her knees together, notebook in one hand, pencil in the other, a fresh vodka and tomato juice on the desk corner. The material of her dress stretched itself against her hips and along the length of her thighs. In Sweeney's eyes as Mandy looked at him expectantly the streaks were much brighter.

"Thanks, honey," Sweeney said. "We can start you on some of the executive work Mrs. Humacher handled for me. Like I'm taking an interest in a job Affiliate Operations is running up north, Bradfarrow, Ontario. Affops is doing the work through an MPI affiliate called Deloro Nickel. The project was chugging along okay before I left, plenty of miscues and foul-ups naturally, Affops isn't the sharpest division in MPI Security. They were at the stage of arranging the details for scenes I had in mind. Where people had to be and at what time, what should be said, the cues and props and choreography. Mrs. Humacher was overseeing that for me. She had a theatrical sense. It's more theatre than business anyway, a territory operation," Gable Sweeney explained. "Writing a theatrical performance and directing the thing from a distance is what it is. People like to have the feeling they run their own lives, so the work calls for flair."

Here Sweeney could see that his secretary was holding a careful attitude of interest, chin up and shoulders straight. However boredom showed in the doe eyes.

Now he wants me to get excited about a native village up near the Arctic, Mandy thought. In fact she knew in her heart that

places outside New York were unreal except for Europe and two
ski resorts in Colorado, and parts of Massachusetts and California.
She studied the man, ignoring what he was saying. This man
could be actually attractive, Sweeney's new secretary decided, if
he tidied the beard and trimmed back the moustache and lost a few
pounds. Short people show it more when they're carrying fat,
Mandy told herself, and then of course they're oversensitive about
appearance. That's probably one of the reasons they talk a lot, to
take your attention away from what they look like.

". . . what we had was two Affops operations on stage,
put it that way. Affops was setting up the people for Flouncy in
Saddler's Springs. Flouncy is the other project I'd like this office
in on directly, a multi-million dollar business selling a product
nobody needs. We have tremendous ideas for that kind of market. Just recently Mrs. Humacher took her eye off Bradfarrow
while she worked on Saddler's Springs. Right now I don't know
how the heck we are in Bradfarrow, whether we're okay or down
the drain or what."

"Where should I start, Mr. Sweeney?"

"Dig out Mrs. Humacher's files and give them a look, you
could start with Deloro Nickel. There's a Joe Kowalski in there,
people named Williams, Palmieri, Huntzagel, Ryan, Melan-
prope." Sweeney said: "And ask Affops to brief you and check
what they're doing. If they haven't lost all control of the territory
in Bradfarrow I'll be pleasantly surprised."

Mandy's phone rang outside. She tried a few switches and got
the call through to the director. "The boardroom's decided on the
Governor of Louisiana in 1992, Louise," Gable Sweeney told the
Ecpolcol chief. "He'll make a superstar president. No, Kennedy
was voted out. This new guy's hair will stay, the doctors tell us,
the teeth are solid. Perfect health record except for a broken leg.
Fighting Tigers against Penn State, Orange Bowl '74. Bachelor.
We have people on the look-out for a suitable wife."

"What you're saying," said the Ecpolcol chief, her lesbian
rasp aggressive and ringing with complaint, "is that first we have
to put him in as Governor, don't we, baby. The last I heard the
Governor of Louisiana was Ed Edwards."

One hand kneading his upper stomach Sweeney said patiently: "I almost didn't bother to pass you the job. The man will breeze in, he's your simplest presidential assignment since Harry Truman. The guy looks like Johnny Carson. Charm to throw away, style, people want to believe him when he makes a speech, they could know darn well he was telling lies and believe every word. A terrific body and we have him on a diet. He has a great smile, no sense of humour. I've seen tapes and they're a hundred per cent, the camera loves him."

"Yes? Well all right, we'll have a word with some Democrats. We can take a few baby steps this year I guess."

"Louise, he'd be a knock-out as a Republican. He can wear clothes. He has manner, Louise, he makes William F. Buckley look like a schoolboy telling a dirty joke. What I'm saying is the directors were kind of thinking Republican for '92 when they picked the guy."

"Well I know politics would dirty your nice clean Wall Street hands and everything," shouted the Ecpolcol chief, her rasping voice ringing even higher in rage. "I wish to God sometimes MPI would get the basics of the God damn country's politics straight when they make these decisions. We have this two-party split, Gabe. President in '92 means he'll have to go in as governor at Baton Rouge in '84. That's all uphill shit road in Louisiana if your dream-boat's a Republican."

The Ecpolcol chief was a consummate political strategist and perhaps the best economic brain in the MPI organisation. She was however notorious for artistic temperament. Right then Sweeney was in no mood to listen and he cut the conversation with the chief short. Feeling the sweat pop out on his forehead even as he dragged the back of his hand across it the security director suspected that he was running a fever. He knew he should go home and catch up on his sleep but there was the SCM to attend. In Sweeney's profession a director who missed two consecutive security chiefs' meetings courted the same risks as an African dictator on vacation abroad with the army on manoeuvres.

Mandy was at her desk outside the office talking to somebody in Affops about Bradfarrow.

"But that's marvellous," Sweeney heard the girl say. "How super. How clever of you. Not in the least corny, it's very creative. I never dreamed a small town could be so busy."

Sweeney looked at his notes of his talk with Bigg Proudfoot and called Public Relations Security division. "We're not convinced no news is good news from Alaska, Beau," he said. "We think we'd like a prevailing mythology for the place."

A pained sigh came down the wire from the PRS chief. He was in his early twenties and a public relations prodigy, an ex-seminarian whose mind was mystically attuned to keeping secrets. "We have the Alaska story wrapped, sealed," he said, "and buried a mile deep in the ground. Nothing short of a bona fide miracle will break our security. What I mean by a miracle, Gabe, is an angel appearing in the clouds blowing a golden trumpet and telling the world the news. Any other way we have the stopper on it."

Sweeney said: "Beau, people have to know the truth. It doesn't matter what they know just so long as they know it's the truth. We need those downbeat stories about Alaskan oil reserves. On a regular basis, with quotes from geophysicists and the rest, gabble gabble. Alaskan oil reserves are good for twenty years maximum at our present rate of consumption, whatever the figures are. We're not seeing enough of that pre-emptive mythology, we're looking at more and more of a mythology vacuum for the territory, the people don't know they know the truth. Say if somebody springs a story that MPI is sitting on wells in Alaska good for two or three thousand years of world supply we might get enough believers around the country to start a few questions."

"Yes, I'm reading your thoughts but I happen to disagree. This is just like the nuclear fusion process, I wanted to bury it, Gabe, remember, you said exactly what you're saying now, give the public something to believe. Well that route just drew a crowd, didn't it. We're having a hell of a time keeping the fusion technique wrapped," said the PRS chief. "We haven't been able to come up with a red herring worth spit for MIT in over a year. Somebody has to decide soon about those German nuclear fusion professors in the Turkish jail. People aren't popsicles, Gabe, you know, they won't keep on ice indefinitely. The electric auto guys in the Swiss sanitarium, we should go one way or the other with that problem too, when we have a minute. It's volunteering information does the damage, that's when you lose your control, pretty soon you can't feel comfortable opening a newspaper in the morning."

"Well maybe you're right. I'm taking some pressure about the silence."

"Silence is public relations' sublimest product," said the PRS man.

"All right. People wearing denim, is that ours?"

"Not any more. Denim's out of control. I don't know if you remember the way the idea came up, denim was folksy, it was a picture of the old days and the work ethic, the community, neighbours, hayrides, *Oklahoma!* by Rodgers and Hart. Now it's off the meter. You can pay two thousand bucks for a pair of Paris jeans. The denim operation's counterproductive and we're taking the blame for the error in PRS division."

"Okay. Can we turn it back?"

"No."

"Another thing, the old-time visuals from the US are down on MPI's Naples monitors," Sweeney said. "They're up for some of the overseas territories. Beau, you'll have to fill me in."

"Well there's an argument about whether it does any good, it's just the idea of nostalgia, Gabe. The message MPI wants to convey is that life was better in the old days, and we get extra points for indirection. We had our troubles with direct programming. We kept *The Waltons* on too long, the Walton kids were all grown up and living at home, it was beginning to look like a pretty sick family. *Little House on the Prairie*, same story, it's taking on adoptees. We've been procuring our propaganda visuals indirectly for the past few years," the PRS chief told the MPI Security director. "The visuals are on the commercials instead of the programs. Say you're making beer chemically with urban river water, your commercial of choice is an old-time propaganda visual, beautiful dray horses, polished leather harness with brass fittings, wholesome malty beer in oak barrels. It makes people yearn for yesteryear, Gabe. You're in Detroit with a product to sell that's made out of beer-cans essentially, rusting before it leaves the factory floor, well except for the gears and transmission which are plastic, okay you know damn well you're going to have to spend money to make the public love this auto. You don't care how much you spend, it's the easiest way. Sooner or later somebody's going to think of that solid auto the company built in the twenties, so there she is in the commercial, the beauty, driving along a country road. Sure the people buy the junk auto but what they really want is the old days back again. We're getting pure gold visuals from the food industry. Cheese, wieners, canned meat, cereal, where the industry's having the product made up in bulk south of the Mexican border they'll usually come through for us, a Kansas farm in about 1912, sunset and golden wheat, some healthy freckle-faced kid eating the crap. What we do is lobby the companies to keep the product quality down, Gabe, and the advertising takes care of our propaganda for us, we can count on a steady percentage of the budget. If the quality bobs up for some reason the count on those old time visuals sinks. That could be our problem at the moment. Hard to say what's gone wrong, that lobby is easy work, usually it runs by itself." He said: "On the subject of TV, Gabe, some of the guys in the division here would like more air time for their stories on TV news. I said I'd check with you whether it was okay to try to put Walter Cronkite on subsidy."

Gable Sweeney did not reply for a moment, wondering if he had heard the question correctly. He was shocked. He said: "Wait a minute, Beau, this is MPI. We're not the Cosa Nostra for God's sake."

"Well I'm just asking. The other way is MPI acquires CBS but that still doesn't guarantee us Walter."

"You want to try to buy Walter Cronkite."

"We'd like to give it a shot. What's the worst that can happen? He says no. It's not such a terrible idea, Gabe."

"No? It's the darnedest proposal I've heard from a division chief since I've been director," Sweeney said angrily. "It stinks. What the heck's the matter with you people in PRS? I can't figure you out, Beau, just because we don't have a shelf of law books telling us what to do doesn't mean we're free to do anything we like."

"I only asked."

". . . I'd be the first to admit this company doesn't make a fetish out of conscience, but darn it, Beau . . . "

After an hour in the new job Mandy D'Arcy liked working in the security director's office. When she put another Jameson and ice at his elbow he glanced up from the phone and said: "Here's looking at you, kid." Already he seemed to need her. Say with a firm tidying of Gable Sweeney's hairiness, Mandy reflected, beginning to plan, he could then use a little tactful coaching about his personal habits. He had graceless tics, like screwing up his face with his eyes shut, combing his fingers through his beard and, the worst one, rubbing his tummy. She did like the informal working atmosphere, never having thought of an office as a place like home. I bet we could have good talks about life too when he's relaxed, Mandy thought. He's probably very relaxed in the afternoons from his drinking in the mornings.

She said to Gable Sweeney when he was off the phone: "We're doing all right in Bradfarrow. Affops has the scenario under control."

His eyes were somewhat filmed-over as well as streaky now, and directed downward as he looked at her instead of straight. Had he been a younger man Mandy would have suspected him of eyeing her hips.

"They know an awful lot about the people in that little place."

Sweeney was not reassured. "Okay. Maybe so," he said. "They don't get a star for knowing about the people in Bradfarrow, though, kid, that's just looking up files. In MPI Security we have a file on everybody in the world," the director explained. "It's no particular secret, so has the telephone company, the credit card people, a few others. We've had the capability for decades, it was always just a question of the leg work. The last few million units came in a couple of years ago," he said. "Bedouins, the deep rain forest people. New Guinea villagers and the stone-age tribes from that part of the world. You wouldn't believe how backward humanity can be, kid, the inhumanity of certain peoples. Some of them didn't even have names," Sweeney said with wonderment. "They hadn't advanced enough in language for names, we had to give them names before our computer system would assign them numbers." He shook his head, his imagination defeated by the backwardness of societies without names. "I think myself we collected personal data on tribes of gorillas and chimpanzees in our product sometimes. We didn't have an anthropological scan.

We sucked in these flimsy dossiers, birthplace unknown, parents unknown, assigned name, a diet of nuts and roots. No languages, no political affiliations, tropical jungle habitat. A psychological profile that shows up high on boredom and fear. Life expectancy of fifteen to twenty years. I wouldn't mind seeing photographs with those. Maybe they're real people. To me they read like Charlie the Chimp."

"I'm surprised we could get Russia and China."

"Well Russia was the easiest file bloc, the work was already done in Russia. They just gave us everything from the Leningrad computers, we had blocs they needed. Hard to tell who got the best deal on the exchange. Sure, we had to put out a little effort for some parts of northern China, but that's a heck of a big country," Sweeney said. "The State Department's highest estimate of the Chinese population was nine hundred million and we collected one thousand million personal dossiers, a billion, no fakes or duplicates." He said: "Well we have this information facility at Mini-People Incorporated Security, we have these files in the bank. We're working under plenty of pressure to use our advantage while we have it, we shouldn't fool ourselves we have anything more than a temporary lead on the competition. Say five or ten years and your local gas station will have the same information. Knowing everything about individuals in Bradfarrow, Saddler's Springs, is one thing, turning over a dollar on the knowledge is what counts. I wish I could feel as good as you do about what Affops is doing in Bradfarrow. How many leprechauns are they using for instance?"

Mandy opened the SCM folder. "Well it doesn't say who's a leprechaun and who isn't," she said.

"That's okay. Plenty of leprechaun country up that way. I guess they're using local resources, which is what they should be doing. Our leprechaun designation tends to apply to the general population," Sweeney said, "not just to Mini-People people. On the other hand not everybody at Mini-People is a leprechaun, not even everybody on the board of directors. If our directors were all leprechauns we'd have a security problem that sticks out a mile. We have the problem now in some professions. Sports are difficult, well horse-racing isn't so bad. The acting profession is insecure, God knows why so many leprechauns go into acting, they have gifts for pretending to be what they aren't I guess. We're equal opportunity of course. The non-leprechauns who work at MPI don't have second-class status or anything, they can make it to the top here, but naturally we keep an eye on them."

"Am I a leprechaun?"

"You'd know if you were a leprechaun, honey."

"You are."

"Yes."

"Well could I be promoted to a leprechaun?"

"Why sure you could, hon," Gable Sweeney said with immediate hearty sincerity. "Personnel designation is all it is. We're not some kind of elite brotherhood working for our own interests in the world. When you settle in and get on top of Mrs. Humacher's routines we'll have a talk."

"I think I'd prefer to be a sprite. That sounds more fun. What was Mrs. Humacher, a banshee?"

Mandy turned over the pages of the green file, leprechaun briefs. She was feeling some exasperation. I'll get my merit badge if I please old Brown Owl here, she thought. Who needs it, she asked herself.

"I don't like Dallahans. They're creepy."

"There is only one Dallahan."

"Well I'm sorry but it sounds so absolutely childish to me, Mr. Sweeney. I'm sure all these people are having a good time, but this is the business world, it's for grown-ups not for play. When I was Wood Elf in Brownies I really believed I was a wood elf. I loved it but I grew out of it. By the time I was nine I didn't want to be a wood elf any more."

But instead of paying attention to Mandy's objection to his world Sweeney was tapping buttons on his phone. "Dan, I stopped over at one or two of your busy places on the way home," he said to the Heads Aprep chief. "I took a helicopter here and there in the Middle East. We can't go along with your Begin proposal, that's the bad news."

"I didn't expect the idea to fly," said the Heads Aprep chief. He was a man with a uniquely detailed knowledge of international affairs. As MPI Security's best desk planner he was practically indispensable. He was a bureaucrat, though, who loved proper procedures and mistrusted anything in the shape of an unorthodox channel or an irregular method. "We don't have any particular investment of policy in a change, it was just a question of Begin's health and personality. We thought we'd like to put in somebody thirty years younger, easier to talk to."

Sweeney said: "Well he's a grouch, he's tough, you're right Dan, you can't talk to the man, but he's the best leprechaun we've got between Alexandria and Baghdad. You'd have to show me somebody pretty special before I'd want to okay a gold watch for Menachem."

"All right. We can live with it, Gabe. So long as we stay on schedule with the guy at Ar Rimal, for the Iranian coup."

"I was about to say," said the director, his fingers moving to his stomach. "I took an extra day to check him out. The good news is they were just rumours, about him drinking French wine by the crateful and ordering Rolls-Royces and the rest."

"Well okay, but we could've saved you the trip, we could've told you that. The man's an ascetic, he doesn't take a dime from the sheikh. He weaves his own sandals. Like he won't even drink coke, twice a day he eats a handful of raisins. On special occasions, say he's celebrating or entertaining, he'll cook up a pot of sheep stew, mostly fat and hardly any meat the way we hear it. He's gaining more support every day."

"Yes," said Sweeney who was watching his secretary again. Mandy had returned to her desk outside the office and was on the telephone, her attitude elegantly alert. "It's the sheep's head and lower legs is what it is, you get bones and grease and the eyes are darn near the only meat in the pot. You know, Dan, I sometimes wonder about the whole operation. Like we weren't in bad shape in Iran in the first place. I can't see that we gained anything terrific from the original lobby. Sure the Shah was a pain in the ass but he's a class A head of state compared to that religious flake you people put in his place."

"The country's going exactly the way we said it would. Our projection was on the nose."

"The way he's running the country doesn't bother me, Dan, what bothers me about the guy is he's unpredictable. In the office here when we put out cash and resources we like to be able to see what we've got."

"We got a nationwide gas shortage."

"Well it was temporary, Dan, it didn't stick."

"Gabe, this Ar Rimal man will work."

"All right. See if you can move it along, would you."

Sweeney said as he put the phone down: "Wow, my darn gut, what an ache." The phone rang. "This is the White House switchboard," a bossy female voice said. "Mr. Gable Sweeney? Hold on, please." Sweeney replaced the receiver and pressed the intercom. "Honey," he said, "I have calls getting through from outside here, give me a break for a half hour, okay?"

"Sorry, Mr. Sweeney. I haven't figured the buttons out yet."

In fact Sweeney needed only twenty minutes to prepare himself for the SCM, reading through the folder his new secretary had assembled. Her work was uncluttered, with a minimum of memos. Mrs. Humacher always included every document, even those of arguable relevance, and stapled memos and reminders to each one, as if he was a robot she was programming for the job. Sweeney liked the freedom of the new method.

The girl continued to be an unnecessary difficulty and a luring challenge for Sweeney. ". . . but I can't see where we make our profit," Mandy was saying a little later, in her learning mode, cost extracts and territory cash requisitions in her hand to support her questions. "Here's another ten thousand to leprechauns in Bradfarrow, the local help isn't cheap labour, is it, twenty-five thousand to the Dallahan in Saddler's Springs, whoever the weirdie is. We're spending all kinds of money."

"Well we reclaim Bradfarrow money from Deloro Nickel of course . . ."

Sweeney wondered tiredly what to tell the girl. Mrs. Humacher had never asked for explanations even when she was new in the office. Indeed much of Mrs. Humacher's strength of personality had been based on the certainty that she understood MPI better than Sweeney did. Mandy's face with the rabbit teeth was intelligent but also doubting, as if she expected to find his answers unsatisfactory, in the way of youth. She stood by the filing cabinet with her paper and notebook, directing a businesslike frown at the director.

He said: "All right, you have to look at the big map first. We don't distribute brochures about it or anything, but we're not in business at MPI just to make money. We're not an organization of mad squirrels gathering nuts," Sweeney told the girl. "I can't speak for the other outfits, the world's commercial empires, but my guess is it's the same story with them. They'll tell you they're good for the country, we're what this country's all about they'll say, any time they talk about it. Well, on the outside, stuffing dollar bills in their pockets, watching the costs, maximizing the profits, checking that marketing has the last word on quality control, what you see on the outside is mostly greed, which nobody claims is good for a country. They're doing something else, they have their particular dreams. In this corporation our vision," said Gable Sweeney, "is to restore the small community to the world."

Mandy did not look impressed. In her experience a small community was a place with natives and a gift shop.

"It's a vision of the older leprechauns here in particular," Sweeney said. "They remember the community, a village community. In a village community a man sees his worth reflected in his neighbours' eyes, put it that way. Well a man or a woman I guess. When his stock goes down, say he makes a mistake, everybody knows, but there's a new day, he can always redeem himself again. Nobody has the monstrous power you see around now, and nobody is worthless either," the MPI Security director said seriously. "Maybe you get a few psychiatric problems. There was a village idiot usually, but you don't get the street violence and the big-time insanity. Where are your muggers and thieves, your rapists? Everybody knows everybody."

"Mini-People would like us all to live in villages?" Mandy asked. What a stupid idea, she thought, there would be nowhere to go.

"The way they see it we haven't been giving importance to a sense of direction. We've made a number of bad decisions already, the world in general I mean, America especially because everybody follows us. We're cruising along nobody knows where.

We're even going backward sometimes. We had corner grocery stores, let's say, and then we had supermarkets to replace them, we had an improvement in the food supply system to the common man on the retail level. Supermarkets bought in bulk and you helped yourself from the shelves, what we had there for a while was a saving in time and money. Now buying groceries can take up most of Saturday afternoon, you have the battle of the shopping-carts in the aisles and then the cash register line-up. And nobody knows where the prices come from any more."

"There weren't so many people before."

"We always had lots of people, hon. We didn't have arrangements for them all to meet at the same time in the same places before. I'm talking about a total system, the system of the community," Sweeney explained. "Leprechauns aren't socialists, not by a mile, what bothers us most is the nonsense factor. We do like to see people working at something that makes sense, which just means behaving sensibly. I happen to like the old corner store myself, somebody running a corner store is doing useful work. But paying sky-high prices to be processed in a crowd through a supermarket like a herd of cattle is nonsense, isn't it. Some of the other guys have other ideas, they like agriculture, farms, meadows, the growing year, the plough, there's a consensus we're putting down too much concrete. The leprechauns of MPI would like people to show some respect for grass."

"What's so great about grass?" Mandy asked, quite impatiently. She said: "I've heard of saving the whales and seals but I didn't know anybody was worried about grass."

"You go crazy when you lose touch with it, that's all. It's a mental health problem. Grass is the planet's skin and we're creatures of the planet, look at it that way. We're supposed to walk on grass, when we don't we're out of our territory. See, we can't see a difference between sense and nonsense if we have ourselves strung out too far from our basic territory. Like a normal intelligent person goes into Flouncy at the age of twenty-five, he gives it everything he has because that's business, ruins his stomach and so on, retires with half a million in stock and cash. Okay, but he hasn't done anything worth a man's life, has he. It was only Flouncy."

"It was big dollars, though, wasn't it, Mr. Sweeney. When I was a girl we had a housekeeper who used to run a corner store and it nearly killed her."

"Sure but she was in her right mind I bet. Concrete and the auto," Gable Sweeney said, "are the worst two things ever invented because they took the guts out of the idea of people living together. All the buildings we're putting up now have the structure of communities but without the guts, you see. Well take a condominium, that's a place to live, plus stores, a pool and a tennis court. It's a village. An apartment shopper, a co-op, they're villages. Except that the sense of community isn't there, is it? That's gone. The folk keep trying to build villages."

Mandy thought about it. Then she said with hostility: "A village would be perfect for me. I can see it all in my mind. I'd be a milkmaid I suppose. I could spend my mornings with cows. I'd have this sensible fulfilling work, churning butter and making cheese all day. Such a rewarding life, such good sense, such excitement. Then when I married the ploughboy of my dreams the local lord would have the right to sleep with me first. Is that the idea?"

"Well of course we're not pushing a perfect way of life," the director said to his secretary. "The thought of building heaven on earth isn't in our minds, but take the auto away and the world breaks down into the ancient pattern again, it was a terrific pattern, agricultural and artisan communities. I see your objection, somebody would have to milk the cows, but darn it think of the fresh air. Or how about seeing hills again, under those concrete snail-tracks we have all over the landscape, drinking from clear streams." Sweeney wiped sweat from his hot and aching brow. "Detroit won it all, no question about that," he admitted cheerfully. "Still, we can turn the game around. Shutting off the gasoline supply is showing good results. Wait and see. There'll be black-eyed susans coming up through the asphalt of the highways when the leprechaun has his day."

Mandy bent to close the bottom drawer of the file cabinet, her manner decidedly cold. Her compliant dress flattened itself along one hip and thigh. Sweeney watched her and shook his head and sighed. Her phone rang.

"It's the White House again, Mr. Sweeney."

"Our troubles began when we stopped thinking horse," the director said, not particularly to Mandy, somewhat feverishly. "The people would be happier in a real life. The people should have fundamental concerns, hunger, disease, love, death. We're going nowhere if the big anxiety is whether we're making full use of the Cuisinart." He said to the phone: "Well, I've been in business long enough not to expect the President, lady. I can give your guy two minutes but I have a meeting coming up."

The voice from Washington was vibrant with youth and savvy. "Lincoln Thorn at the White House, Mr. Sweeney. We're chasing down a rumour about Defense Department contract work. There's supposed to be a move afoot, one big multi-national is manoeuvring to sweep all the defense budget."

"Heck, that's news to me," Sweeney said. "I guess we're not close to the source of these Washington rumours. I hope there's no truth to it. MPI handles some contracts for Defense if I'm not mistaken."

"It's not a Washington rumour, it's a whisper we happened to hear in Washington," Thorn said. "This isn't Washington's fault. We don't know how some of these fairy-tales get started either, but they upset people. Right now General Electric is seriously perturbed. I've never seen General Electric in such a state."

"GE's credulous if you want my opinion, the technology outfits are like that, a little naïve for the world. I can't see it myself, one company cornering all the Defense gravy. Nobody's big enough." Gable Sweeney's mind began to wander ahead to his meeting. I'd better fine-tune that darned Bradfarrow scenario with Affops, he thought.

"Yes, that's how we figure the position too. A few facts of life and the story falls down. Just looking at the raw materials end for a minute, even among the multi-nationals, raw material sources are spread around. This one company would need all the available supply, though."

"Well it couldn't get that, Mr. Thorn, you're right. The holes in the ground are staked out."

"Except in Russia, of course," said the youth with an aggressive bark of laughter, bearing down on this emphasis: the White

House had to worry about Russia even if nobody else did. "We have to take total world resources into account."

"Sure we do. But it sounds, well, let's be kind and say imaginative, Mr. Thorn. Who knows about the Russians? Nobody knows what the Russian government will do, they're an enigma." Sweeney said: "Defense buys manufactured goods, doesn't it, steel and electronics systems and so on. The last I heard they weren't interested in ores and minerals as weapons systems. Or whatever else it is they spend the taxpayer's buck on, the country's industry is standing in the way. What you're checking out is just another big bad monopoly scare, isn't it, Mr. Thorn. I guess it's a long day in Washington, lots of time to stop and smell the flowers."

"We have to do this sort of thing," Thorn said. "If we don't, who will? Now when you assume raw materials, some new source, the idea does come within imaginable limits, there's that. We're more realistic than you give us credit for, Mr. Sweeney, we're not treating the rumour seriously of course. But a multi-national which made the sweep would be a hairsbreadth away from taking over the country. Okay, so it's not unreasonable to spend a little time. Assume the raw materials from abroad for the sake of argument," Thorn said analytically, his tone of bright respect for ideas suggesting recent practice on a school debating team, "everything except nickel in the case of Defense, and US Steel for instance has sixty per cent of the necessary manufacturing capacity. MPI has all the electronics products capacity, computers and communications. We don't even have to include General Motors. Any time Mini-People looked like getting together with US Steel, you see, we'd have something to start worrying about here at the White House."

"That's what we miss, you know, Mr. Thorn, in the private sector, the wild horses of the mind," Sweeney said, bad temper welling up again. "Making conjectures and playing the game of what-if, during business hours. In the free market-place hardly any of us have the leisure to do that. We're too darn busy with the practical stuff, making the country function, earning a crust of bread for our families. Paying the government its fat taxes, lad."

"The reason I mentioned nickel is it's a particular case. Somebody trying to hog all Defense's money would need some new domestic source, I might as well tick off that possibility while I'm doing this," Thorn said, undiminished in self-confident brashness. "So how about MPI for that thought, Mr. Sweeney, anything new happening in nickel exploration that you know about?"

By the time Sweeney had got free of the boy on the phone Mandy was ready to go to lunch. But she wanted a word with Sweeney before leaving the office in case he spent the lunch hour believing her to be an idiot. Look at the man, he's really dishevelled already and it's only noon, Mandy thought, he's a sweaty hairy person who needs to be taken in hand and groomed.

Sweeney could see considerable peevishness in his new secretary's eyes behind the oversized glasses with rose-coloured lenses she had put on for the street. She said: "Mr. Sweeney, I hope what you were telling me just now was a joke, that garbage about villages and so on. Because I don't believe a word of it. I'm not a conservationist or any kind of a radical, Mr. Sweeney, I had a good upbringing. I've been in villages, they're boring and stupid. What do small-town people do besides gossip about each other? Maybe everybody knows everybody, but you'll still get muggers and rapists, won't you, Mr. Sweeney, it's what people do. Somebody who was born in one of those stupid places had to stay there and die before the invention of the auto. The invention of the auto was the *best thing* that ever happened in the world, Mr. Sweeney. And the invention of concrete was the second best thing. We can hardly build anything without concrete, can we? Unless when we're all put into villages you'd like us to live in mud huts?"

"I wonder whatever happened to youthful idealism," Sweeney said in some depression. This was fifteen minutes later, however, and he was talking on the phone to the Mini-People Incorporated president Bigg Proudfoot. "When I was a kid we believed you could improve human nature by making a few drastic economic changes. Idealism is supposed to be an endemic condition of youth, isn't it, sir, sort of an acne of the soul; not with this young lady, though."

"Your people have always been imponderable as far as I'm concerned, Sweeney."

"Well, sir, they're a heck of a bunch of guys, you can't take your eye off them for a minute but the morale is magnificent. Put it this way, we have a locker room atmosphere any owner in major league sport would pay a million for. Keep my people busy and they'll give the company a hundred and ten per cent every day. In security we live the job," Sweeney told the president.

"I didn't call to hear commercials for your section, Sweeney," Bigg Proudfoot said in a reverberating tone from far distances. "I have larger matters to occupy my mind. There's a distressing plot being hatched in the murk of your section apparently. A plan to try to corrupt Walter Cronkite. Do you know anything about that?"

"Yes, sir. I've already switched it off."

Even across oceans Bigg Proudfoot's relief was palpable, and most intense. He said gladly: "You have? Oh, good man. Excellent work. That's just splendid. Caught it in time, did you."

"Yes, sir. Enthusiasm is all it is, sir."

"Well, my dear Sweeney, look, I'm pleased. Security is doing a first-rate job."

"They're a heck of a bunch of guys, sir."

"Absolutely, I agree. Goodbye, Sweeney. Oh, and do give my warmest best wishes to your wife too, of course."

Gable Sweeney was a bachelor but nevertheless he felt somewhat better after this conversation with the president. He saw himself surviving the day. He settled down with the Deloro Nickel file and turned the pages over slowly. Puckish glee spread across his dark and hairy face. "That Joe Kowalski," he chuckled once and slapped his knee. "What a boy. Son of a gun."

Nine

Killer

1

"Chief Williams, please. Central here."

"Williams."

"Car 23 has your subject, Chief Williams, he's at the Raven-wood Golf Club. Ninth hole. French and O'Dacre are hauling him into the clubhouse there."

"Well you took your sweet God damn time, didn't you, Central. I told you to check the golf club first."

"We've had our eye on the clubhouses, Chief Williams, he hasn't used them. We had to send men out to search the course. Near as we can figure he's been shooting golf for eight days."

Chief Williams banged the telephone down. It rang. "Mr. Williams, a treat to hear your voice," said Percy Grant with a hearty and reassuring laugh. "Boys in blue gave me the message. Mr. Williams, you're upset."

"Upset, yes. You're damn right I'm upset. Listen, Mr. Grant. A neighbour of mine named Graveley was evicted last week. The Italian wreckers pulled his house down. Trevor Graveley thought he was safe because he wasn't on that fifty acres owned by the Little Sisters."

"Little Sisters, yes," Percy Grant said soothingly. "I've heard of them."

"A scruffy order of Irish *bog nuns*, Mr. Grant, and those greedy whores," said Chief Williams, firmly raising his voice as he sensed Percy Grant's drifting attention, "were able to steal fifty acres of the costliest real estate in Bradfarrow because Corcoran and Craddock's conveyancing documents were incompetent."

"Dear dear."

"Now I'm wondering where Equity Mortgage and Trust got the authority to pull down Graveley's house. It's not far from my house, that's what worries me."

"Well we checked your title, Mr. Williams, big rush job a month ago, you remember. What's to worry about?"

"There is this to worry about . . . Are you listening?"

" . . . and splashed right into the water. Sorry. Go on."

"There is this to worry about, that you are Trevor Graveley's lawyers, Mr. Grant, he's a client of Nesmith, Buchanan and Grant. That wouldn't mean anything, except that he isn't on the fifty acres owned by the Little Sisters, I mean he wasn't. Mr. Grant, do you remember the Good Neighbours?"

Chief Williams heard a throated moan, like a yawn made aside. "Yes? Yes, go on. I'm listening."

"What I'm trying to tell you, Mr. Grant, is that you have a serious crisis at your office. You should be there right now."

"But haven't you heard?" Percy Grant asked, with his full attention, incredulously. "I thought everybody knew. You haven't heard, oh my dear. Mr. Williams, I've made the cut in the Canadian Open. I'm shooting in the sixties and low seventies. Lofting on to the green like Nicklaus, my dear man, and putting like Watson. How do I need to be at the office? Look here," said the lawyer, in the authoritative manner of somebody who sees an immediate way out of a tangled situation, "why not talk to Enoch about this? I'm on the ninth hole, playing Knudson and only one stroke down. Two of your policemen dragged me into the clubhouse. Concentration's all shot to pieces now. I could go under before I have it back, Mr. Williams."

"I can't get hold of Enoch. I'd be very happy to talk to Enoch. Where is he?"

"Oh yes, that's right. I'd forgotten. Poor Enoch. Well I don't see that I can help you with these anxieties of yours. I was never much of a psychologist, a bedside lawyer as they say. Plain law, right and wrong, innocent or guilty, good people and bad people, I try to stay with those, Mr. Williams. Now I'm sorry that the mail hasn't reached you. You wouldn't believe how busy we are at the office. One of the clerks is off sick. But everybody else is pulling to break that logjam, get caught up on it," said Percy Grant, and there was the sound hiatus of a hand placed on the receiver. ". . . with a nine iron," the lawyer said happily. He said to Chief Williams: "Leave a message at the main clubhouse here if you need me again and I'll try to get back to you, okay?"

"Look, Grant, I think Equity Mortgage and Trust aren't acting for the Little Sisters any more. They could be acting for the Good Neighbours now. You should be doing something about that."

"Really?" Percy Grant said, interested suddenly. "Really?"

"Yes. Well it's just a suspicion I have right now. I hope I'm wrong. But get the hell back to the office and handle it, would you."

"Really? I don't believe it. By God, you're right!" said Percy Grant warmly. He was not speaking to Chief Williams, though. He said to the chief then: "Guess what? *Arnold Palmer just walked into the clubhouse.* See here, we'll have to do this another time. We'll have a good long talk, promise, but I must let you go now, Mr. Williams. It's Arnie. Oh and the green warden says to tell you, no more policemen on the putting surface." He hung up.

Chief Williams told his secretary on the intercom: "See if you can arrange an appointment for me with Cohen and Liebowitz, lawyers, Prince Albert Street, please. Today." He put a call through to the office of Nesmith, Buchanan and Grant next. On the fifth ring a sulky female voice said: "Yeah?"

The chief gave his name politely. The sound of cracking gum came over the wire. "I've just been talking to Mr. Grant."

"Lucky duck."

"May I speak to the senior person there, please?"

"Yeah?"

"That's you, is it," Chief Williams said with the utmost

courtesy. "Very good. Mr. Grant tells me that my deed hasn't been put in the mail yet. I wonder if you would mind finding it for me. This is urgent."

"Outgoing mail. That's outgoing mail, right?"

"I imagine so, yes."

"Okay, well, outgoing mail, except invoices. Know how long it's been, eh, since anybody even *looked* at outgoing mail, except invoices? Three weeks. There's only me and Ginger here. Ginger's doing briefs to counsel and we ain't taking no more civil suits, not until Deborah gets over the 'flu. Contracts, I'm so far behind drawing up contracts it is to laugh, so you can forget about outgoing mail, eh?"

"I'm sorry, but I must have it today. I'm putting my affairs in the hands of another firm of solicitors. If it would be more convenient I could drop by and pick it up."

"Yeah, well nothing's convenient, is it? I'm paid to be a typist, so this isn't convenient for me, preparing legal opinion and like that. Nobody's picking nothing up on account of we got the office closed. We ain't particular to answer the phone either except the Supreme Court's sitting until four. Have a nice day," the sulky girl enjoined Chief Williams and disconnected.

The chief was thus in a distinctly aggrieved mood when Sergeant Brock entered his office with paper work for signature and routine matters to discuss. Sergeant Brock sat down, his tranquil pipe clamped between his teeth. "A sort of a heavy week this week," he said, glancing at the chief's empty desk. "The underwriters' and the fire department complaints about the arson committee, that's come up again. Break and enters in the cottage country over the winter, the provincials made more arrests this year but our convictions are down."

Chief Williams's thoughts were elsewhere. "And why is that?"

"The economy's good. More valuables in the cottages, the villains can afford a top-notch defence." He said disgustedly: "Everybody in the CA's department is running for office so I suppose they don't have the time."

Sergeants, the chief told himself, in despondent observation of Sergeant Brock's bulking ease, were intended by nature to serve officers and discipline men. They were the natural lightning rods in the chain of command. The sergeant was meant to be feared and hated by the men, enabling the officer to be popular and respected. But Sergeant Brock had no sense of this role. He had allowed the men's ill will to bypass him completely. How good it will be to have a hard sergeant in place of this soft one, the chief thought.

". . . needs your signature, and our memo to the spending committee on last month's personnel reductions. The investigation of Joe Kowalski for the Police Commission, that needs your approval."

Letting me become the hated one and using me as a rubber stamp too, Chief Williams told himself. He turned over the pages of the Kowalski file, taking his time. He said finally: "A medal, is that the idea?"

"Don't get you, sir."

"We're recommending Kowalski for a medal, is that the idea? This isn't any kind of an investigation, sergeant."

"Sure it is. That's a complete report."

"Where's the evidence for the felony? I asked for evidence."

"I did a full investigation. There isn't any evidence. I can't give you evidence that Kowalski took a bribe, the main reason there being because he didn't. Put it another way, there wasn't any felony, you see, chief."

"That's a pity. You can't give me evidence because there isn't any. I see. Brock, the other matter here, where Kowalski harassed Mr. Sieracki. This isn't what I asked for either, is it. Look at all this drivel. The murders by August Amundsen, search for August Amundsen. What's that for?"

"Well it's background, chief, so that the commission will understand Joe's reasons for arresting Albert Sieracki."

"I see. It's a new idea. The police briefs the defence." Chief Williams threw down his pen and opened a desk drawer. He took out some papers. "To be frank, sergeant, I'm finding it more and more difficult to work with you. You personally," he said, talking down to the papers he was turning over. "You're not doing what I order you to do. You have interests of your own, which aren't my interests. I don't seem to be able to depend on your loyalty."

"Sometimes, you know, before I get up in the morning," Sergeant Brock said, "I look at myself. Half asleep, that time there. I think about myself, how old I am and what I've done. Some mornings I want to stay in bed for the rest of my life. I wouldn't make it out of bed pimping revenge for you and your wife, chief. I couldn't rise to the day. I don't have that particular brand of loyalty you're asking for. But if I found any facts that said Joe Kowalski's a villain I'd've come down on him like a ton of brick."

"But that's just sanctimonious shit, isn't it," the chief asked. "Fact of the matter is, you want Kowalski off the hook. I want him to pay the price. I'd like it done my way. I wrote a covering letter to go with the report of your investigation to Commander Ridgeway. I went to the trouble of outlining the salient facts, fortunately. Let's see, skip the personal part, *delighted to hear that you can come to dinner on the twelfth*, blah blah. Right, here's an important connection to think about, the connection between the Riordan bribe and Kowalski's behaviour afterward. He became brave and lippy, our friend. *'Erskine, I'm impressed by the fact that Constable Kowalski's behaviour since the Hornblende incident has been flagrantly contemptuous and independent as if his career on the force, including his need of salary and pension, had suddenly become unimportant to him.'* Anything wrong with that, sergeant?"

"Well, everything. Joe's always been the same. He had the bad luck to cross Mrs. Williams a couple of times lately, that's all."

"It's an important connection I'm making. It explains the man's behaviour, sergeant. A pattern begins to take shape. *'This to my mind, Erskine, was a case of malicious assault, by a police officer who could afford to snap his fingers at consequences, having amply secured his future. Kowalski had a long-held grudge against this merchant. On numerous occasions he refused to act upon Mr. Sieracki's complaints although Mr. Sieracki in these instances had been the victim of theft.'* Those occasions should have been listed in your report, sergeant, by the way."

"I guess I didn't notice the depravity. Joe has a blind spot when it comes to old people. He has two old aunts. He tried to talk Sieracki out of charging grandparents a few times."

"'Kowalski's vendetta was so persistent and intense that Mr. Sieracki has often pleaded with the duty sergeant not to send that officer to his place of business.' True or false?"

"Sieracki prefers Ryan. That's as far as that goes."

"Now this pretty little scene. 'Shortly after his release of Seamus Riordan, very shortly afterward, Kowalski accosted Mr. Sieracki in the street outside his store, abused Mr. Sieracki in front of witnesses, handcuffed him violently and took him into custody. Kowalski did not have an arrest warrant and was, he claimed afterward, acting to apprehend a fugitive and so did not need one. Checking Kowalski's story about a fugitive took four hours. So what Kowalski succeeded in doing, certainly, was jailing Mr. Sieracki for that four hours, with the consequent infliction of distress and humiliation.'"

"Amundsen is a homicidal psycho, chief, and Joe had reasonable suspicions. Maybe Joe rushed at it without thinking, but he wasn't too far out of line, you know, bringing Sieracki in for a check."

"Nonsense, sergeant. Everything ties back to Riordan. We have a circumstantial case for bribery there, even in my view if the ten million dollars is never found. The men we've had to let go for budget reasons," Chief Williams said, "are a whining bunch. The public is afraid that there won't be enough policemen to keep the peace. TV and newspapers conducting their courts of enquiry, are we cutting into bureaucratic fat or law-and-order muscle? That sort of thing. No harm in it, not much need of it either. Strictly political. At a higher level than the force. Still, we know who the pennypinchers are. They're in now, somebody wasn't minding the store, but I daresay our crowd can take them out soon enough. Some of my wife's friends are making plans. Those newspaper and TV interviews are becoming very boring, though. Whining about this and that. Cliques and back room conspiracies, interlocking influence, too many of the same families in the positions of power in Bradfarrow. Bird piss."

Sergeant Brock sat forward watchfully. "Yes?" he said. "I'm trying to keep up. I don't have a picture yet."

"It's an accusatory form in the media right now, isn't it? Men who were fired telling any ridiculous story they can think of. Very hysterical in some cases, these stories. I never know what to expect when I open a newspaper. I'm a Russian spy, that wouldn't surprise me."

"Got you. I'm slow as a tortoise today," the sergeant said. "Say you fire somebody who saw you doing something scandalous, jumping rose bushes in the nude with a crowd, let me put it that way, he couldn't do you any harm by getting the story into print."

"It would be just your word." Chief Williams picked his pen up again. "So we'll add one sergeant to the staff reduction memo. I really am very sorry, Brock — but I must have a sergeant with a sense of reality. Changing the political position round shouldn't take too long. Nobody likes economies, do they, well not for themselves. One recommends spending cuts for other people, that's the way to economize. Naturally we'll be in touch with you again when the situation changes for the better. See Sergeant Pulthorpe for now, though."

There was a pause. "Joe Kowalski saw those jumps too."

"Yes," Chief Williams said without looking up from his writing.

Sergeant Brock was uncomfortable. He put his pipe in his pocket, thinking hard, and began to rise. He sat down again.

"All right. Suppose there were photographs."

The chief looked up.

Sergeant Brock said anxiously: "I'm not saying there are photographs. Blackmail is criminal. What I'm trying to work out," the sergeant explained, "is a distinction between office politics, the jostle and pressure you get there, and blackmail. A threat is legitimate office politics, I think."

Here Chief Williams and Sergeant Brock looked into each other's eyes. The sergeant's were amicable, raised in worried enquiry, not without guile however; the chief's were searching, sceptical and wary.

"You're saying you have photographs."

"No. I'm saying, suppose there were photographs."

"Photographs of me and my wife and my niece Helen, with Ryan?"

"That is correct, chief. Jumping the rose bushes, say."

"As we were, without clothes?"

"Could be."

"Let's see them."

"They may not even exist."

"Good day, sergeant."

"I could be using diplomacy. I could be having a hard time getting my threat across. I could be having the normal trouble dealing with little men, you have to get down on your knees to make them see eye to eye unless you want to kick them in the teeth. I could be a liar, just starting out on that now, a life of falsehood. As a blackmailer I could run off a few dozen copies of any photographs I happened to have. I could send them to your wife's committees. I don't know, though. Maybe I'm trying to have my cake and eat it. I never did care for a holy Joe type of cop myself."

"It's certainly very theological."

"I'd like to think it's just office politics."

"We don't have photographic equipment in cruisers, that's one idea."

"That idea would only be good if I was saying I might have taken photographs myself. Suppose I say instead they might have arrived in the mail."

"What I'll do is this, I'll go along with the position," said the chief, whose skin had become a grey colour, "that if you had photographs you'd be slapping them down on my desk now without these scruples. That's because every pietistic humbug I've ever met was always able to act like the worst shit whenever the need arose and forgive himself for it too. God damn insolence. You have a God damn nerve, calling me a little man. This is a curious day in my career," Chief Williams said. "First Ryan with his boots on my desk and now you with your weaselling sermons, well it seems the po-faced peasantry feels free to walk all over me today. I mean to say the mongrels and illegitimates. All the toading street-reared nobodies in Bradfarrow, what I'm getting at, sergeant," the chief said, "is that every farted pismire on the constabulary strength seems to have been lolling in this office today laughing in my face and taking it for granted that I'm a half-wit. I'm talking about the slum sweepings and immigrant layabouts who pass as policemen nowadays, people like yourself, and Poles, Irish, Italians and worse." Chief Williams asked sincerely: "How can we keep our standards that way, if we have no values left, just people breeding like rabbits?"

"I'll have to think about what to do," Sergeant Brock said. "I'll give it some thought and get back to you."

In his own office a few minutes later Sergeant Brock unlocked a drawer and took an envelope out. It was an OPP envelope from Peterborough detachment with the green confidential stamp. There was an unsigned note scrawled in ballpoint: *Thought you might like to get working with these right away. Will call in with some other material soon.* There were a dozen black-and-whites. The anguished faces of the rose bush jumpers showed up clearly on every one. Being of the same group doing much the same thing, the prints were boring as a photographic portfolio. Perhaps anticipating that, the unknown photographer had sought novelty angles: one shot for instance appeared to have been taken from ground level and had caught, beneath the pained faces, four clefted moons sailing overhead, two of them with cometing peaks.

On the whole Sergeant Brock thought that Chief Williams deserved to see them. But he still had not come to a decision an hour or so later when the switchboard called through with the message that a detective-sergeant from the Peterborough provincials wanted to see him, named Burty.

The sergeant had thought he knew all the Peterborough provincials. Detective-Sergeant Burty was a stranger with narrow-set eyes and a horned, hooked nose. The nose and eyes gave him the appearance of a carrion bird, a crow. He placed a briefcase on the floor, extending a sort of clawed hand.

"I've just come from a meeting, we've been talking about you, a couple of the lads are worried, Sergeant Brock," he said. "The hard chaws. I'll tell you the truth, there's some feeling getting around that you're the soft fellow yourself." He made himself comfortable and opened the briefcase. "No reflection on your intelligence or integrity, nothing of that nature. Now I have some odds and ends of documentation on your man August Amundsen." There was something odd about Detective-Sergeant Burty that Sergeant Brock could not place.

"The hard chaws tell me you have a conscience and suchlike

disabilities. My people," the provincial said, as if speaking of a famous and antique race, "have a tradition of not being disabled in that manner. We aren't bad people," Burty said, his crow eyes assessing Brock, seeming to look for censure. "We would prefer the world to be perfect, but since it is as it is we act in the belief that most of the people in it are farts. When the world becomes fragrant I've no doubt at all we'll cultivate consciences, revive honour, principles, and so on. It's just that we're not sitting on our hands and waiting for it." He took a newspaper from the briefcase. "One of the lads works undercover at the Bradfarrow *Times*."

Sergeant Brock took the paper and was surprised to see Chief Williams on the front page, with Mrs. Williams and Helen and Ryan, naked, leaping the rose bushes. The caption said: *An enjoyable get-together at the home of Mrs. Mavis Williams.*

"We slipped her in, and for my money we should leave her there. Williams has been begging for a shot like this. But my instructions are to tell you we can pull her out before the press runs tonight. We'll put back the other picture, the mayor giving somebody a cheque. They told me you'd be too soft to show your man the photos I sent you."

"I'm still thinking about that. I don't understand what's going on here, Sergeant Burty."

"Show Chief Williams the photos, get the bastard's mind straight on his position. Do that or else he'll be seeing himself in the *Times* tomorrow. You're not making our work easy for us, Sergeant Brock, with these arsy-farsy notions of morality. We had to go to considerable trouble. We had to put on an elaborate performance in Regency Gate in the dark of night."

"How come Peterborough OPP is acting in BCP jurisdiction like this, taking photographs and running a man inside the paper?"

"You people aren't doing the job. The villain Joe Kowalski arrested is August Amundsen."

"No, we checked that. He's clear."

"Albert Sieracki is August Amundsen," Burty said unexcitedly, morosely even, with an avian hunch of his shoulders, as if settling his feathers. "Simple computer foul-up. Wonderful contrivances they are for engendering trust, computers. Like the prodigal son they are, every day of the week somebody is forgiving one of the wayward things for its transgressions and restoring it to his affection."

"Sergeant Burty, the dates are wrong, the fingerprints don't match."

"Exactly the problem. What happened was the accidental bursting of a bubble memory, or a diode died maybe, God rest its soul, there was the disintegration of an integrated circuit in it. Two of the codes they used changed places, the fingerprint one and the dates for the murders, so while the machines were still chattering to each other they had stopped talking sense from a law-enforcement point of view. An eight-code fingerprint transmission in a date modality gives you June of last year and January of this year for the murders. An eight-code date will be a difficult fingerprint to match with man or beast."

Here Sergeant Brock reached for Detective-Sergeant Burty's papers. "Can you prove that?"

"At Peterborough detachment," Burty told Brock, "we did something archaic, we wrote a letter. In an envelope with a stamp on it, you understand, asking National Homicide Division, National Police Headquarters, Stockholm, for the particulars on August Amundsen. We got back correct dates, on paper, and Amundsen's fingerprints, the ink dabs themselves with all the necessary little whorls and ridges. We had to explain to the Swedes that we were backward Canadians. They are a kind people."

"Are you sure of these dates?" Sergeant Brock turned the pages, stunned. "It says the murders were reported in the Swedish papers last June. Have you got those Swedish press reports on file?"

"Hell, the Toronto *Globe* had the story, sergeant. We keep our brains outside our heads these days, that was our problem on this."

"God almighty," Sergeant Brock whispered. "'Mrs. Ellen Bochner, Scarborough Drive, Creek Pond. I was looking for soapstone near the tailings . . .'"

"Mrs. Bochner says she saw Albert Sieracki, that would be Amundsen, dropping a heavy sack, *that* would be Sieracki, into one of the shafts of the old Creek Pond talcum mine last November."

"Did you search the shaft?"

"Well it's not our jurisdiction," the provincial said, becoming vague of a sudden. "We don't want to be muscling in on your territory, do we. No, we just put in a few hours for Joe, it's all yours now." He drew a small paper bag from his pocket. "Sunflower seeds? Good for you. I eat them a lot." Burty's nose moved up and down as he chewed the seeds with his front teeth. "Oh yes, here's a thing, a nurse saw Amundsen hanging around the Bradfarrow General a month ago. We have the feeling he's thinking of killing nurses again. I suppose he needs to do that as himself. We've had our eye on him since then. We have a hard chaw watching him, a very hard chaw indeed. He has a particular sympathy for nurses, this lad, and strong prejudices against people who harm them. We think it might be a good idea for you to get Amundsen back under lock and key before this hard chaw lad of ours beats him into jelly. Bites his head off and so on. The lad isn't too stable."

"Joe had him, didn't he?"

"The farther we get away from men like your man Kowalski, the worse off we are. As policemen."

"As people," Sergeant Brock said, blushing.

"That's too deep for me," said the provincial policeman. "In that serious vein, though, since you're in a confiding mood, I am myself a humanistic socialist by persuasion. It's a matter of evolution. By the time people are ready for my kind of socialism they won't need it." He leafed through his remaining papers, dealing some across the desk and keeping others. "This isn't such a bad day." He closed the briefcase and looked at Sergeant Brock with his bird head cocked, fondly yet irascibly. "I was wondering if you think you could handle the chief's job here?"

Nice surges of excitement were lightening Brock's spirits as he scanned the windfall documents. He said: "This is it. This is big time. We're on the map at last. Bradfarrow arrests August Amundsen." He said to Burty: "Yes I could, and so could any other cop in the building. Chief Williams is good for another twenty years, Sergeant Burty."

"Not," said Detective-Sergeant Burty, his face dark as a

crow's again, "if he keeps getting up my people's noses he isn't. There's a lot of sensitivity about him among the lads."

The two sergeants shook hands affectionately. Brock saw what was odd about Burty, that he was undersized for a policeman, gnomish for the provincials who had a minimum height requirement of five eleven.

"Gino," Sergeant Brock said on the telephone. "Could I see you for a minute please, we have a big one."

"These are the photographs I told you about, chief," the sergeant said to Chief Williams later. The chief gave them his attention lazily and then looked through them with animation.

"Negatives, are there?"

"That would be my guess. I can't see anybody making prints like these and, you know, chief, destroying the negatives, with you holding the prints."

"What a wretched bastard you are, Brock."

"My options were closed off on me. On the other hand I don't mind doing this, really. I don't feel bad at all. I feel pretty cheerful to tell the truth."

"It's pornography and obscenity. This could ruin me. Has anybody thought of that? Do you see now," Chief Williams asked, "what I meant earlier when I spoke of loyalty? This, these photographs, what you're doing here is personal disloyalty to me. I've put my trust in you for fifteen years, and am I to understand this is how you show your thanks? God, but people are all the same," said Chief Williams who customarily made this remark with the understanding of himself as an exempt observer. He thought for a little and then he said: "You'd like to keep your job here, was that the idea?"

"Right, chief, that's all of it," Sergeant Brock said. "That's all that concerns me, keeping the job and the pension, supporting my family, paying the food bills. It's just a practical matter as far as I'm concerned."

4

"Your call to Sheriff Burns, Grabe Pass, California."

Sergeant Brock's feet were on his desk. "Staveley, good

friend, a hard time getting through," he said. "Somebody using the Grabe Pass party line I guess. Not too bad. No I'm meeting the payments on the igloo okay. Winter was fine, we didn't have to eat any of the huskies this year. Listen, Stave," the sergeant said contentedly, tamping tobacco into his pipe, the phone under his ear, "you know that killer at large somewhere, could be anywhere in Europe, the American continent, well there was a report he was seen in Australia, August Amundsen. Guess what, Stave."

Ten

The Ox Problem

1

Joe Kowalski stood in the bus line at the Quinte Mall with two
bags of groceries in his arms. It was Saturday afternoon. The
buses that serviced the mall were mostly full when they turned
into the ramp and he was near the back of a long queue. Rain blew
across the parking-lot in gusts. The morning radio forecast had
promised clear skies and Joe was dressed in just slacks and shirt.

A battered little old Renault cruised by. Dave Cardozo leaned
over to open the offside window. He seemed surprised. He said:
"What are you doing, standing there?"

Dave Cardozo wore a tee-shirt and denims. He too was wet,
much wetter than Kowalski indeed. Along the bus queue the
people who made their own decisions in the morning about
weather were dressed for rain.

"I'm waiting for a bus, Dave," Kowalski explained.

"A bus. Gosh, are you? Hey," Dave Cardozo said, getting an
idea, "would you like a ride home, Joe?"

"Well, terrific."

As they drove away from the mall parking-lot Dave Cardozo
kept glancing at Joe Kowalski. Cardozo's wet hair swung lankly.
Kowalski could not see his eyes.

Kowalski liked Cardozo. "How are you doing, anyway?" he asked. "I heard you were after a private security job. Metropolitan Life was it, Sergeant Brock said."

"They had just the one opening at the Met. I mean, the cops looking for work now."

"Well that's too bad, Dave. Hang in."

"Sure. I have a job in House Hardware." Dave turned to stare at Joe Kowalski, awe on his pale face. The curtain of wet hair practically reached Cardozo's nose. The hands on the steering wheel showed fingernails bitten down to the blood line. "What I don't understand is," he said, "how come you were waiting for a bus?"

Kowalski thought about the question. "I had to get the groceries at the mall," he said. He added: "It's too far to walk."

"Listen. I'm in the know. You arrested August Amundsen."

Joe Kowalski eased his backside on the small car seat. The wiper on the driver's side wasn't working. He wondered how Dave could see the road, when he looked at it.

"The Amundsen case was top of the list for Interpol, wasn't it. We were getting all that urgent stuff from Saint-Cloud. Every police force in a hundred and thirty countries, and all the state cops and the OPP on this side. A hundred and thirty countries."

"The cops in those countries weren't looking for Amundsen all the time. He had to be somewhere and he was here."

"And you arrested him. August Amundsen."

"I go in House Hardware sometimes," Kowalski said uncomfortably. "I was in there looking for spikes, they don't stock spikes, or brads either. They just stock the popular size nails. I don't know what kind of guy they stock nails for. He never uses anything smaller than half inch or larger than four inch. Nothing comes apart on him that isn't medium size."

"Well I just work in the warehouse, Joe. *The FBI*," Cardozo said with reverence. "The US Federal Bureau of Investigation. The US Treasury. It's that big. You arrested him."

"Jeez, Dave, he was down on Harbour in The Magic World toy store. I didn't like track him all over Africa. US Treasury doesn't count," Joe Kowalski said. "The Treasury was only on the case for Interpol. You already mentioned that."

"How come you're just standing in the rain, waiting for a bus, after you arrested Amundsen?"

Usually Joe Kowalski's conversations with Dave Cardozo were better than this. Cardozo, Kowalski felt, was a sophisticated kid, good taste in TV, a smart cop. However, these questions now were baffling Kowalski.

"On Saturdays I have to get the groceries at the mall, Dave. I buy a little treat for my aunts too, fruit, English tea, anything I can see," Kowalski said. "They look forward to that, so on Saturdays they get me out early. If we had an earthquake I'd still have to go to the mall, that's the only way my aunts understand Saturday. Okay, now I brought Sieracki up from Harbour and booked him in," he said, "and that was trouble. I know because I've been doing the same sort of thing for, jeez, nearly forty years. You get to recognize the signs. It's a big headache, whenever I do something like that. Sure enough, I brought him in, there was a whole lot of shouting. He was the wrong guy and everything."

"But you stuck to your guns."

"Well the way it usually happens, I don't have any choice you understand, about what I do myself," Kowalski explained. "The desk-man and the officer in charge are shouting, the CA's office is on the phone or they send a guy down, what I have to do myself is stay clear, Dave. Then Sergeant Brock might fix the thing. Or sometimes it depends on the CA guy, if he gets tired and gives up you're okay. But they pretty near always change back whatever I did. Say it was drug-selling, they release the pusher. Or they let a thief keep what he stole, say. This time with Sieracki it worked out my way in the end. They all agreed with me, Sieracki was Amundsen. All right, I was out of trouble, that didn't mean I won a Cadillac," Kowalski said. "They don't give you an auto for making an arrest they happen to agree with. They didn't make an arrangement for somebody else to pick my groceries up, and the treat for my aunts, if it was raining."

"The Swedish police turned over every house in Sweden. Look at it this way, the police organizations of Europe failed to capture him."

"Well he wasn't there, Dave, that's the only reason they failed. He was here."

The Renault swished through the rain. What could be seen of Dave Cardozo's face was set in awe still.

"Instead of brads, for small jobs you used to be able to use glue," Kowalski said. "You could use hide or case glue. Case was a powder, hide came in strips, you had to soak hide. Sand the thing you were working on down, glue it, clamp it, a team of horses couldn't pull the join apart. The glue was just glue, for sticking jobs, it couldn't hurt you. The glue you get now at House Hardware is instant," he said. "Sticks instantly, takes maybe a day or two to come apart again. Bonds skin and eyelids. Probably does a great job on those. On old furniture you may's well use spit. They don't have hide or case glue at House Hardware any more. Like the doughnuts at the Gee Yummy, same thing."

"What?"

"Gee Yummy Country Donuts's the same problem. Do you go in the Gee Yummy, Dave?"

"The Gee Yummy. Oh sure."

"Always nice and clean. You see that big doughnut on the roof, you know the place is clean. Their coffee isn't bad. Perce Donniker's Eat Here used to be where the Gee Yummy is on North Front. Everyone said the booze would kill Perce in the end, he was over eighty by the time it finally did, though. He used to make just two kinds of doughnut, sugar and plain. Trouble with Perce was he used to roll home-mades when he had the shakes. His tobacco got on the doughnuts. Or you could find mustard on your doughnut, say somebody ordered a hot dog. Well, it's improved now, they have fifty flavours. Three chocolate flavours, dairy milk, mocha and mousse," Kowalski said. "Only you can't put the doughnuts in your coffee. You could dunk old Perce's doughnuts. These if you put them in the coffee they melt. You're drinking doughnut coffee."

Cardozo said: "He had the Mounties beaten here, Joe."

"Who knows about the Mounties," Kowalski said. "I mean, what they do, how good they are as cops. Nobody knows. They don't know themselves." He said: "Now you're getting more hole than doughnut too. Having all those flavours to choose from isn't so great either because the doughnuts are all too sweet. You can still buy the kind of doughnuts Perce used to make, on Oldham

Street, at the Oldham Gourmet down there. The only difference is the price, and no tobacco or mustard. Exactly the same doughnuts."

Kowalski said a minute later: "You can buy case glue too, or hide, but you have to send away for it. You have to order it from Halifax. Paint's another problem."

While Dave Cardozo drove Kowalski home through the rainy streets of Bradfarrow, Joe Kowalski continued to chat about things that had been improved beyond usefulness or palatability, having got on that track. He spoke of paint, cut lumber, electrical plugs, strawberry jam and cough medicine. Dave did not respond much to Joe's conversation. He paid somewhat more attention to his driving. Still he glanced to the right at his passenger often as if unable to believe that Joe Kowalski was riding in his car.

At Kowalski's house Cardozo took a BCP notebook and a pencil from the glove compartment.

"Joe, do me a favour. Sign your name in here."

Kowalski took the notebook amiably and wrote his name on the first page. A thought occurred to him then. "Hey, is this my autograph?"

"Yes."

Kowalski looked at his own signature. "Jeez, that's great, Dave. Thanks a lot." He chuckled happily. "How would it be, let's see now, if I wrote underneath, arresting officer, the August Amundsen case."

"All right. You could put the date."

Joe Kowalski felt a definite surge of pride in his chest. He wished he had signed his name in a larger hand. "Now how would you like, to my good friend Dave Cardozo?"

Dave Cardozo demurred though, wanting his notebook back. "All right. But don't write anything else. That's enough, what you've got now."

Kowalski stood for a moment in pride outside his house with the groceries in his arms after Dave Cardozo had driven away. *Kowalski*, he thought, the name that stands for law. A name the worst villains respect, Kowalski. Kowalski is just a regular cop — with a difference. He saw the curtains of the front windows move.

Both his aunts were standing at the window waiting to see what treats he had brought them from the mall.

2

The Kowalski patrol in the region of Cambridge Mews was careful these days. He would pass through the area on nimble feet. He was surprised to come upon a demonstration at the bottom of that street. Kowalski had not seen a crowd protest in ten years. The house on the corner was in much the same state as the Graveley house had been when he had last seen that, a relic site, a shell halfway demolished.

Well-dressed men shook their fists at Alex Palmieri and Alex's cheerful Italian levelling crew. There were women with little dogs on leashes also. From time to time an expensive auto would pull up and let out another indignant person.

This was at five o'clock. The workmen who had already razed fifty acres of Regency Gate property were putting away their tools for the day. Alex stood on the box of a truck, reasoning with the crowd.

"Is a democracy we got here, you understand," Alex lectured. He brought his shoulders up to his ears and turned out his palms to show helplessness, which made him look excessively Italian. A spontaneous growl of rage ran through the audience when he did that. "Somebody here doesn't like what we're doing, you use the democratic process. You got to vote for a man represents your interests, you see, change the laws, that's the democratic way. Not a mob rule, you understand, ladies and gentlemen, in this democratic country of ours."

"Whose? Whose country?" many voices asked with resentment.

"I happen to be a provincial court judge," one austere man with silver hair said, although in truth he had become a magistrate as a pursuit of ambition and not by chance. "I warn you, sir, that you people are abusing the judicial process. Our court system does not exist to be manipulated by special interests who can afford to spend vast sums of money."

"No, eh?" Alex Palmieri asked in surprise. "Since when was this new rule?"

The magistrate added: "I'm not commenting on any specific matter now before the courts. You people aren't going to get away with this, though. You people are violating our rights. You people . . .

"You got a complaint, write a letter to your member of parliament, mister."

A tubby, busy man wearing a carnation the size of a hockey puck in his buttonhole pushed his way forward then, indeed the parliamentarian for Regency Gate in the provincial jurisdiction. He said as the crowd yielded: "Sorry, Tim. Hey, nice to see you, Meredith. Way through here, Harold. Mrs. Dalgleish, excuse me . . ." He said to Alex: "Allow me a few words with my friends here, eh."

Alex joined Joe Kowalski on the fringe of the mill. "They don't work, you see," Alex told Kowalski. "They sit on chairs all day, a desk in front to lean on. Now I got this fellow with the flower standing on my truck giving a speech. Hands soft like a baby's hands. If you ask me, Joe, their brains are soft too. When a man doesn't work, his brains get soft. He starts thinking funny. We should make them work, Joe, for the good of the country. That flower guy, he's going to have to move off that truck when gramma gets here. Gramma don't like anybody fooling with the equipment."

"She's a nice woman," Kowalski remarked. "She does a good job watching the sites."

Alex was a family man but he was realistic. "She's a not nice, Joe," he said. "She's a good cook and a great gramma, but nice, no, sir. When the boy came to tell her she should be in the union to have the nightwatchman job, Joe, she nearly killed him. A Mareschi he was, the union should've known better, you don't send a Mareschi boy to tell gramma something like that. Then the bastard union gave gramma the idea of axe handles. She never even thought of axe handles. She was using her, you know, Joe, her teeth and the nails of her fingers, a little biting and spitting, some kicking sometimes. You could fix somebody up with band-aids. Then they sent a man with an axe handle, this dumb Italian union, a Sicilian dirt picker, Joe. Gramma took the axe handle away from him and busted his thick farmer's head. You tell me what I should do now, Joe. Gramma's got the axe handle. These people, these baby hands, they don't think they're stealing. They think they have good taste, picking through garbage. A plank of rosewood, a dozen glass doorknobs, we're foreigners so we don't know what they're worth. Now she's got the axe handle and these garbage pickers with good taste are gonna have, you know, splitting headaches, Joe."

". . . my personal assurance that this extraordinary destruction of private property will be thoroughly investigated," the provincial member said. "I am seeking urgent consultations and demanding a public enquiry." His phrases rolled over the ardent mob like a cooling wind. People grumbled and talked indignantly together and moved away toward home and dinner.

"We got the rest of the house here, then the swimming pool. Pull out the concrete, fill in the hole. Dominic will make it all smooth like a meadow. That's tomorrow morning. Hey, Joe, listen, in the afternoon then we start on your police boss, Chief Williams's house."

Well, jeez, that's going to make the chief mad, Alex," Kowalski said. "He loves his house."

Alex Palmieri nodded in agreement. "Sure thing. I understand, nobody likes to lose his house. Would you, eh, Joe? Still, it's the law. Ten o'clock tonight the bailiffs come, throw his furniture out in the street. Throw him out in the street too. Any cats, dogs, birds in cages, out. The bailiffs aren't bad fellows but they're, you know, ugly. I'm not saying it's a nice. We all got a job to do, that's all."

"Yes, well. We're getting plenty of complaints about those bailiffs. Nobody expected bailiffs around here. I mean the Chippewa from the reserve were breaking into empty houses up near Rutger's Distillery and the old tracks. That's how we got the ordnance. You can ask anybody in Regency Gate, they'll explain it to you. They don't think it's fair to use that law against them. Everybody understood at the time the law was meant to apply to the Indian squatters up there at the north end.

"That's a your democracy, though," Alex said, yawning, tired from the hard day. "What can we do, eh? Change the law back for Regency Gate, the Indians move into the houses again. Then whoever owns the houses, he's unhappy again, you can't please everybody, Joe. All the time somebody is unhappy, no matter how you work it. Some bastard's always bitching and complaining, so what the hell, eh. Try to please everybody, you end up pleasing nobody."

"What I think I'd better do," Kowalski said, "I think I'd better get back here tonight in case the chief decides to make trouble for those bailiffs. He's going to be mad as a hornet."

3

Mrs. Elizabeth Sigurjonnson, the Williams's houseworker, was a competent middle-aged lady who, like Sergeant Brock, had no sense of role. She would not wear a white apron, explaining that it made her look like a servant. The Williamses had given up calling her Betty, since whenever they did she would realign the relationship at once.

"You could do the downstairs windows today, Mrs. Sigurjonnson."

"Sure thing, Mrs. Williams."

"Oh and Betty, the french doors too."

"Right, Mavis."

After dinner Mrs. Sigurjonnson brought coffee into the library. This room had shelves on two walls with old brass and copperware exhibits that winked in the light, and some books too. Chief Williams poured brandy. Their houseworker returned with her hat and handbag. "I'm off. Dishwasher's full, start it up after you put the cups in. I'll need help with that new door gadget getting out."

"Goodnight, Mrs. Sigurjonnson," said Mrs. Williams, smiling. "Thank you so much."

"Yes, certainly, I'll see to it," said Chief Williams, and followed her to the front door. He unclasped the stout bar-lock which had just been installed. "Do have a very good evening. See you tomorrow."

"Not if the bailiffs get in here tonight, though, eh?" Mrs. Sigurjonnson said and laughed. " 'Bye. Don't get drunk."

The chief made a tour of the other doors and windows to check the locks. He took Sergeant Brock's envelope from the desk in his study and gave it to his wife in the library.

She looked through the photographs with interest.

"Helen isn't bad," Mrs. Williams said. "With her clothes on and those glasses she looks so frumpy. Oh these are terrible of me. Frank, I must take some weight off."

"What do you think of Ryan?"

"He comes out very well. Of course the grapes are ridiculous."

"I mean," said Chief Williams, studying his wife carefully over his coffee cup, "in the matter of any scandal arising from these photographs. We can depend on Helen, but then there's Ryan."

"He's your policeman, Frank," Mrs. Williams said. She seemed to be engrossed in the photographs. "I suppose he'll do what's in his own interests."

"I'd like to put Ryan on the list."

"What?"

"I can't stand the bugger."

"Alisha wants him promoted."

"Very good dinner from Mrs. Sigurjonnson tonight. Stuffed chicken breasts with oysters and artichoke hearts. They do it at Morley's. Did you know that? Any day now, Mavis, Ryan will be asking me out for a beer."

"I promised Alisha."

"Hard to say how that would work out, though, Mavis. With Brock, I mean. Say I fire Brock and move Ryan into his job, Brock might make a lot of trouble. I expect he could convince himself that there was an important principle involved. We should leave Brock where he is for now. Ryan's the problem."

"Well obviously you could depend on Ryan if you made him a sergeant. I think you're being difficult, Frank. I know you can't increase rank personnel right now but I'm sure you could move some other sergeant out to make room for Ryan. It doesn't have to be Brock. I almost think," Mrs. Williams said, "that you're using these photographs against Alisha. She doesn't often ask you for a favour."

"I have this personal difficulty, you see, where he's almost asking me out for a beer and calling me Frank, as a constable. I have to think ahead to Ryan as a sergeant, fetching his coffee for him, polishing his boots, those are the sort of things I worry about, Mavis."

"I see. It's just behaviour, though, isn't it, Frank, there aren't any real obstacles?"

"Well behaviour is real enough, Mavis. Ryan has to tighten up considerably in that department."

"He could be told that."

"Yes. Say in a week or two, then, when I've had a chance to see how he handles himself, I'll let you have some word for Alisha. I won't do anything for now. The lunches will have to stop of course."

"What?"

"Ryan is taking too long at lunch these days."

"Well I'll tell her, Frank, I'll explain the situation," Mrs. Williams said, not too pleased. "I know she'll think you could be more helpful if you wanted to be. Can I say he'll be a sergeant?"

"No. We're just talking about letting him stay on as constable. He's in over his head as a constable. He has this simple investigation to do, finding out who's behind Equity Mortgage and Trust. He's writing me reports that look like stock exchange lists of companies. I'm getting better information on Equity Mortgage and Trust from the morning paper. Also he's got himself stuck on nickel. I'd say at the moment that Ryan's the BCP's foremost nickel expert. We don't need a nickel expert on the force. What I'm asking you," Chief Williams said, "is whether we can depend on the bugger if Brock makes trouble for us with these photographs." He took a sip of his brandy, lifting his glass in an affable toast to his wife.

Mrs. Williams sifted through the photographs again, paying more attention to the shots of Ryan than those of herself. She said irritably: "No, you're being selfish and obstructive, you know you are. I'm not asking for the moon, Frank. I wear myself out helping you, there's a homicidal maniac living in your jurisdiction, under your nose, and you put yourself on record to the Police Commission with a letter saying the man's a respectable merchant, a good citizen, a victim of false arrest, and God knows what else. I had a terrible time getting that idiotic letter to Erskine back from Cecil at the commission office. How poor Mr. Sieracki was harassed by Constable Kowalski. Such a stupid letter to write. Then the incinerator in that place isn't working, I had to tear all those papers up in the ladies' room and flush them down the toilet."

"The Police Commission should buy itself a paper shredder," Chief Williams suggested. "We have two."

Mrs. Williams did not reply to this but drank her brandy with a surly face.

"Morley's for God's sake, Mavis," Chief Williams said.

"It was just once at Morley's."

"All right. I can put Ryan in as a sergeant in Traffic at the north end, and that's the best I can do. Traffic is the only division that shows a profit. I can tell you now that Ryan won't like the work. See him up there, not down here. Would you let me know, please, when you get tired of him. I'd really prefer somebody intelligent in that traffic job."

Mrs. Williams's manner became immediately sunny then. "That will do very well, Frank, thank you," she said. "That will solve the problem, at least for me. I don't care whether or not he's happy with the promotion. He's a dreadful little thug."

"I know. I think up at the north end you get a lot of drivers stoned out on liquor they make at home from peaches. Macedonians or something, they want to pay their fines in chickens, that sort of thing. Ryan will have to take his pay-offs in poultry." The chief looked at his watch. The evening was not going badly for him. "Then there's Kowalski. RCMP Murder and Missing Persons will take a while with the Amundsen interrogation. He might have killed other people besides the real Albert Sieracki, and they have to check his movements against their murder and missing files. The Swedes want him back of course. We'll be able to arraign Amundsen here in about three weeks. The reporters will get the story then. Say two weeks to be safe before Kowalski becomes a Bradfarrow hero, TV celebrity on the networks and so on. I imagine our friends on the council will give him the freedom of the city."

"Well, I had a talk with Erskine. We'll hold the commission hearing next week and decide whether or not he took that bribe. If we wait, the Amundsen publicity will just confuse everything."

"Good. I'm sorry we couldn't come up with any of the money."

"Maybe it will turn up later, in a year or two," Mrs. Williams said. "I've been thinking. The Vaniers had that marvellous stained glass in the dining room. Set into a screen with the light behind it, do you remember? Probably the Italians have smashed it up already. I thought I might slip down there after your men come and see if I can find any pieces that aren't broken in the rubbish."

"All right. Wait until I have the men in place." Chief Williams checked his watch again. "The bailiffs are supposed to come at ten but they could come earlier of course. I imagine they try to catch people unprepared."

"You know, Frank, it could be nice in Regency Gate from now on. Now we have all that lovely green open space."

"Yes, but not if it goes too far, Mavis, use your head. Living in Regency Gate is nice, yes. Maybe living here with the green space will be nicer, but if they knock down too many houses after they go round us we'll be alone for God's sake, won't we. We'll be surrounded by countryside. We won't be living in Regency Gate then, we'll be living in the country. Who wants to live in the God damn country?"

Chief Williams's argument here was interrupted by the sound of a vehicle on the gravel outside. The chief went to the window. A cattle transport had arrived. A long-haired man, young and grubby, dressed in a check shirt and denims, descended from the cab. The man lowered the transport tailboard and pulled on two ropes, shouting: "*Out*, you ugly bastards." Four gigantic horned beasts swayed indecisively down the ramp in file. The man went into the transport then and began to unload sacks and barrels.

"Mavis, keep an eye on the driveway and the back."

Chief Williams opened the front door with all caution, leaving the heavy bar-lock chain secured. The man approached on steel-toed boots and drew a bunch of papers from his pocket. "Mr. Frank Williams?"

"Get those brutes off my driveway."

"Four oxen for you, as per agreement," said the man. "Delivery from Equity Mortgage and Trust for Mr. Frank Williams. I take it that you are he, sir? Four prime oxen, animals with hearts of oak," the man said, staring challengingly at Chief Williams. This man's experience was that the customers became absurdly upset when their oxen were delivered. The people took the money readily enough, and the rum, the flour too and even the cedar. Not the oxen, though, which was why he liked to put the oxen to them first and up front. "Half a sovereign." He dropped the coin into Chief Williams's hand. "Twenty cedar rails as specified, one hundredweight of flour, one hogshead of rum which is to say three twenty-one gallon barrels, there's many a good song in there, sir. One fiftieth of fifty acres, one acre's price duly delivered. A nice little spread you had here, Mr. Williams. I don't need a receipt. Any questions," the man asked uneasily, "about the oxen, sir? I have grooming and feeding information in this booklet, *The Ox, Nature's Tractor*. That's free of charge. I'd be lying if I told you they were intelligent, and they don't respond to affection, but you wouldn't believe how strong they are, Mr. Williams," said the man.

"I don't believe this," Chief Williams said. "Now you'd like me to move my furniture out and hand over the keys to my house, would you?"

"I just do the deliveries," the man said, and looked around him at the porch, driveway and lawn, as if expecting to see moved-out furniture. "Though you should've seen to your furniture before you got the oxen problem, hard to work near the animals, you know. We have an anomalous situation here," the man said apologetically, "whereby I make the delivery to your house, which thereupon becomes the property of Equity Mortgage and Trust. They're on a tight schedule. They'd like your oxen off their property before nine tomorrow. The Humane Society aren't taking any more, and whatever there ever was in enthusiasm for oxen," said the man, "in the country around Bradfarrow is pretty well dead now, with this glut in Regency Gate. Enjoy your rum, sir."

When the man had driven off the oxen remained standing like statues on the gravel facing Chief Williams. They raised their heads together and bawled at the chief, seeming to expect something of him. Three police cruisers pulled in and the animals made a lumbering turn to watch the arrival. Four policemen got out of each cruiser. These were remarkably large policemen, tall men massively built, wearing truncheons on their belts instead of revolvers. A sergeant, the tallest of the tall, tried to pat one of the bawling oxen and jumped back in time to avoid a vicious hook of a horn to his stomach.

The men entered the house with the bashfulness of all large men, their caps in their hands. Mrs. Williams led them to the kitchen, which was actually a commodious work-room of the old style built to accommodate the presence of many servants. The heavy squad overfilled the room. The huge sergeant saluted.

"Six on guard outside, Sergeant Derby," the chief said. "That's one on each door, the other three patrolling. I want you to keep the front door secure, men at every other door and window inside too. I'll show you the lay-out."

Sergeant Derby, the giant, who had a cropped head and a battered line-backer's face, agreed with this strategy. He was a jovial and talkative person by temperament. "Suckers are in for a surprise," he said. "Eight o'clock now, chief, we'll take two-man breaks. Your good lady wife could man the Mr. Coffee if that's okay," he said, looking at the bubbling pot left by Mrs. Sigurjonnson. "May's well get the team working together if we're having this duty regular, make it easy on ourselves."

Here, though, the sergeant's agreeableness met resistance from Chief Williams who did not see a need for rest periods, his house being at risk; and from Mrs. Williams who refused to be a coffeemaker for the squad, and who indeed removed the coffeepot to the living-room.

At dusk Mrs. Williams put on old slacks and stout shoes and a dark sweater and went off to see what she could find of intact stained glass in the rubble of the Vanier house at the corner of Cambridge Mews.

The wait for the bailiffs was awkward time. Inside the front door Sergeant Derby was not his jovial self. He was silent in the wait and his battered face was closed.

Once he broke the silence to say: "Some of us are down the Doctor's Hotel around now. A beer would go down okay with the men, sir."

"I don't keep beer in the house," Chief Williams said.

Kowalski made his appearance at nine-thirty, on foot, wearing an old grey cardigan darned at the elbows and baggy slacks, his TV-watching outfit.

From inside the house Sergeant Derby and the chief recognized Kowalski's voice.

"What's this, Wilf?"

"Special job for Chief Williams."

"You in charge here, Wilf?"

"No, Darl's inside the house. Why don't you go on home, Joe."

The doorbell rang.

Chief Williams said: "Ignore that, sergeant."

However Sergeant Derby unlocked the door. "It's only Joe Kowalski," he told the chief.

Kowalski's face was set in hard lines. He looked at Sergeant Derby, then at the chief. "What's this, sir, all these cops?"

"My life isn't my own any more," Chief Williams said, partly to himself in amazement. "I don't know, I have the feeling I must account for myself to every passer-by who shows an interest."

"There'll be bailiffs with a legal warrant here at ten, Darl," Kowalski said to Sergeant Derby. "Like anybody tries to stop 'em's breaking the law. It's the same as the Indians up by the old tracks, when the band gangs up on the bailiffs there."

"This is different."

"No, it isn't. It's the same."

"I'll tell you what," Chief Williams said. "Sergeant Derby, kick this dumb bugger out of my house. Kick his ass the hell out of here."

"Hold up, chief. Look Joe, I mean this is Chief Williams's house. He's no Indian," Sergeant Derby said. "He's the chief of police. He can put us all on the cutback list."

Chief Williams said: "That's right."

Kowalski said: "Well it surprises me that bothers you, Darl. You're a cop, just like me. In this particular incident here tonight the chief is Mr. Citizen. What he has in mind is against the law. Next time around he'll ask you to rob a bank, I guess, steal a few purses for him in Zwick's park. This house here is the worst house on the beat for disturbances. I already gave Mrs. Williams one warning. I got stopped from doing my job here before, when they had their orgy," Kowalski said to Sergeant Derby.

The giant sergeant asked: "So what was your idea, when these bailiffs come?"

"Nothing. Verify the warrant, then nothing. Keep the peace."

"Supposing some trouble starts."

"Darl, I have to arrest anybody causes trouble. We always arrest the Indians."

"There's me, and the guys outside. We have some other guys around the house. Big, you know, Joe, big guys."

"Anybody causes trouble has me to deal with."

Sergeant Derby unlocked the door and went outside. Joe Kowalski stayed in the house with Chief Williams. Now and then the chief stared at Kowalski, trying to understand him. Otherwise Chief Williams made the inside rounds and kept an eye on the driveway and pretended Joe Kowalski did not exist.

The bailiffs, four in number, arrived in two trucks. The backs of the trucks were piled with mover's boxes. The bailiffs were big enough but ill-conditioned. One seemed to have more paunch than muscle. Another had a stump of cigar between his teeth and coughed through the smoke. Chief Williams was pleased. He noticed that the bailiffs parked some distance from the oxen, showing the respect of familiarity, and circled the animals at a wary distance to approach the house.

Sergeant Derby chatted with the bailiffs outside the front door. The outside squad was good-humoured, and sounded to Chief Williams as if it was allowing itself far too fraternal a mood. Laughter floated in from outside as the doorbell rang.

"You intend to take some action now, do you," the chief said, without looking at Kowalski. "I believe you have a psychological problem, constable. Get somebody to explain to you about people who enjoy hurting themselves." He opened the door on the chain. "What is it, Derby?"

"Everything's under control, chief. We have to deal with Constable Kowalski. We'd like him out here."

"What do you think now, Kowalski?"

"Well Darl Derby's an okay guy, chief," Kowalski said with a tolerant shrug, misunderstanding the question apparently. "Talk your ear off if you give him a chance of course, but that's Darl."

The chief said politely: "Good luck, constable."

When Chief Williams undid the chain to let Kowalski out the door was pushed all the way open by Sergeant Derby.

"Muscle power," Sergeant Derby said to Chief Williams. He looked down reproachfully at the chief from his serious height. "That's what we're good for, isn't it, chief, muscle work. We're just walking muscle." He brushed Chief Williams aside. Men tramped in cheerfully, police and bailiffs. "So we'll give these guys a hand to move your furniture out, since we're here," the sergeant said. "Any other way we'll be here all night. Teddy, you go upstairs and tell Burt to start taking the beds apart. We'll leave that mother of a piano for now but get the sideboards and stuff out of the kitchen there, we want a track through."

Sergeant Derby said to Joe Kowalski: "I had a talk with the guys. I don't know what's the matter with me. I must've got my brains rattled hitting the books."

"Nobody told me you were out here, Darl."

"It didn't seem such a big deal, one way or the other. I was in two minds there."

"Like if I knew some cops were going to be here anyway I could've saved myself the trip."

"He didn't even offer a cup of coffee. I think I could've been bought for a beer."

Chief Williams stepped in front of Sergeant Derby to address the men but the sergeant lifted the chief by the coat collar and stood him against the wall out of the way.

"Comes as a surprise to you I suppose, me talking about my brains," he said to the chief. "Somebody sees somebody big with muscles, they never think he might be brainy. No, sir, they never do. The old heave jobs, hump, shovel, lift. Muscle is useful, right.

Somebody sees one of us and right away he thinks there's a guy's useful to have around. The little buggers are all accountants and like electronic technicians on the force, they're in public relations and visiting schools and nice jobs like that. Well me and the guys don't have any future on the force, when you look at it. We're too useful to waste us in good jobs. Over the winter I took political economy course four-oh-four at the university night extension. I hit through a pile of books. Nobody mentioned that to you I suppose."

Chief Williams, quite dazed, watched one of his own policemen strolling by carrying three dining-room chairs in each hand.

"No, nobody did, eh. All anybody needs to know about me, I'm six-seven, three hundred pounds. That's all's important, correct, chief?"

"Listen, sergeant," Chief Williams said. "I don't think you understand what you're doing. I'm ordering you to order the men to put my furniture back in my house. Do you understand the order?"

"Well it's difficult because of these muscles I got and everything, understanding something like that," Sergeant Derby said. "We're only up to multi-national corporation cost projection techniques on the course. But the way I was thinking tonight it could've bounced either way. Like I was on your side. You might've held on to your nice house tonight. For a cup of coffee. For a beer. Even," said Sergeant Derby gazing down at Chief Williams with self-righteous sentimentality, "for one kind word."

"I have to use the telephone."

"Leave personal clothing, personal effects, luggage, Wilf. Like they have to pack, so they need that stuff inside." One of the bailiffs went past with two avocado trees in brass planters on his shoulders. "You better start packing the linen and stuff in the boxes, Dougie. Dishes too, doesn't matter if you break some, we're clumsy." He said to Chief Williams: "A guy reaps what he sows, ever hear that said? You could've had your house for a smile. We would've thrun those bailiffs out for you. Say a few beers, a couple smiles, potato chips, say you didn't turn up, Joe, and a bag or two of peanuts with the beer."

"I'm going to have your badge for this," Chief Williams said, "and the badges of every one of your gooneys into the bargain."

Sergeant Derby turned away from Chief Williams to one of his men who was carrying out a sideboard. "Burt, those bailiff pussycats are goofing off, going by here with little pots of plants." He addressed Chief Williams again, showing teeth the size of a horse's in a smile: "We'll have you all moved out pretty soon. Shouldn't take long now, with sixteen guys. Hump hump hump."

"I could be at home with an ale," said Joe Kowalski, who was beginning to feel a little bored.

"I guess we'll all be ready for a few cold ones when we're through here. Usually I'm down at the Doctor's tonight, but this came up. Just as well anyway with training started. We might do okay this year, we have a quarterback who can throw the football for a change. We ran all season last year, a whole season eating grass. Made the semi-finals and got tore up by Lindsay. No phone calls," the sergeant said as Chief Williams tried to break clear. He gathered the chief's collar in one hand and stood him against the wall again. "We're putting all your good stuff over on the lawn so's the wreckers won't drop any of the house on it. Could rain though, you should get some tarps."

Up against the wall, a smile broke out suddenly on Chief Williams's desperate face. He stretched a hand up and laid it on Sergeant Derby's shoulder. "I have rum," he said. "You people like rum, don't you? Believe me I'm sorry about the beer. I'll break open the rum. Send a car for a couple of cases of coke. Rum and cokes for everybody. We'll talk football," the chief said. "Or, I have an idea, let's get a good brainy conversation going, give ourselves a treat, me and you and the fellows, I've always wanted to know something about political economy. Later on we could phone out for a few pizzas."

"Too late for that now, Frankie boy," Sergeant Derby said. He said to Kowalski: "Would've worked like a charm at eight o'clock."

When the men were carrying the final items by, rugs and carpets, Mrs. Williams came unsteadily up the driveway uttering little bird-like cries of distress. Black and blue lumps stood out on her forehead. Her face was streaked with dirt. One eye was puffed and she had lost her shoes. She clutched to her chest two panels of stained glass, however, which shimmered rose-red and green in the light from the house. "Help," she said.

Two of Sergeant Derby's men ran to her at once and grabbed her elbows to support her. This loosened her clutch on the salvaged panels which fell and tinkled into small bits on the gravel.

"All right, we have an injury. Injury drill, Dougie, let's see what you remember. Lay her on the porch front up for now. Got her wind knocked out looks like. Bring some ice and towels, Pete. A jug of water, somebody."

A couple of the men spread Mrs. Williams's arms and legs and kneaded her shoulders and her thighs, while the sergeant ran her through the eye movements for signs of concussion.

"We should strip her down and do a finger-check on the ribs and hams," said Dougie but the sergeant shook his head. "Cramp, running cramp here, bring her to and she can walk it off." He threw the jug of water in her face.

Sergeant Derby set Mrs. Williams to tottering back and forth on the porch with a plastic bag full of ice cubes on her head. All the policemen and the bailiffs watched her critically. Presently her eyes focussed, on Kowalski's face as it happened.

"Somebody is going to suffer for this," Mrs. Williams said, when she had got her breath.

Eleven

Willy Woolly

1

With examinations over and the pain-racked groaning forms in denim withdrawn, the public library was under quiet rule again. It was the morning following the Williams's eviction. The librarian, Abe West, sat at his own little table in a corner of the reference room reading without enjoyment a number of reports— from the Hastings County Zoning Appeals Committee, the Land Use Commission, the Department of Natural Resources and Bradfarrow City Council, among others. The reports ranged in appearance from fancily-printed brochures in colour to smudgy stapled pages, according to the affluence of the bureaucracy that produced them.

The librarian winced but did not look up every time Redmond Ryan's boots rang like shots on the parquet between his table and the magazine file racks.

Ryan was on the track of a link between Auto Aluminum Hybrasing Ltd. and Mini-People Incorporated. Then, as Ryan saw the investigation, it would be just a matter of connecting both these companies with Allegheny Dry Docks. Allegheny came under the Deloro Nickel Holdings umbrella.

"How far do you go back," Ryan asked, his voice echoing from the walls, "with this thing from Sudbury, *Nickel Industry Journal?* I'm looking at 1970 here."

The librarian drifted across the floor on soft shoes. He mimed whispering with his lips as he whispered, to get the idea of quietness across. "I'm sorry, officer. We only file the nationals."

"Like, you and me are alone in this place," Ryan said, still loudly, staring at the librarian with speculative contempt, with a man's man's loathing for an unmanly man. "Unless we shouldn't be waking up any fairies you have sleeping around here."

Since Sergeant Brock's visit with questions about leprechauns the librarian had developed strong affection for the Bradfarrow City Police. They were splendid men, Abe West felt. One could talk to them about fairy folklore. He had become aware, certainly, that he was not receiving the same intelligent response to the subject from the blond airman constable as he had from Sergeant Brock. Still he was a professional librarian who dealt with students regularly and was accustomed to that central phenomenon in the life of the custodian of knowledge, hostile reaction to interesting facts.

"Most of them aren't even fairies," Abe West said. "Outside that group you have your vry and your niffy, who are agricultural. Turning milk sour, making cows barren. The kelpy, the hobhoulard, the dunny, quite complicated beneath their simple artisan appearance. The dunny for instance," he said, "is basically a wirrikow."

"Oh yes? Is that a fact? Blow me down," Ryan said. "I found this company that treats aluminum parts for the auto industry, and I want to know why they have an office in nickel town."

"We don't have direct information, you see. This is research. In language groups, the chittiface is interesting. Medieval roots, hardly any vowel sounds. If you prefer a flatland wight, as many do. Our friend the gytrash is mountainy, and so is the hodgepocher. Strong gutturals. Everybody and his brother's heard of the hellwain and the bugbear, lots of sightings, like UFOs. Waffs and puckles, not so many. Down the east coast, mumpokers, firedrakes and hobbits. Bodgarths all over the place in Georgia, plenty of jemmyburties up here. And leprechauns of course."

"I didn't believe any of that eyewash even when I was a kid."

"Yes, you get nonsense too, naturally. The melchdick. You won't find many serious people supporting the idea of the melchdick, or any other kind of ditch sprite," Abe West said, falling in with the policeman's scepticism. "The gallytrot too for that matter, a shaggy white dog, he comes out of the same bottle as the pink elephant if you ask me. Too much drink taken, too long a walk home late at night. Keeling over into ditches with a bellyful of ale."

Ryan put away his notebook. He continued to bear on Abe West an unfriendly policeman's scrutiny. "You guys should get more fresh air and exercise," he advised. "Hanging around the Harvest Moon all night, noses stuck in books all day, no wonder you go that way."

"But we could be lucky with leprechauns soon. We could have leprechauns in Regency Gate. The houses are all off the old rath now. There's a chance the leprechauns have been living deep underground in the sidhe-barrow. Maybe they'll show themselves again."

"Well the little buggers are going to be out of luck when Deloro Nickel moves in," Ryan said, amused. "You're going to see a lot of digging and blasting and drilling in Regency Gate soon."

"They won't need to do that, for a sheep-farm."

"How do you mean, a sheep-farm?"

"That's what we'll be seeing in Regency Gate. A hundred-acre sheep-farm."

"Oh yes? I've been on this for a month. Everything I find says nickel, but if you've got better information," said Ryan, thumbs hooked in his belt and with a condescending glance around at the library shelves, "I mean if this *book study* you do here gives you an edge over me as a street cop I'm ready to listen."

"Soon you'll see the barns and feed silos going up. Fences around the hundred acres, fences are important with sheep. I don't know whether they'll leave a house intact on the property or put up a new farmhouse. I'd be inclined to put up a new farmhouse. One of those fancy mansions would look out of place in a rural setting."

"Sounds like a great money-maker. Where did you get this dumb information from, a fairy book?"

"The County Planning Authority. They say it's a sheep-farm. They know. Put it another way, in the Zoning Appeals Committee report it says that the Land Use Commission has given proper notice to the County Planning Authority, designating a sheep-farm. That isn't something you can argue with, officer. Designated use is all locked up now."

"That can't be right. It's a multi-million dollar operation. Who's going to spend millions of dollars to make a sheep-farm?"

"People can surprise you, though," the librarian said comfortably. "They do odd things. I was just researching this for the Historical Society. Most of it is secret, but you can always find out what you want to know. With shared jurisdictions often the bureaucrats will publish each other's secrets. Very dull reading of course. Sheer slogging boredom to tell you the truth. You take somebody like the secretary of the Zoning Appeals Committee, I don't know what to say about his writing style. He uses the same sentences every time. He can put together different reports using exactly the same sentences. It's like building different things with Lego pieces. I can't figure out how he does it."

Ryan understood only some of this. In Ryan's view of written material company records were power and money and were real, as were newspapers. Books were unreal except for pornography. He understood books but knew nothing about bureaucratic reports. He said: "We like to deal in facts. What I've been doing myself, I've been checking back from Equity Mortgage and Trust to find out who they're acting for."

"Yes. That's no good. You'll get yourself into a daisychain of interlocking companies."

"Yes but I found nickel!" Ryan said, shouting like a thwarted child.

"You aren't doing sound research, I'm afraid, officer. You have to read these reports made out of Lego. The Bradfarrow Historical Society likes to keep an eye on the reports, so I get copies here. People are always plotting to tear down historical landmarks, put up a taco franchise, something the community can use."

Abe West, looking into Ryan's blank face, added helpfully: "Say Wonder Value Supermarket buys a historical building, nine times out of ten what they have in mind is to tear down the building and put up a supermarket. Okay?" The librarian thought that the policeman was somewhat naïve. He seems to be a really decent kid, though, Abe West thought. "Well, the Historical Society likes to know. Say a group called the Heritage Preservation Foundation buys the building, the Historical Society likes to check that this isn't another name for Wonder Value Supermarket. It's just a routine we have in the library here."

"You have a report, do you, saying that whoever owns the hundred acres will be using it as a sheep-farm?"

"Over there on my desk. Mr. Kowalski."

"What?"

"Mr. Kowalski owns the hundred acres."

"Not Mr. Joseph Kowalski?"

"That's the name."

"Let me see," Ryan said, "that God damn report."

The librarian found the report and the page. Redmond Ryan looked at it and his world suddenly became perfect for him.

"The ten million," Ryan said out loud. "Kowalski had it all the time. I knew he had it. He had it. He bought a sheep-farm with the ten million he got from Seamus Riordan, the dumb Polack. Can I have a copy of this?" A radiant smile lighted Redmond Ryan's noble face. He was much moved by emotion: the joy of the lucky break, the happiness of being proved right at last. *He had found the money.* He said: "Thank you."

"No sweat," Abe West said cheerfully. Solved a homework problem for the kid, the librarian thought, we do useful work in this library. "Fifteen cents a page, officer."

2

One of Ryan's willowy girls was in the bathroom taking a shower. He spoke over the noise of rushing water.

"The Four Seasons must be chock full of Regency Gate people I guess," he said. "No trouble making up a crowd for bridge or tennis. Put Frank on, will you, tweetie-pie."

"What did you want to talk to him about?"

"Me, where I'm going on the force, things like that. I have a few, you know, demands."

"He's very busy, Redmond, we both are. We've had the lawyers here all morning."

"Yes, well. That's your business, isn't it. I'd like to talk about me. Sergeant in Traffic, I don't know, Mavis. I'd have to work out of the north end. I don't speak any of the languages."

"You're forgetting what I said about your attitude."

"No, I remember. What *you* forget is, I'm me. I've got to be me, Mavis. If I'm not me, who am I?"

"Oh God. This is a wretched week."

"I'd be interested in detective, staff sergeant, detective-sergeant, maybe I'm even worth inspector or deputy chief. We'll have to see how the negotiations go, if you wouldn't mind putting the chief on the phone, Mavis."

"I'll get Frank."

"Ryan?"

"I found the ten million. From the bazooka hold-up in Montreal."

There was a silence.

"Are you sure of that, Ryan, you've found the money?"

"Yes."

"I want to see you right away."

"I thought you might. Frank."

"What's that?"

"Something else, Frank."

"The hell is it now, Ryan?"

"The Equity Mortgage and Trust investigation. I've broken that case too. I know who had the houses knocked down in Regency Gate. I know who got your house, Frank. I know the name of the person responsible, the man who got your house."

"Good God. Report over here right away."

"I don't know."

"What do you mean, I don't know, Ryan?"

"About getting over there to the Four Seasons. It's a lot of trouble. I have a guest and everything. I don't like the tone of your voice, either, if you want to know the truth, Frank."

Another silence occurred, with tense whispering at Chief Williams's end of the line.

"Redmond?"

"Yes, Frank."

"Say I drop by at your place, Redmond, how would that be?"

"That would be better, Frank."

The willowy girl came out of the bathroom towelling her hair. "Who's on the phone?" she asked jealously.

"Just the frigging chief, eating out of my hand," Ryan told her. "I'll put a few beers in the fridge," he promised Chief Williams.

3

"Well we have to go by the book, in this case the Bradfarrow police articles. We have to take him before the Police Commission under arrest, lay the charge if the commission approves. We can throw him in jail then," Chief Williams said. "He's a free man until the commission meets, though."

"Very well," Mrs. Williams said angrily. "Please send somebody to arrest the bastard right now. We'll hold the hearing this afternoon."

"I see. You can arrange that, can you."

"Yes I can, Frank. I most certainly can. He hired those Italian ruffians. *The man destroyed my beautiful house*. I can arrange that very quickly indeed."

They were in Chief Williams's office at the station. The chief occupied a visitor's chair while his wife sat behind his desk with her own paper work spread in front of her.

Chief Williams rang Central and ordered the arrest of Joe Kowalski. "I guess it will be just a formality, the hearing," he said. "He has the ten million. The sheep-farm is in his name."

"Well. No meeting is a formality, Frank. Meetings can go wrong. Sometimes somebody will make a stupid speech and everybody will agree with it. People get upset or confused, and then they vote the wrong way."

"Or they go to sleep. Teague nods off."

"But he votes with me. He's old, he has to be picked up and taken home, he hardly ever understands what's going on, but I can always be sure of Judge Teague's vote."

"I know Kramer is solid. I thought you said that Mott is in with the new crowd on the Council now."

Mrs. Williams tapped out a number on the chief's phone. "Mr. Mott always votes with the majority. He's a weak young man, a nuisance on the Council of course with these new people in control, but he's perfect for me on the Police Commission. Cecil, Commander Ridgeway, please. It's Mrs. Mavis Williams speaking."

"Us, you mean, Mavis. Perfect for us."

"Us, Frank. I'm sorry."

The voice of Cecil, the clerk, came to Chief Williams across the desk, tinny and peevish.

"Commander's on the other phone, Mrs. Williams. Call back, eh."

"I swear that shabby old fool is getting senile," Mrs. Williams said without covering the mouthpiece. "At once please, Cecil. This is urgent."

"Brock has some explaining to do, and I suppose we'll need Ryan, the man who broke the case. My new buddy Redmond."

"Yes, tell them, Frank."

"Detective-Sergeant Ryan."

"He was in a very strong bargaining position."

"That didn't make it any weaker," Chief Williams said, "when you said, name your price, Redmond. Anything you want, Redmond."

"Within reason, I said."

"I didn't hear you say within reason, Mavis. I have a new murder case on my desk there, happened in Brampton. This man killed his wife it seems," the chief said, bored, as at routine matters to take care of. "I'd like to go over it before the hearing. So I'll order you a car now and you can pick me up here after you collect Teague."

"All right. I should be back with Judge Teague by two-thirty. Wait for us downstairs at the main entrance."

"He got tired of his wife for no apparent reason," the chief said. "This Brampton man. Turned himself in after he did the job. Strangled the lady. Happiest couple on the block according to the neighbours, married nine years."

Commander L. Erskine Ridgeway, bad-tempered enough when he came to the phone, was enraged when he heard the news about Kowalski. "Foul, corrupt scum and wearing the BCP uniform, the dear old blue," the commander shouted, choking on his words. "Treacherous villain, he's disgraced us for ever, Mavis. By God, Mavis, we'll make an example of the fellow. By God, a pity we can't flog the greasy-fingered swine. A ten million dollar bribe, by God, for shame, the stinking dog, the scoundrel."

"Just a short hearing should do, Erskine," Mrs. Williams said. "So would you call Mr. Kramer, please. I'll let Mr. Mott know and bring Judge Teague."

"Be glad to. Comes of letting rough-scuff with funny names on the force. Three o'clock, eh?"

"Thank you, Erskine."

On his way out Chief Williams said: "You and I and Erskine would be enough, wouldn't we, Mavis, according to the rules. We've done business before with just the quorum. I have work to do. The more people you call up the less chance we have of a short hearing."

"Yes but I don't want any more mistakes now. Remember I let you make the arrangements for protecting the house. I should have taken care of it myself. This has to be done right. If we hold the hearing with just the three of us, on paper you and I control the meeting two to one. That's a family affair, and there's too much talk now about influential families. The news people could say that Mr. Kowalski was condemned by the Williams family." She said: "Judge Teague, please. Mrs. Mavis Williams speaking."

Mrs. Williams had an opaque but satisfactory conversation with Judge Teague. The weak Mr. Mott too said he could attend the hearing. As she fitted her papers into her briefcase Mrs. Williams experienced a feeling of well-being, pleasure from work that is going well. Even the loss of her beloved house was diminished as a calamity in her mind. A humming noise came from her chubby mouth involuntarily, then words.

". . . your sunny side up, *up*," Mrs. Williams sang, "let the laughter come through, *oo*. Stand up on your legs! Be like two fried eggs! Keep your sunny side . . ."

Indeed Mrs. Williams was in such a glad mood that she found

herself speaking kindly to the man at the wheel of her police cruiser.

"We're going quite far west, to Ravenwood." She gave the man Judge Teague's address. "A long drive there and back for you I'm afraid, constable."

He was an odd-looking peasant, the driver. His neck seemed to be sunk deep into his shoulders in the manner of a resting vulture. All that Mrs. Williams could see of him, as she settled herself in the seat behind, was the constable's cap that was apparently sitting on his uniform collar.

"Yerrah, but a much longer drive back than going for you and himself the judge," said the strange man, putting the cruiser in gear. "Much, much longer, lady." He said this in a voice that told of deep gloom.

"The hills are alive," she sang to herself, "with the sound of mu-U-sic . .." Mrs. Williams never paid attention to the conversation and individualities of drivers.

4

The committee room had dark blue carpeting and beige curtains, with wall panelling assertively imitative of some exotic wood, perhaps teak. Most of the chairs were stacked against the walls. A row of a dozen or so on the floor faced the dais, a step up, a forum of elevated deliberation. The board table on the dais was unoccupied except for Cecil, the clerk, a weary-faced middle-aged person wearing an old suit who was hunched over his papers and his tape recorder.

Joe Kowalski sat with Sergeant Brock in the middle of the row of chairs. Constables French and O'Dacre, who had Kowalski in custody, were on guard outside the door. The only other person in the committee room for the moment was Redmond Ryan. Ryan was of course not in uniform, being now a detective-sergeant. He wore a dark-grey business suit with an outsized white handkerchief spilling from the breast pocket. He paced the carpet, studying his notebook from time to time. He sat down now and then too, away from Kowalski and Brock, looking successful and righteous.

Joe Kowalski was depressed, though not by his immediate circumstances. As usual Brock was perplexed by Kowalski whose worrying, if not random, certainly did not respect priority. Though Brock worried about his daughter Sally almost constantly, he could forget her now and then too when the day's concerns pressed.

The aunts were the weight on Joe Kowalski's mind.

"I bet we have millions of people in the country with the same problem," Kowalski said to Brock. "They can't do anything rough, games I mean or disco, one broken bone and that's it. Millions of people with nothing to do."

"I suppose it's a question of money, Joe," Sergeant Brock said. "I don't imagine it's a rich market for anybody to go after, that age group."

"One broken bone and you have the nursing home problem, at a basic rate of seven hundred dollars a month. That's the bottom rate. That's no private room, no physiotherapist, what you're talking about is boiled egg and toast for breakfast, tuna fish casserole for dinner, nobody gives a damn what you do in between. It makes me mad, sergeant. It isn't their fault they get old."

"Well, come on, Joe," said Brock. "We're not barbarians after all, are we. We have a system to deal with the situation."

"I'd like to know what it is. What's the system?"

"*I* don't know what the system is," Sergeant Brock said, still feeling that imminence should give a problem priority in a man's thoughts, even Kowalski's. "I'm not up on the arrangements we have for old people. I know we have a system. We have pensions and so on. Go out in the street and you won't see a lot of old people lying there dying. Right? So they're in houses, aren't they. You don't read in the paper where they're starving to death either, that means somebody is feeding them. We don't spoil them, I'll agree there."

"I wish we could get something better going, though. I wish it didn't have to be macaroni all the time. I wish I knew what that system is, where we, you know, pay them back some of what they put in. The way it is now, jeez, I'm glad nobody's figured out a way of making them into glue. They did the work while they could. They aren't stray dogs and cats, are they. If you don't die along the line you get old. Okay, so you're still you, it could happen to anybody. There isn't a system where they can hang on to some of what they had before, say a little pride."

"If they get food and shelter that's the best deal they can have, Joe."

"Well if I could be sure of that, the food and shelter. But seven hundred dollars a month, supposing Myrtle takes a cup too much Scotch and goes down. I could pay the seven hundred for say two years, then all three of us are wiped out. It doesn't make any sense."

"They can watch TV. They can do that."

"Why should they like TV? I mean some guy down in Los Angeles with his hands tied, he has to blow up ten balloons to win a set of golf clubs, why should they care whether he makes it or not? Some lady must tell the people what she liked best about her honeymoon, my aunts would prefer not to know, sergeant. They can't relax watching the shoot-outs either, they get headaches."

"You were thinking of pets."

"A couple of Labrador puppies I thought."

"I don't know. Puppies could get under their feet. You could be into that seven hundred dollars a month thing, Joe. How about something easy to look after, a tank of tropical fish?"

"I tried that before. Fish aren't any good. I mean fish don't even know they're pets. The big problem with fish," Joe Kowalski said, "is that they don't know what the hell's going on outside the tank. You can give them names and say they're cute, but they don't know anything about it. Like what my aunts need is something difficult to look after, not something easy. They have all day. With those last fish it was feed the fish, feed the fish, all day long. We had five fish, I forget what their names were, Arnold and Swishy were two I remember, you could look at them for maybe a minute swimming in there, then you needed something else to do. The first day I couldn't see through the water when I got home with this fish food sludge, and the five fish belly up on the top. The aunts shouting at each other too of course, which of them killed the fish. I had to deal with that."

"What do you think's going to happen, Joe?"

"I think I'll give the puppies a try. The way the aunts are now I have to take chances."

This conversation between Joe Kowalski and Sergeant Brock was taking place at four o'clock. They had been in the committee room with Ryan and the clerk Cecil since three. Of the commissioners, Commander Ridgeway and Mr. Mott had arrived in good time. They left again, however, when a policeman brought a message for the chairman from Chief Williams. In fact the message was that Mrs. Williams and Judge Teague were missing. The chairman and young Mr. Mott were at a telephone in another room, waiting for news from the chief who was directing a police search for the vanished pair.

"I mean what's going to happen here," said Brock. "This hearing, Joe."

"Well I don't know. We'll find out when they get started I guess."

"Can you think of anything," Sergeant Brock asked tactfully, "that they might be mistaken about. Say there's something that looks bad for you, well really terrible, but you have a good explanation for it, can you think of anything like that?"

"Letting Timothy Hanrahan go."

"Seamus Riordan."

"Letting the little guy go. Problem's I don't have a good explanation for it."

Chief Williams came in then looking airy, with Commander Ridgeway and Mr. Mott. The chairman had a narrow face and an equine head, a horsy appearance. He had lost all of his hair except at the temples where it was grey and frizzy. Liver spots, the chloasma of Florida sun, stood out on his upper brow and crown. Bands of chrome bridge work flashed in his mouth. With his silver-wire spectacles, the regular impression Commander Ridgeway made was of spotted malevolence and a metal glitter. Mr. Mott, in his late twenties, had beady-brown, drifting eyes. Sandy hair curled over his ears and collar, casually leonine though actually locked in place by fast blow-drying. He was a good-natured person, with the innocent ambition of succeeding in politics and becoming important.

The chairman, stepping seriously toward the table on the dais, halted to confront Kowalski and Brock wrathfully. "Which of you is the bad apple?" the chairman asked. "You," he said to Kowalski. "You don't have to tell me. I can smell you. I can smell the corruption, Mister Kowalski. I can smell the corpse of honour and integrity, but you'll pay the price." Then Commander Ridgeway mounted the dais and went into conference with Cecil.

Intercepting Chief Williams, Redmond Ryan asked about Mrs. Williams, fittingly grave and worried. The chief, however, did not pretend that the new detective-sergeant's concern was based on any feeling tenderer than self-interest.

"Well, this could be damnably unlucky for you, Redmond," Chief Williams said quite candidly. "She's disappeared. OPP says she's not on the highways but they're checking the side roads, the ditches, they have death-spots they look at in cases like this. We've been all over Bradfarrow, hospitals and so on. She picked Teague up and vanished. Career-wise you could be all out of luck as of now."

"I don't understand how come you're so calm, Frank."

"Well I'm in control of my emotions, you see. We were taught that where I went to school. I don't allow my anxieties to rule my behaviour."

"If somebody asked me I'd say you look happy even. What if something bad's happened to her?"

"I shall have to see how I feel then, Redmond."

"We could be worrying for nothing. She could walk in here any minute."

Chief Williams smiled civilly at Redmond Ryan.

"Gentlemen," Commander Ridgeway said. "Places, please. What's your wish, Chief Williams, an adjournment, we all understand your distress?"

Mr. Mott and Chief Williams took their seats at the table on either side of the chairman. "No reason why we shouldn't get this done now we're here, Erskine," the chief said. "I know I have the chairman's assurance of a brief hearing."

"By God, you have that, Frank. We can just go into session, hear the evidence, no speeches, vote that we indict our villain, the punk cop sitting out there. That's all we have to do this aft. But are you sure you're up to it, old man?"

"Grateful for your consideration, Mr. Chairman. I'll be fine."

Mr. Mott said: "We could have it over and done with while we're talking."

Commander Ridgeway turned slowly on his elbow to Mr. Mott. "When I need that kind of snotty-nose, disruptive remark from you, sonny," he said, "I'll tell you. I'll tell you something else first, though. Make an enemy of me in this town and we'll see how far you go. I don't want to tell you again. Do you understand what I'm saying?"

Mr. Mott became still at once. "My apologies, Mr. Chairman."

"That's okay, sonny. Just watch that smart mouth, eh. All right, Cecil, let's begin. Not that I think my time is more valuable than anybody else's, but I have other things to do today."

"Bradfarrow Municipal Police Commission, L. Erskine Ridgeway, Chairman, now in session. Present: Commissioners F. Williams and W. E. Mott. G. Kramer, where's he?"

"All right, Cecil, swear in Constable Redmond Ryan. That's a nice suit. Where's your uniform, constable?"

"Detective detail, sir. Detective-Sergeant Ryan."

"Congratulations, detective-sergeant. Good work well rewarded. You found our bad apple for us and we're all proud of you."

"G. Kramer, present or what?" Cecil asked. "I have to keep a record here. Slow down."

"Kin *fuss*. Mrs. Mavis Williams told me to call Mr. Kramer. I forgot. I forgot to call Gerry Kramer, if that's okay with you, Cecil. The instruction slipped my mind. Not too long ago we had a clerk with this commission who'd remind me, not any more. Kin well fussing like a God damn old woman, let's get the hell on with it, eh."

"We have another item first, under Kowalski. Harassment of Mr. Albert Sieracki, businessman, Harbour Street."

Chief Williams said sharply: "No, we're just hearing the bribery case."

"Let's move along, gentlemen."

"Sieracki?" Mr. Mott asked, brow all wrinkled in concentration.

"Complaint of the chief here, a letter and reports. I had a big bundle of documents, sir," Cecil said.

"Oh for God's sake."

"Submitted to the chairman. Then somebody swiped the

documents. Strangest thing you ever saw, one minute they were sitting on my desk, next thing I know Mrs. Williams is inside the ladies' flushing the toilet. She must've put a thousand gallons through the system."

"Well we're off the track. I don't remember that complaint. Could we have the bribery hearing, Erskine."

Commander Erskine stared at his clerk Cecil, glinting metallic hatred. "What the hell business is it of yours how long Mrs. Williams spends in the washroom, and how often she flushes the toilet?"

"Three days later she indents for a paper-shredder. Right hand on the book, detective-sergeant."

"The Swedish nurse-killer maniac," Mr. Mott said and snapped his finger, happy with his memory effort. "I thought the name was familiar. I had it from a friend in the CA's office, Albert Sieracki aka August Amundsen, Mr. Chairman. We got him here in Bradfarrow."

"Erskine, my wife is missing, I have a major police operation under way. Can we get this done, please?"

"I offered you an adjournment, Frank," the chairman said, bending a decidedly cold look on Chief Williams to his left. "I want to know why this villain of yours was *harassing* Amundsen. The move to make there was to *arrest* him. What was the complaint, Cecil?"

"The clerk doesn't have a complaint from me. I told you."

"I do, though," Cecil said. He withdrew the Bible from under Redmond Ryan's hand. He opened a file, his fingers spreading paper in aloof satisfaction. "Toilets flushing all over the building, I put documents through the xerox when I open the mail. I get an indent for a paper-shredder, I order a new X-100. That's the only way to survive in the paper world," the clerk explained to the commissioners.

"All right. I'm withdrawing the complaint, Erskine. We'll do it that way."

"Just a minute, Frank."

" 'Kowalski accosted Mr. Sieracki outside his store, abused him in front of witnesses' — this is from the chief's letter, Mr. Chairman — 'and took him into custody.' "

The chairman looked at Kowalski. "Hey, good work, fellow," the chairman said with glee. "I didn't know you were the cop who put Amundsen in the birdcage for us. Nobody bothered telling me."

"Abused and handcuffed Mr. Sieracki, that's the complaint."

After an uneasy moment of silence at the board table the chairman said: "All right, abusing a suspect, I like to have heavy medical evidence for a police brutality complaint as you know. Broken bones, ruptured parts. The general run of these people doing the bitching are criminals. What do we have on this, Cecil?"

"Verbal abuse."

"Eh? Since when do we have to talk nice to people we're arresting, Frank?" Commander Ridgeway asked, his wrath out of control again. "What the hell, eh? What the hell kind of police force are you running for us over there? Great God, asshole councillors are screaming about my spending, any little fart the civilians elect can cancel my chauffeur, you and your bossy wife were supposed to be handling that end. You were supposed to keep them out. They're counting Cecil's paper clips, they put Morley's off limits, I have dockets that go back two months but I'm down to peanut butter sandwiches on my expense sheet. The *shit* you mean, handcuffs? What's so bad about handcuffs, Frank, eh?"

"With your indulgence," Chief Williams said. "This particular misunderstanding can be cleared up privately. Move we adjourn, Mr. Chairman."

"Mr. Mott."

"Yes, sir?"

"You're picking up four thousand a year stipend as a police commissioner. Say something."

"Well I'd like to second Chief Williams's move to adjourn."

Commander Ridgeway turned on his elbow to Mr. Mott. Light striking down from the tubes overhead flashed on the metal in the chairman's face.

"But I can't, in conscience," Mr. Mott said. "I don't grasp exactly why Constable Kowalski should be in trouble for bad-mouthing the killer. That sounds like the old do-gooder's lament. It's let's-be-kind-to-our-unfortunate-killers week again, I suppose. The constable called the killer nasty names, maybe gave him a few little pushes. Well, I'm sorry to say, Mr. Chairman, that that doesn't bother me. Our police are out there on the front line. So thanks to the bleeding heart crowd, no capital punishment. We can't keep criminals in jail any more either, we have the parole boards setting them free. A guy can rob a bank and get the same slaps my kid gets for not putting his toys away."

"There's a move to adjourn," Cecil said tiredly. Now that his own grievance had been aired the clerk was bored.

"Very well put, exactly my own feelings, that's the kind of talk I like to hear, sonny," the chairman said to Mr. Mott. "We're doing okay here, forget about adjourning. You with me on the vote, lad?"

"Bet your life, sir."

Detective-Sergeant Ryan at this time stepped up to the table and spoke urgently into Chief Williams's ear. "I'm going to check on the search for Mrs. Williams, chief. We need her," Ryan whispered. "This clown is all out of line and we're going down the drain, for God's sake."

"Motion to adjourn defeated."

"See here, Erskine, we're short three commissioners," Chief Williams said. "To tell you the truth I'm not feeling well." He stood up. "I'm taking off home now. I'll call you if anything comes through on Mavis."

"Sergeant Brock, guard that door."

Ryan had reached the door and was turning the knob.

"Where do you think you're off to, in the new suit there?"

"Who, me, sir? Well, just an errand, sir."

"People who are up before this commission can't walk in and out whenever the fancy takes them. Sit down. That goes for you too, Chief Williams. Sergeant Brock, nobody leaves this room, tell the constables outside."

Cecil said: "We can do the business any time you like. We're clear to go."

"Good. Thanks, Cec."

"But I'm not up before the commission, sir," Ryan said with smiling charm and grace. "I'm the police witness for the bribery hearing. I'm Detective-Sergeant Ryan. Constable Kowalski is over there, sir."

"Who says you're not up before the commission, Constable Ryan?"

"What? Look, I'm a *witness*. Ask Chief Williams. Chief Williams and Commissioner Mavis Williams ordered me to be here for the Kowalski case. I'm the police officer who found the bribe money in Kowalski's possession, that's all, sir. That's the only reason I'm here."

"Well if that's what you think you have a big surprise coming. Sit down. I've been chairman now for what, seven years," Commander Ridgeway said, lounging back on his vinyl boardroom chair as if in idle conversation with the commissioners on either side, "taking orders from Big Blondie, our friend the plump circus lady with her whip and whistle."

"Mr. Chairman."

"I'm referring to your wife Mavis, Frank. All wisdom was with her, to hear her tell it. We do know what's going on, though, don't we, Cecil?"

"Eh? Oh to be sure, sir. We have files."

"One on Ryan, do we?"

"Illegal break-in and search at Constable Kowalski's house, authorized by Chief Williams."

"Always starts there, an illegal break-in and search. Your first sign the team's making up its own rules, by God. The act that says everything's not copacetic with the guardians of law. They've turned on their own people, the citizens. Rule of moral superiority goes out the window. That's when you have to burn them root and branch, Frank. Old friendships notwithstanding, for the good of the citizen population. You let an illegal break-in and search go by, other crimes follow as the night the day."

Chief Williams said: "Mr. Chairman, I've never in my career attended such a malicious, arbitrary and irresponsible Police Commission hearing."

The chairman stared at Chief Williams, somehow offended by the protest. "An orgy, Chief Williams," he shouted, trembling with disgust and other emotion. "I suppose that's responsible, is

it? Eating grapes on the run, nudity, fertility dances. This commission is acting legally, Frank, and by God it's asking for your
resignation what's more."

"Move to accept Chief Williams's resignation," said Cecil,
whose eyes were half closed. "Mr. Mott?"

"God. Suppose Mrs. Williams walks in that door."

"Mr. Mott."

"Give me a minute."

"Good meeting so far," Sergeant Brock said to Joe Kowalski,
both men being alert and interested.

"I'm getting older here, Mr. Mott. My own darn little weak-
nesses," the chairman complained, "are known to all of Bradfarrow. Vengeful, how would you fellows like that kind of a
reputation?"

"I'll second the motion. God."

"And I can't take a young female protégée to dinner without
starting telephones ringing everywhere in town. Oh yes, deco-
rator beige TouchPhone Contempras in Regency Gate ringing
off the hook. I wouldn't cry any tears if somebody cleaned out the
rest of that viper's tangle, send our wop friends back in there I say.
The new diet, what's on sale at Holt Renfrew, she's young enough
to be the old goat's daughter, chatter chatter, it's their whole lives,
and now they're all libbers too, they have a cause just like real
people. Anybody's not involved, it's like wearing last year's shoes.
You can't pay a compliment at a party any more but some miser-
able female starts screaming sexist in your face. Hardly ever an
evening goes by these days but some broad or other is jumping on
me and calling me a male chauvinist swine. That's not a sexist
remark, I suppose. That's insight, it's okay to drop that into the
conversation, you're a male pig. Sure, yoghurt and white wine
and insulting guys to their faces. I can't wait for the great day of
freedom to dawn, myself. That's when I stop smiling at ugly
broads who call me names. They start getting popped on the
mouth by this little piggy, when that day dawns . . ."

Chief Williams was by now pale of face and in a good deal of
shock. "I imagine you'll be conducting the hearing some time this
afternoon, Erskine," he said, interrupting the chairman's mus-
ings. "The purpose of the hearing is to decide whether or not to

lay a charge against Constable Joseph Kowalski, in case you've forgotten. The police can prove that Kowalski is in possession of a bribe from an armed robber named Riordan, who is still at large. Proceeds of the robbery of a Brinks armoured car in Montreal, ten million dollars in cash the approximate figure."

". . . always the uglies, you'll notice, the good lookers have all the power in the male world they need. Before we had Cecil here," the chairman said, nodding at the clerk in old clothes who was almost asleep, "we had a child named Bimbo handling the job. That was before Mrs. Mavis Williams got herself appointed to this commission, Bimbo's time. Nineteen years old. The moppet loved being nineteen. Enjoyed every second of her life, dear little Bimbo, lovely charmer. That's unusual, nineteen is an insecure age. She had a lot of heart, that's what I'm saying. A laugher rather than a giggler if you understand me. A man could love her company without a randy thought in his head. Our meetings were beautiful in those days. Our words were golden, you see, because we knew they were going into Bimbo's precious little ears. Then the circus lady came on board. We got Cecil instead. Do you mind my asking how old you are, Cecil?"

"Forty-seven, sir," Cecil said sleepily and with definite resentment.

"Yes? I would have said middle fifties. What do you think about forty-seven, Cec, do you enjoy it?"

"Mr. Chairman."

Cecil shrugged. "Now and then."

"That's the size of it, Cecil, now and then. Forty-seven doesn't make any sense. Twelve is like that too, and thirty-four. Forty-seven is my own age, and I'm like you, Cecil, I have to work at forty-seven full time in order to enjoy it now and then. Nobody's blaming Cecil, gentlemen. Though God knows it's hard to care what words go into Cecil's waxy old ears. But we haven't had any golden talk around this table since we lost dear little Bimbo. Fortunately I was able to set her up in another line of work."

"So what would you like, should I swear Detective-Sergeant Ryan in?" Cecil asked.

"Seven years under the whip and whistle, by God it's good to be free. Sure, swear him in if he has something I haven't seen, if he has evidence that Kowalski took Riordan's cash." Commander Ridgeway looked through his papers. "All I see here, though, is proof that Kowalski owns a lot of money, maybe more than ten million. I don't see a smoking pistol, gentlemen. How about it, constable?"

"He means you, detective-sergeant."

"Well let's start saying constable, get the fellow used to hearing it again," the chairman said to Cecil, avoiding Redmond Ryan's eye. "Do you have evidence that Kowalski took the money, constable?"

"That he *took* it? Mr. Chairman, we *knew* he had it. We searched everywhere. Our problem was figuring out where he *hid the money*. Then I *found* the money."

Commander Ridgeway delved into his briefcase. "Mini-People Incorporated, that's one of the companies in my investment portfolio, a dear old reliable," he said. "The New York guys are celebrating their centennial this year. Funding centennial projects all over the world, not a problem for the shareholders, charity deductibles of course, but they're spending money like water. Universities in African swamp and jungle, we're going to have cannibals with good table manners, endowments, memorial scholarships by the bushel. Let me read you part of a letter here. 'We have included in the Centennial Celebration a memorial to Willy Woolly and his popular trademark friends, and a special celebration of the I Wish I Had a Willy Woolly era in our history. Certainly nobody could forget Willy Woolly, or Wimple Woolly, or indeed Woofy Woolly. The memorial seems appropriate, though, since the days of the domestic homesteads that made those great products possible are now, alas, gone for ever.' "

I've made a terrible mistake, Chief Williams thought. I'm washed out. First meeting without Mavis and Erskine's taken over the shop.

" 'As a memorial tribute to Willy Woolly and his friends we are arranging to endow in your area a hundred-acre sheep farm, one of those proudly independent homesteads now seen no more. We are particularly anxious that the endowment will be a wish come true for somebody who, when he was a child, might have gazed up at a bright star on a cold winter's night and dreamed: *I Wish I Had a Willy Woolly*.' "

"Point of information, Mr. Chairman. What are we talking about?"

"Children's stuff, Mr. Mott. The Willy Woolly was a kid's woollen suit, mitts attached. They were popular about fifty years ago, Willy Woollys. The Woofy Woolly was a dog, a great favourite before Snoopy came along. I don't have information as to the Wimple Woolly."

Kowalski raised his hand. Sergeant Brock tried to wrestle it down.

"That's all right, Chief Brock. Yes, constable?"

"Sergeant Brock isn't chief yet. We haven't done that part yet."

"A helmet, Mr. Chairman, like a balaclava."

"Did you have one when you were a child, Constable Kowalski?"

"No, sir. They were a parents' thing. A kid had to be tough, wearing something called a Willy Woolly, maybe with the Wimple Woolly too. If you weren't tough you got punched out all the time. I never had them myself, no, sir."

"So it could be possible in fact, as the president of Mini-People Incorporated says in his letter to me here, that when you were a child you might have gazed up at a wishing-star and said: 'I Wish I Had a Willy Woolly.'"

Joe Kowalski looked uncomfortable and morose. He let his breath out between his teeth with an anguished hiss, thinking.

"Well?"

"No, Mr. Chairman. Jeez sir, *nobody* wished he had a Willy Woolly. Like I said, the advertisement was for parents. I don't know how many parents believed it, after they put their kid to bed he hopped over to the window and looked up at the star and said that. On account of it some guys I know remember rotten Christmas mornings. It could spoil most of grade school for you, the Willy Woolly. Every winter up to when I was ten my aunts wanted to buy me that stuff, I had to talk 'em out of it once a year at least. The kids today don't know how lucky they are, with snowmobile suits."

"Kin people won't be helped, will you?" Commander Ridgeway shouted at Joe Kowalski. "I should know better by now. Breaking my ass trying to do you a good turn, and you're too

God damn sanctimonious to play along for the record here. What I'm explaining, constable," he said more quietly, though with metalled teeth clenched and bright loathing eyes swimming, "is an act of pure philanthropy by the officers of a great multi-national. I'm talking about *New York sentimentality*, Constable Kowalski. But that's too sophisticated for you, isn't it, nostalgia for an advertisement, pretending that just once as a child you might have looked through a window at a star and said something simple and unforgettable like *I Wish I Had a Willy Woolly*."

"He's sorry, sir," Sergeant Brock said.

"All right. Well the word from New York is clear enough. Chairman of the centennial celebration committee announces the name. Chosen from thousands, etc. As little children, wished they had a Willy Woolly, but I guess we can stretch a point. You get the sheep-farm, Mr. Kowalski."

Joe Kowalski sat back in his chair.

"No doubt the politics of what's happening here will become clear to me," Chief Williams said. "I never heard of a garment called a Willy Woolly. I don't believe there ever was such a thing as a Willy Woolly." The chief had been thinking about committee tactics. "Let me point out that if you vote to throw me off the commission you won't have a quorum, so you can't ask for my resignation as Chief of Police. If you do it the other way round, and ask for my resignation as chief first, then I'll just resign my position as commissioner, and that puts you in exactly the same spot, you can't touch me. I'm appalled at this exhibition of chicanery, Erskine, you vengeful little bastard. We're in Bradfarrow not in Russia."

"Maybe he's right," Commander Ridgeway said to the clerk Cecil, looking somewhat troubled. "This could be too damn Gilbert and Sullivan to work. What do we do, Sergeant Brock and Chief Williams here go outside the door and change clothes? Brock is Chief of Police and a Police Commissioner, and the chief goes down the snake to sergeant. Something along those lines you have in mind, is it?"

"Did you hear that? *Little* bastard, he said," Sergeant Brock remarked to Joe Kowalski. "He is little, isn't he, the chairman. I never noticed that before."

Cecil said: "No. We give the mayor a call, get him over here, and he appoints Sergeant Brock to the Police Commission. Then the commission appoints Brock Chief of Police. Like I'm assuming Brock has enough sense not to vote against that, but you never know with these people as you said yourself, sir."

"All right. That's near enough what I thought. Then Frank goes down to sergeant. Sergeant Frank Williams."

"No. He's not up to standard morally, sir. He just gets booted off the force and off the commission."

"He lost his house and his wife, Cec. Have a heart. Can't we fit him in anywhere?"

"No sir. We don't have a vacancy for a bugger of no moral principles, that I know of. We don't have an opening at the moment. Too bad he lost his house. But he doesn't get any sympathy from me on the missing wife occurrence. That's a stroke of luck, the way I read it, if it holds for him."

They argued this point amiably.

"What would he be, the chairman, say five foot two. Is that about right, Joe?"

"Right for what, sergeant?" Joe Kowalski asked.

Sergeant Brock was silent.

"I don't get you, sergeant."

"You want me to say it."

"I'm not sure I understand the question. Honest."

"All right. Is that about the right size for a leprechaun, Joe, five foot two?"

"Oh, for a leprechaun. Well, sure, that's a perfect size for a leprechaun. I mean, if you believe in leprechauns. Lots of people don't. Say, sergeant. When he stands up, take a look at the guy arguing with the chairman, Cecil. He's even smaller. I don't know about the mayor," Joe Kowalski said. He put his meaty elbow into the sergeant's ribs and closed one eye in an exaggerated conspirator's wink. "We'll have to *size him up*, the mayor, when we see him, eh, sergeant. We'll have to take his measure, okay?"

"This is one hell of an afternoon."

"No, this is pretty good. I like it. I've always wanted a sheep-farm, you know. Hey, you'll make a great Chief of Police, sergeant, congratulations."

"Thanks, Joe. I'm fairly sure none of this is happening, though," Sergeant Brock said.

The mayor was called, rather snappishly, by Cecil, and the commissioners made other dispositions for an hour or so. The mayor was in fact a large man. He was not in the least co-operative to begin with, and argued against the unprecedented step of making an unknown sergeant both a Police Commissioner and Chief of Police. There were better men available, he said. He had known the two deputy chiefs since he was a child, and had been on the football squad at Western with one of them. Commander Ridgeway talked privately with him, glancing at his watch while he did so, grudging the time. The mayor then appointed the sergeant to the Police Commission, and the commission voted for Brock's promotion. Frank Williams was given his full pension, over Cecil's bad-tempered objections. The former chief showed no gratitude. He had stopped listening, and would not speak again, and he wore a remote smile. The commissioners dropped the burglary complaint against Ryan, upon his promise to undertake six months of expiatory community work. The new chief and the retiring constable, Brock and Kowalski, were officially wished the best of good fortune in their new endeavours: a wish that was devoid of sentiment and somewhat hurried, since the chairman was anxious to get away and dress for a dinner date.

Twelve

The Arrival of the Martians

1

The maples along the streets of Regency Gate had put out dull orange boughs, ready to break the trees into their autumn fire. Chief Brock parked his car at the farm gateway. He followed the broad grass path that had once been Cambridge Mews. An eye of memory could see the matrix of former habitation under the pastureland: wolds where houses had sat on commanding rises; little valleys winding where roads had been; and streams that drained the land into pond and marsh, formerly pools and stretches of lawn.

The Kowalski farm was the regular type commonly seen in the country around Bradfarrow, built in days when farming was a practical business yielding a good living. The farm-house was red brick with white-painted shuttered windows, a tin roof, and a solidly-built verandah. The clustered barns and silos, some distance away, were large against the sky and cast long shadows. While farms of this kind that had survived in the countryside were usually decrepit, the Kowalski place sitting in its reclaimed pastoral expanse was spanking new.

About two dozen fat sheep grazed on a slope to Chief Brock's right. As the chief walked by a small black animal broke furiously from the fence on his left, hurtling at roly-poly speed toward the sheep. Instantly the chief heard the buzzing of a bee-swarm. A man crouched over the handlebars of a trail-bike crested the hill behind the grazing sheep and descended upon the attacking animal, a poodle dog. The rider showed good manoeuvring skill in staying with the poodle, which though it dodged and turned still wanted to reach the sheep. When bike and dog converged, the rider reached a short shepherd's crook from the bike's rack-straps. The crook swept under the dog's collar in a precise capture, and the bike spun to a dead stop at the same time.

The man then cuffed the poodle dog smartly. "That's your two, Givenchy," the man shouted at the dog. "One more run puts you in the lock-up."

With the miscreant dog under one arm the man rode the trail-bike toward the fence that separated the wild grass of the sheep-farm from the tame back lawns of Regency Gate.

"Good work, Redmond," Chief Brock called out sincerely.

Redmond Ryan turned and saw the chief. Ryan's hair was longer, and bleached to white by the life out under the sun. He wore an old woollen sweater, fuzzy with dog hair, and leather gaiters for protection against bramble and thistle. He snarled above the bee-swarm noise of his vehicle, going by.

". . . you, Brock," drifted to the chief from Redmond Ryan on the autumn evening air.

Chief Brock pushed tobacco into his pipe with his thumb and continued his walk. The pity of it is, Ryan makes a first-class shepherd, the chief reflected. Nature made the occupation of shepherd for people like Ryan, a life of honest use among dogs and sheep, away from vulnerable humanity. But too soon now Ryan would take his wholesome good looks back into the world, where everybody trusted and believed in them.

Chief Brock liked the spacious breadth of the new farm buildings, their lay-out and solidity, which for him was like revisiting the Bradfarrow of his past. He stopped to greet Kowalski's aunts as he went by the paddock. They both looked busy enough. Aunt Caroline was stirring something in a metal trough. Aunt Myrtle, working separately, was hosing out a wooden barrel, stopping now and then to scour the inside with huge handfuls of steel wool.

They returned Chief Brock's greeting courteously. "If you had some idea of what is necessary work and what is *unnecessary* work," Aunt Caroline said to Aunt Myrtle then. "We have certain chores that take priority over others."

Brock was a little surprised by dozy Aunt Myrtle's zealous attacks on the barrel with the steel wool. I guess life in the open air has woken her up, the chief thought.

Aunt Myrtle said: "You've worn a mantle of virtue all these years, haven't you, Caroline. Now I'm working quite as hard as you are and the best you can do is say that my work isn't strictly necessary. I don't remember ever questioning whether you should be vacuuming or dusting, or which was more important. This isn't the least difficult to do. I expect gardening is even easier and shovelling snow and the rest of your silly fuss."

"I'm mixing the sheep-dip, which we need," Aunt Caroline said to Chief Brock, loudly enough for her sister to hear over the water-rush from the hose. "We save farm expenses with a scratch mix, you see. This is an excellent batch." She handed the paddle to the chief. "Would you mind breaking up some of the lumps for me, Mr. Brock. Joseph is running the wool-washing machine. I'll tell him you're here."

A sulphurous stink rose into Chief Brock's nostrils from the sheep-dip. It was a bluish, gluey substance. He could barely move the paddle in it. He pushed and pulled with straining arms, breathing through his mouth, while Aunt Caroline headed for the machine shed behind the farmyard. The paddle tended to stick in the bottom silt as if now and then seized by a giant hand down there.

"I've never objected to work in my life, Mr. Brock," Aunt Myrtle explained, her voice echoing as she peered into the barrel's cavern looking for areas of grime, "except that so much of it is unladylike of course, but I do find the self-righteousness of people who have the working obsession unbearable, don't you. I believe it's a form of hysteria."

By the time Aunt Caroline returned the chief had his knee on the trough edge, trying for some leverage. Aunt Caroline looked severely at the paddle, stuck upright in the sheep-dip.

"Thank you, Mr. Brock, that's most helpful," she said. One sweep of her skinny arms rippled the paddle the length of the trough. "I think I'd like some more water in this now, Myrtle, please," she said, "when you're through playing with the hose."

A minute or two later Chief Brock accepted an ale from Joe Kowalski in the kitchen. They sat at the table.

"She gets tougher every day, your Aunt Caroline, Joe. It's my personal opinion she'll live forever."

"The life suits her. I hope she goes another ten years anyway, chief," Kowalski said seriously. "I don't see how I could run this place without her, the taxes I pay."

"Deloro Nickel still trying to buy you out, are they?"

"I had two of their what they call resource development men here last week again. That's an outfit won't take no for an answer, Deloro Nickel."

"We got some news on the telex today, Joe. I don't know how you'll feel about this. Seamus Riordan's been captured."

Joe Kowalski looked interested, in the warm way a retired man likes to hear about the earlier career. "Nice going."

"He's been on my mind, Seamus Riordan, since I've been chief," said the chief, feeling his way toward a thought that could be unpopular with his friend Joe Kowalski. "Riordan had a gift for organization, especially for organizing other people. He could make people do what he wanted them to do. He turned a pious Presbyterian into a bank robber, from what we know. Say you're talented like that, and you have ten million dollars too, you could do nearly anything in this town, Joe, if you had a mind to. I thought maybe Riordan wouldn't have the ten million, if he was ever arrested. Sure enough he didn't."

"Well jeez, chief, it's been nearly nine months. What's he going to do, keep the money in the trunk of the car for nine months?"

"Sure, I know, it was just a thought I had. He'll be older than your aunts when he gets out of jail, that's all, he could bargain for a shorter sentence with the money but he isn't doing that. He says he was never in Bradfarrow, by the way."

Kowalski uncapped another two ales.

"It doesn't bother you, Joe, does it, the news about Riordan? You don't think, do you, that you'd recognize the villain if you were face to face?"

Joe Kowalski tried to understand this and failed. "Well, Hanrahan looked exactly like the photo, chief, but I never met Riordan."

"Okay," Chief Brock said. He took a pull of ale, eyes distantly reflective, thinking his own thoughts. "Well that's just fine by me, Joe. I'm not arguing. I'm a reasonable man, though, it's the only way I know how to handle my life. Most other people too, if you gave them a choice, they'd see the thing my way I bet, it's a question of peace of mind. Doing it your way there's nothing to depend on, we don't know where the hell we are."

"I remember once when I understood everything, chief, I was in second grade, five years old. A grocer down on Riverside was carrying stock into his store from the delivery waggon. He had a spring on the door, and he asked me to hold the door open for him. He gave me a packet of Juicy Fruit gum. Well, that gum scared the life out of me, chief. What I wanted most in the world was to chew the gum. I'd never even tasted it, gum. The kids in my class, their jaws were moving all day long, but there was this thing about my teeth. Aunt Caroline said, no gum, Joseph, *your teeth*. You'd have to see her face when she said that, all scrunched up, like somebody was going to stick a knife in her. Well that was how I understood what was going on, by putting together the teeth, the gum, and Aunt Caroline looking so frightened. I knew when I chewed the gum my aunts would die." Kowalski, with his elbows on the table, let both arms flop down, to demonstrate two aunts toppling over. "They'd drop dead, just as soon as my teeth touched the gum, down they'd go like bowling pins. It was all clear as daylight to me. I've never been so sure of anything in my life since that time on Riverside, with the Juicy Fruit in my hand like a bomb," Joe Kowalski said and sighed.

"Well, did you chew the Juicy Fruit?"

"What, and kill my aunts? Of course I didn't, chief. I threw it away. I didn't chew a stick of gum until I was six. That was what I got the only time in my life I was certain of what was going on, I got cheated out of a whole year of Juicy Fruit and Doublemint."

"I think I follow what you mean," Chief Brock said, nodding while he stared at Joe Kowalski. "Basically what you disagree with is somebody being certain. I mean, of anything. I'm beginning to wonder about myself, though, since you got this sheep-farm, ever since I was made chief in fact. Well, just this summer, the . . ."

"Leprechauns."

"Yes, the . . . Well, take our trip down to Grabe Pass, I've been looking forward to it more and more. Sunshine in the deep of winter, March say. All right, Grabe Pass, armpit of the world, what I had in mind, though, was to make them *eat* the Amundsen capture down there. Two hicks from Bradfarrow, refugees from the snow, but we wouldn't have anybody asking where's Bradfarrow, not this time."

"I've been working on it," Kowalski said, somewhat guilty and anxious. "Probably I'll be able to take the time off okay. Snow's on its way, and there's a lot to do, winter doesn't give you any breaks in this business, it's a tough dollar."

"Well you can relax, we're not going. I wouldn't enjoy the trip. Tell me how this can happen. Riordan was arrested in Grabe Pass."

Joe Kowalski remained silent in sympathy, blinking sadly at the chief.

"Out of all the towns on the map. Riordan was driving through Grabe Pass and ran a red light. And don't say nothing's impossible, Joe."

"I wasn't going to say anything, chief."

"All right. You see that's something I won't understand until the day I die. Well, no damn way I'm going down to Grabe Pass, I mean they were bad enough up to now, bragging about their big-time arrest twenty-one years ago. Now they're out of their minds. The sheriff's been on the phone to me three times since he sent the telex. I have to take the calls. I don't have any choice. Phone's probably ringing for me at home right now. They're planning to add a message to their signs for the tourists, Stave says, Grabe Pass, Crime-Fighting Capital of the World, something like that. They weren't exactly modest before so it's going to be just sheer hell for visiting cops down there until about 1999."

"Jeez I'm sorry, chief."

"Yes, well. You haven't put up the TV mast, I see."

"Something I haven't got round to yet. I'll get her up before the snow flies I guess. Maybe I won't put it up at that. Those new shows don't do much for me, the sex comedies. They took *Kojak* off, did you hear? I don't know, chief, it seems hardly worthwhile watching TV, now Old Baldy won't be on any more. I can't see myself watching those sex comedies with the barns full and Aunt Caroline too busy to sit down."

"This is a good brew," Chief Brock said. "I noticed on the way up, Myrtle's pitching in now with Caroline. I guess farm life's changed her habits."

Kowalski shook his head. "Aunt Myrtle's too old to change her habits," he said. "The thing is right now, she's had this project of her own going since the doctor cut her Scotch off. Down near the creek by the birch copse. She's been hauling rock and putting something together, looks like a fireplace. She's swiped a whole lot of copper pipe from the workshop too. Well she better not be building what I think she's building. Any time I see her collecting bottles and barrels I'm going down there and break it up."

Chief Brock said nothing for a while, tilting his chair back to look through the kitchen window where the shapes of tiny houses could be seen far away in mist. "Nice view of the town you get from up here. I bet in the early morning you can see most of Bradfarrow." He slid his empty bottle across the table to Kowalski. "Snap another one open for me there, would you please, Joe," said the chief. "It's been sort of a dry day."

2

Sergeant Dave Cardozo was in Chief Brock's office when a call came through on the chief's phone from his mother. He jotted down the items she wanted picked up at the supermarket. "I can't now, mom, I'm not in my own office," Dave said. "I'll call you back later and read it to you."

"I have the paper right here, Dave."

Chief Brock opened his copy of the Bradfarrow *Times* and folded it to the feature "Gardening Dreaming" by Francis R.

Williams. The sergeant then read the former chief's poem for that
day to his mother, naturally with some self-consciousness:

> " '. . . evening when I weed the beds
> Gratefully they nod their heads
>
> Shasta daisy, dusty miller
> Favourites of the gentle tiller
> Hardy poppy, flower of Spain
> Hyacinth and winterbane
>
> Abatina, heartsease, rose
> In September starwort grows
> Narcissus and asphodel
> And ranunculus as well
>
> Winter's snow is cruelly laid
> On the garden that I made
> Polyanthus, aster sweet
> Tread the snow with careful feet
> Flowers are sleeping underneath!'

". . . touches me too, mom," said Cardozo. "He's very sensitive. Sure, I'll save it for you." He said to the chief when he put the
phone down: "She's a big fan."

"I don't know anything about poetry," Chief Brock said
impatiently. "I'm a gardener, though. He's bogus, he doesn't
know what he's talking about, like starwort is *Stellaria*, and that's
another name for aster for God's sake, Dave, or 'aster sweet' if
you're looking for a rhyme for 'underneath'. Flowers don't sleep
under the snow either. They're dead under there, what you have
is mulch. Even perennials, the *flowers* are dead."

"Well, if you want to get all technical," said solemn-faced
Dave Cardozo. "Anyway, poets are allowed to do that, my mom
says. She's a gardener too and she likes him."

"Well I like the scientific truth, Dave."

"I bet he really enjoys his garden."

"No, he doesn't. He doesn't have a garden. He has an apartment on the eighth floor with two spider plants. Frank's just as big a fake as he ever was."

Right then the door was opened suddenly and urgently by Sergeant Derby, who spared an instant to grimace an apology at the chief and then shouted desperately to Sergeant Cardozo: "*Martians, Dave, Martians!* They're on their way up 62 to Cormac!"

"Martians? Oh God. Can I have a cruiser, chief? We've got to stop them."

"I'll say," Chief Brock said, feeling eerie. He punched his phone buttons. "Central, this is all cars. What do they look like, Sergeant Derby?"

"Green and blue."

". . . all cars, and I want roadblock set-ups on Highway 62 from Cormac south . . " Here the chief stopped, seeing the puzzlement on Sergeant Cardozo's face. "Sorry, Central, cancel the all cars, please, we've had a false alarm here."

". . . just the one cruiser, it's the Bradfarrow Braves against the Marmora Martians tonight, chief, see Darl and I train the Bradfarrow Braves. The Martians didn't get the new schedule so they think they're playing the Cormac Chieftains."

"They aren't real Martians," Sergeant Derby explained to Chief Brock.

Joe and his leprechauns have done this for me, Chief Brock thought, sweating a little. Now I can believe in Martians when you jump me.

"They couldn't be Martians anyway, it's too hot on Mars, out in space it's either too hot or too cold for life," Sergeant Derby said to Sergeant Cardozo. "Anything like us'd be burnt to a crisp, or else we'd be a block of ice."

Dave Cardozo's hair was combed smartly sideways, out of his eyes. His fingernails were still blunt but beginning to show timid growth. "I wonder if that's right, Darl," he said. "What does anybody know? Nobody knows much, do they. I mean the more they discover about what's out there in space the less they understand."

"It's big, I guess," Sergeant Derby conceded. He held the door open for Cardozo and said: "I can take the cruiser out and head off the Martians if the chief needs you, Dave."

Chief Brock was watching Dave Cardozo, worrying. He's still awful green, the chief thought, I won't be doing him a favour if I bring him on too fast. When his mind was elsewhere the chief sometimes called his sergeant Joe instead of Dave.

He said: "Thanks, Darl. I'd appreciate it."

Dave Cardozo asked: "So why do you suppose we're always so certain of everything? Nothing's certain, is it? Anything is possible. Right, chief?"

Sergeant Derby at the door turned to hear the chief's answer too so Brock gave the question a moment of honest thought.

"Yes."